Editing by: Brenda Williams

Published by Cauldron Press

info@cauldronpress.online

Visit www.ansage.ca

AETHERBLOOD

The AetherBorn Saga, Book 3

A. N. SAGE

CAULDRON
PRESS

"It was night, and the rain fell; and falling, it was rain, but, having fallen, it was blood."
-Edgar Allen Poe

PROLOGUE

D emas watched the boy's body wriggle and twist, trying to escape from the grasp of the smoke that threatened to crush his lungs. Tears streaked his face in dirty lines that might have resembled war paint if they weren't so pathetic. He twirled a black curl around his finger before looking away. "How much longer is this going to take?"

"What's wrong?" His sister asked, "Not having fun anymore?" The boy cried louder as her fingers danced.

"If you keep this up, he'll wake up the whole neighborhood."

"This was *your* plan, brother. Don't blame me for trying to bring some joy into our lives while we work." She grinned, "What is it the humans say? If you love what you do, you'll never work a day in your life?"

Another grin as she straightened her fingers

allowing the boy to take a gulp of air. His eyes watered, and he clasped at his throat as if he was trying to decide between screaming and breathing. His mouth opened but before he could let out a sob, she clenched her fist, yanking the air from his lungs.

His knees shook and he beat at his chest, his body drooping over itself with heaving, shallow breaths. She let go and the boy screamed. A desperate cry to no one in particular. His eyes darted around, looking for a way out despite knowing full well that escape was futile.

"Just hurry up with it already, we have to move on."

There was another flick of the hand, followed by more screaming, and then a loud thud. The boy's body dropped to the ground like an anvil hitting water. His open eyes made Demas groan with disgust. There was really nothing beautiful about these creatures. Nothing poetic. They lived, they died, and that was the end of it. How blasé.

Not having fun anymore, he repeated in his head. He tried to remember the last time he'd truly had fun. Eirene's twentieth birthday snapped to mind. He had brought her to a clearing, away from the elders and covered the entire thing in shadow. Their own private oasis. She was so happy, twirling and singing in the grass. Her eyes never leaving him. That was the last time he remembered smiling, the day that turned into night then into morning again. The day their daughter was conceived.

He shook the thought away and walked to the boy's body. "You're sure it's done?"

"Do you really need to ask, brother?"

"I suppose not."

Demas stepped over the body and leaned on the wall in front of him. His hand pressed against the brick as he looked down, patting the stone lightly.

"Is everything quite alright?" he heard his sister ask from what seemed like miles away.

Eirene's face flashed before him. Her smile, eager and innocent, melting away in the darkness of the night. He straightened his back, twirling to face his sister.

"Everything is splendid. Time to go."

CHAPTER 1
ASH OR SOMETHING

"Fish! You gotta see this!" Shaylah's voice rang through the apartment with a tone that resembled a dolphin's mating call, "Hurry up!"

The morning light had just started to coat the ceiling of Ruby's bedroom in twirling slivers of pink and turquoise. Reflections bounced off her vanity mirror, and she lazily studied the patterns while stroking Liam's heavy arm on her stomach. She looked at him, slowly roaming her eyes over his bare chest, only to catch him staring back at her. Ruby could read his current state of mind without pause; his expression caught between amusement and annoyance.

Since Liam had officially moved his things into her apartment, they had spent most of their time trying to find moments of privacy; but her roommate made it difficult, if not entirely impossible, for them to have any semblance of a personal life. It wasn't that she disliked having Shaylah around, more that she missed the silence of spending quiet evenings with her boyfriend. Her theatrical friend was many wonderful things but quiet had never been her strong suit.

Liam nudged her side with his shoulder as if to wake her up from her thoughts, "Think she'll give up if we pretend to be asleep?"

"Fish! Come on!" Shaylah yelled, as if on cue.

"Guess not. Nice try though." Ruby bounced up to sit, leaning over to give him a quick kiss before making her way to the living room. "I'm coming! Calm down!"

She tugged at the strings of her robe, tightening it around her waist, and sluggishly dragged her feet out of the bedroom to find Shaylah cross-legged on the couch, her hair a giant mess of slept-in curls. The television was on, and she was fumbling with the remote to get the sound louder. *If this girl got me out of bed for another cat video, I'll kill her,* she thought and sat down on the edge of an armchair. The sleeve of her robe rolled up as she settled in, and she pulled it back down quickly to hide the rough scars on her arms. Despite her ability to heal, the cuts on her arms had not disappeared entirely, and she hated the constant reminder of her last fight with Demas. A little gift from Tartarus himself to make sure she never forgot him or his final warning when they met in the Aether Plane that night.

War is coming.

She turned the words around in her mouth, tasting their bitter and spiteful remnants. Why couldn't he just leave them alone? Her and Liam were finally in a good place in their relationship, the AetherBorns had settled in nicely at the center, even Jake had started to come around more– though his attitude towards Liam bordered on toxic. They were so close to living a normal life, as normal a life as half-deities can have at least. Why was Demas so intent on ruining it for them? On ruining her?

"Are you seeing this?" Shaylah asked, tugging her attention back to the television.

"Sorry. Still waking up, I guess. What's this now?"

Shaylah's hand clicked the remote rapidly, blaring the volume even louder. "They found that guy that disappeared last week!" She yelled over the television, "The one in Dalhurst! Remember?"

"Yeah! So that's good, no?" Ruby yelled back and grabbed the remote from her hand. "Can we turn it down a little?"

"Oops. Sorry. But look!" Shaylah's freshly painted red nail pointed at the television as if accusing it of a crime, "He's dead!"

Ruby's eyes blinked rapidly, fully awake now and concentrated on the news coverage. Shaylah had been obsessing over this case lately and had taken any excuse to bring it up in conversation. She wasn't sure why her friend was so interested in the disappearance of someone on the other side of the country that she'd never met but was glad for the distraction. The more time she spent talking about this with Shaylah, the less time she had to worry about what Demas might be planning next.

"You guys want some coffee for this screening or what?" Liam walked out of the bedroom, flashing his teeth in his usual charming smile.

"Yeah, sure!" Shaylah's eyes only briefly glanced in his direction, "And maybe put a shirt on. Like we get it, you're hot." She rolled her eyes at Ruby then turned her attention back to the news.

"I'd love a cup. Thanks, babe." She shook her head at him, smiling, completely fine with his undressed state. "So, do they know who killed him?"

"Nope. They have no clue. The idiots. It's been like a week; you'd think they'd have something by now. I mean, what have they been doing?"

"I'm sure they're working on it, Shay. Why are you so obsessed with this anyway?"

"Are you kidding me? It's the only thing everyone is talking about! Have you been living under a rock?"

Ruby raised her robe sleeve slightly and pointed at her scars.

"Oh, right." Shaylah smiled, "I forgot."

"So, the cops actually have nothing?"

"Well, not nothing. Just nothing useful. It looks like they found a bunch of ash or something around the body. But like who cares? They should spend more time figuring out who killed this guy and less time worrying about the housekeeping." Shaylah huffed, the air billowing tendrils of curls off her face. "Morons."

She couldn't help but laugh at Shaylah's frustration. If she didn't know any better, she would have thought her roommate knew the victim personally. Shaylah had a tendency of getting much too attached to murder and mystery cases. More often than not, she would act like she could do a better job at solving crimes than the entire police force combined. The excitement usually lasted for a few weeks before she would get bored and move on to the next flashy case plastered all over the news. Regrettably for Ruby and Liam, they were caught in the middle of this latest obsession.

"Hey, you think this might be one of your little thingamajigs?" Shaylah asked.

"My what?"

"You know, your AetherBorn stuff."

"Why?"

"I don't know. Ash, Fog. Never mind, I'm probably reaching."

Was she reaching? They still had not seen any hint of Demas, and she'd been going crazy wondering when he would strike next and what he would do. If he came back at all. Ruby wasn't entirely convinced that the murder in Dalhurst had anything to do with her or the Elementals, but she couldn't rule it out. Nothing was out of scope for Demas, and it was highly possible that Shaylah's assumptions, out of context as they may be, were in fact correct. *I should run this by Liam.*

Before she could try to think of some excuse to get away, Liam appeared at her side. "Hey, can I steal you away for a sec?" He asked, shoving a steaming cup of coffee in her face.

"Definitely!" She said a little too eagerly and followed him back into their room. She perched next to him on the mattress, her mouth twisting to whisper a quick thank you when he looked up at her. "What's up?"

"Nothing huge, just wanted to give you this." His hand extended to hold out a black, velvet box. "Thought it might cheer you up."

Ruby slowly opened the lid, her heart leapt into her throat as she peered inside to see a large Onyx stone intricately carved into a beveled hemisphere. The stone sat in the center of a silver frame that connected on either side to a delicate chain. She ran her fingers over the Onyx carefully, feeling every ridge as her lips parted into a smile. "Liam! This is amazing!" She yelped, "It looks just like it!"

She couldn't believe how closely it resembled the necklace she'd had made from her piece of the Sword of Enuma. It didn't have any of the power the original necklace possessed but just seeing it again made her feel stronger. It was a nice reminder of the unyielding energy she had pulled from the sword just a few weeks back. Her gaze met Liam's and she leaned in slowly to touch her lips to his,, grateful for his thoughtfulness. "Thank you," she smiled and unbuckled the chain lock. "I love it."

"I figured you might need a little reminder of how amazing you are."

She slipped on the necklace and straightened her back, feeling the weight of it press down on her shoulders. "So how do I look?" She teased and shifted her shoulders around to pose.

Liam's arm reached for her. He pushed a few loose hairs off her face, resting his other hand on her cheek. "Absolutely beautiful." He whispered.

"You think Shay might be onto something?"

"About how gorgeous you are? What did she say? I'll kill her!" He joked.

"No. About the Dalhurst murder. She mentioned something about the ash being connected to– "

"Demas?"

"Well, yeah." She bit the inside of her cheek, "I'm kinda shocked he hasn't come back yet."

"Rue, he might never come back. You're going to lose your mind thinking about it every day."

"So, what do you suggest? We just pretend everything is fine and peachy until he strikes?"

"*If* he strikes."

"When." Ruby huffed a trapped breath of air out,

"We both know he's coming back. You don't just leave behind a plan you've been working on for ages over one lost battle."

Liam's face beamed, a sly smile tugging the edges of his lips. "You do when you know you'll lose."

"Either way, I think we should ask the rest of the elders what they think."

"Oh, I see," his hand reached around her waist. "One elder isn't enough for you?"

"Trust me, you're plenty enough," she said just as his arm tightened and he swung her around to his lap.

Her breathing faltered and she could feel her legs begin to tingle, eager for his touch. She wrapped them around his waist, pressing her hips down to pin him to the mattress. Her right hand raised, she reached inside of herself, pooling her powers into a concentrated ball of energy. The palm of her hand flicked slightly as she shot a gust of wind toward the door, slamming it closed on command. Liam's full lips turned at the corners into a sly smile, the same smile that drove her mad with wanting. There was nothing else in that moment that mattered more to her than the man in her bed. The man that she would follow to the end of time if she could.

Liam's hands traveled from her waist to the now loosely tied belt of her robe. She watched him with the hunger of a predator as he undid the ties and pulled the fabric off her shoulders. He dropped it on the floor in one swift motion and flipped them to lie down on the bed in another. Her legs still wrapped around him, she pulled him in, erasing any space between them.

Ruby would do anything for more mornings like this. Mornings without her twisted worries about the future. Without thoughts of Elementals or AetherBorns and the responsibility she carried for their safety. Mornings without fear.

She wriggled under his weight, using her toes to push his joggers off. Surrendering to the freedom his body offered.

Freedom if only for the moment.

CHAPTER 2
A COUPLE ON A TRAIN

T he train rolled to a slow stop, sitting at the platform for a few seconds before opening its doors and letting the cool air rush into the car. Ruby breathed it in, grateful to have some relief from the heat of the crowded space. She leaned her shoulder against Liam, instantly regretting the puddle of sweat that formed where their bodies touched. It was a surprisingly hot fall day for Westerlake, and their ride to the Elemental Center was starting to feel unbearable. She was regretting not taking Liam up on the cab ride he had offered earlier as more people piled into the already full train car.

"It's a hundred degrees in here," she sighed and rearranged her purse to sit in her lap.

Liam's hand wrapped around her, pulling her closer to him seemingly oblivious to the blazing heat. Being a

Fire Elemental was proving to be especially useful in this situation and Ruby wished she could tap into even the smallest amount of the comfort he held at that moment. "It's just a few more stops," He said, wiping a bead of sweat off her forehead. "Next time, we're not doing the train."

"I get it, you were right." Ruby rolled her eyes, "You know, you're worse than Shay sometimes."

"Speaking of Shay, have you told her about school yet?"

"Not yet. Waiting for the right moment." She frowned, "She was really excited about starting the semester together. I just didn't have it in me to break the news."

"Rue, if you're planning on taking the year off, you should probably tell her. Doesn't it start next week?"

"Ugh, I know. She's just so eager about it. She keeps asking me about my classes and if I get to spend more time in the studio this year."

"And you're sure you don't want to go back?"

She thought about his question briefly. After everything that had happened during the summer, the idea of going back to school should get her excited. Instead, her life before the Elementals was a constant reminder of the person she could never be again. The normalcy that would never return as long as she stayed an AetherBorn, as long as she stayed with Liam. She wanted to tell him all of it. Every doubt she had about choosing to become their leader, their so-called queen. Confide in him her every fear. "Positive." Was all she could utter on the over-packed train. Not just because there was only so much she could discuss about this life of theirs in public but because admitting the uncertainty might make it seem like she wasn't sure of what they had together, and their relationship was the only thing she could never doubt. "Never been more sure of anything in my life."

"Afraid you can't handle the workload?" He teased.

"If I can handle your massive ego, I can handle anything." She joked back, elbowing him in the ribs. "It's just not who I am right now. Maybe I'll rethink it later, but who knows. It's like–" She paused to choose the next sentence carefully, "The photographs were what I needed to escape. To build some kind of world that was more than what I had."

"And now?"

"Now I think I need quite the opposite. With the center and the AetherBorns, I have enough around to keep me pretty busy for a while. Besides, we still don't know if Demas is coming back. For all we know, he could be out there right now, doing God knows what with Lord knows whom."

"But we don't know that," His squeezed hers in assurance, "All we know is that he hasn't shown his face yet and who knows? Maybe he never will. Maybe he's fine just hanging out with his family forever."

"He hates his family."

"Everyone hates their family sometimes, Rue. They're still family."

"That's exactly what I'm afraid of."

The train bucked from side to side, almost knocking her purse off her knees. Ruby's hand reached for the Onyx stone, forgetting for a moment that it was just a placebo. She knew having the sword back together made it a much more useful object to possess but the underlying worry about it still resonated in her. They had taken every precaution now that they knew what Demas was capable of, guarding it behind symbols of protection that were sure to detract his thieving hands. Ruby even checked on it herself a few times each day, both physically and by connecting to the bond she shared with it. Just to be on the safe side. Still, she craved its power after the Onyx stone was no longer tied around her neck. After she channeled the energy of the deities in the Aether Plane, her connection to the sword intensified. It was as though it became a part of her. Not some foreign object she controlled but a piece of her very body. A limb, really. Without it in her hands, she felt as though someone had sliced a part of her away.

Liam turned to face her, tuning into her discomfort and sneaking a kiss on her cheek. As much as Ruby's powers grew, his own did as well; and there were times where she was certain he could read her every thought. An impossible situation for a girl still trying to keep some mystery in a relationship.

"You know what we need?" He asked, shining a perfect row of teeth her way, "A quiet night alone with some pizza and a few of those horrible movies you make me watch."

"Yeah, good luck getting Shay's ass off the couch and away from the news!"

They giggled at each other, attracting attention from a grey-haired woman across from them. The whoosh of the train passing through the tunnel muted their laughter and Ruby noticed her smiling at them. Taking pleasure in their young love. It was strange to her that with everything they'd been through– all the torture and death they had endured– that they could still be happy. If only for a brief second, she saw them through that woman's eyes. A couple on a train with not a care in the world.

CHAPTER 3
TWISTED ARMY OF DOOM

Ruby's hair reflected the blue glow of the lamps as she walked down the center's hallway. When they finally arrived, she rushed to the cafeteria to gulp down what seemed like an entire barrel of water. She felt as though she had spent days lost in a desert.

Next time we're not doing the train. She repeated Liam's words and laughed.

This morning was no different than any other since the day they had welcomed the large lot of Aether-Borns into the center. The two of them arrived before the classes and training started, parting ways by the greenhouse so Liam could meet with the rest of the elders. In just a few short weeks, he had really grown into his role as the Fire House elder. She had thought it would take him more time to adjust, especially having to replace his aunt in her untimely death, but it seemed that he was determined to put the Elementals first. He barely even cringed anymore when someone mentioned Alice, and she often wondered if Elementals were just better at compartmentalizing their feelings.

Ruby was thankful for the times she had while he was in his meetings. Spending the hours walking the halls of the center to check in with everyone she encountered, Elemental and AetherBorn alike. Even though Liam had continuously reassured her that the transition went over smoothly, she needed to see it for herself.

She made a sharp right turn past the library and ducked down low enough that the top of her hair bun didn't leave a trace in the windows above the two metal doors, taking every precaution to make sure that Liam did not think that she was spying on him while he was inside. Creeping by in a crouch, she bolted upright when it was a safe enough distance away from the doors and almost bulldozed Nola to the ground.

"Shit!" the AetherBorn yelped and hit her back against the wall.

"Nola! I'm so sorry!" Ruby mouthed, somewhere between a yell and a whisper. "I'm an idiot."

"Hiding from Liam again then?" Nola reached down to help her off the ground. "You know you can just take the other hallway, right?"

"Yeah, but then I won't get the rush of almost killing

you every morning. It's better than coffee!" She laughed, grabbing Nola's hand and hoisting herself up to stand.

There were dozens of AetherBorns that had decided to take a chance on her after she had freed them from the hold Demas had on them. Most of them stayed in their quarters with the exception of food breaks, taking their time to get acclimated to life underground in the center but a few others accepted their new lives with open arms and inquisitive minds. Nola was one of the first to come out of her shell, making sure to introduce herself and her mother to Ruby the first chance she got. She was fearless and it was one of the qualities that made Ruby connect to her instantly. She reminded her of Shay in a way, the same fire boiled in her, making her say things without having to have a filter. If it wasn't for her very short, platinum bleached hair and black eyes, Ruby would have sworn her new AetherBorn friend was just Shay wearing a different outfit.

"Yeah, okay. If it wasn't for your little boy toy, I'd be sure you were hitting on me."

"More like actually hitting you, Nola." She laughed, noticing the slight figure behind the AetherBorns shoulders. "Hi, Beatrice! Almost didn't notice you there with your daughter always in the way."

Unlike Nola, her mother was a quiet and polite individual. When they first arrived at the center, Ruby was not even aware that Nola was here with a relative until they were introduced. She wondered how much of Beatrice's shyness could be attributed to having spent most of her life with Demas. She couldn't even imagine what that life could have been like. Spending your days with a monster that convinced you to give everything up to follow him. Worse, to bear him a child just to help his evil plan.

In her weeks making the rounds each morning, Ruby's heart nearly broke from some of the stories that were shared with her. They had opened the center doors to dozens of AetherBorns, all of whom were either coerced or physically forced into following Demas. When she first started getting to know them, she had a hard time accepting that anyone could believe his lies enough to join his twisted army of doom. Her own grandmother had chosen to end her life instead of being with him. But after hearing some of their tales she began to understand their choice more. When Ruby found out that she was an AetherBorn, she had Liam and the other Elementals to help her understand her powers and who she was to become. Being surrounded by others like you, being promised a family, would be a hard thing to turn down. And she had to admit that Demas could be very convincing when he wanted to be. Enough to persuade these women to give up their individuality for his cause. To live in some perverted version of a cult, multiplying his numbers with lies and calculated pregnancies. The thought of letting him touch her made Ruby sick.

Beatrice was one of the women Demas had impregnated, Nola being the outcome of that union. The AetherBorn had often referred to a few of the other offspring as her sisters but Ruby couldn't imagine that they had any bond between them that true sisters might have. The only thing that tied them together was their hatred for the man who had fathered them. In a way, Ruby could say she shared that same connection with every AetherBorn in the center.

"Morning, Ruby." Beatrice peeked her head from behind her daughters' broad shoulder. "How are you feeling today?"

"Pretty great! Excited to get the day going. I was thinking of maybe getting some training in today with Nola, you can come join us if you'd like." She nudged Nola's arm enough to make her tumble.

"Oh, you girls have fun. I promised Zag that I'd help him out in the greenhouse today."

"And she doesn't want to see me pummel you." Nola added with a smirk.

Ruby laughed before saying her goodbyes and moving along down the hallway. She had a feeling that it would be quite some time before the AetherBorns joined any of them in training. Not that she could blame them, they had likely had their share of fighting to last a lifetime. At least Nola was always up for a good practice run. It was hard for Ruby to be comfortable enough with new people to develop true friendships but something about Nola made her feel safe and at peace.

She thought more about her new friend as she made her way through the center, stopping occasionally to chat with passersby. Despite weeks having passed, Ruby still had a hard time believing how many people called the center their home now. A home she built by sheer hope alone.

The blue light danced lazily on the walls as she took each step, admiring the sound of friendly chatter in every room around her. Maybe Liam was right, and Demas had chosen his own family over his obsession with the Elementals. If this is what family was, she would select it above all else. Ruby picked up her pace and walked back to the library, suddenly thinking that her and Demas had more in common than either of them would like to admit.

CHAPTER 4

HIS WRATH IS THAT MUCH
GREATER

"Do we all agree the murder in Dalhurst is not something to worry about?" Elena asked, swirling the last of the champagne in her glass. Today's elder meeting was running long, and one look told Ruby that the mayor was ready to end it.

"We don't all agree on that Elena," Harvey thumped a fist on the table in defiance, but the weakness of his shaky hand left something to be desired. "The ash around the body is concerning."

"It could be a clue." Myriam chirped.

"Or it could be nothing," The mayor continued, "Besides, a clue of what exactly? We don't even know who this poor boy was. They won't divulge his name on the news. I feel we're jumping to conclusions out of fear."

Ruby had listened to them argue about this all

morning and every time she thought they reached a consensus and were going to let it go, someone flipped their opinion, igniting the debate once again. "What do you think?" She turned to Liam who was particularly quiet this meeting.

"Me?" His eyebrows rose like he had been called to the front of the class, "I don't think it's anything to worry about yet. But we shouldn't rule it out either."

"So, it could be something or it could be nothing? That's helpful." She didn't mean for her tone to come out dismissive, but Ruby was annoyed with his lack of support. She didn't care whose side he was on, just that he would pick a side to begin with.

"I'm sorry. I'm simply saying that while it may look like nothing, we can't rule out the fact that it could be Elemental. We've already made the mistake of disregarding signs before with…"

He didn't have to finish the sentence for Ruby to know exactly what he was referring to. The signs they had received from Demas that they chose to ignore. Signs of his presence in the center, his powers that were beyond anything that they had encountered before. Signs that could have helped prevent so much heartache and death. Alice's death.

Liam saw her expression fill with pain and reached for her hand under the table. She was reluctant to accept it, fearful to show any weakness or favoritism in her position, but eventually her fingers laced his and squeezed. "Maybe we could just keep watching more closely for now." He added, slipping back into the neutral ground that infuriated her.

"And if it is Demas? What do we do then?" Cyril's cold eyes cut through his words until each letter crumbled on the ground beneath them. "How do we protect our people? Not sure if anyone noticed but we have quite a few more now to worry about."

"The AetherBorns can take care of themselves." She offered through clenched teeth.

"I'm not saying that they can't, just that if it is him again, there is a chance he might come after them. Demas is not the forgiving type."

"I'm the one he can't forgive. If he's coming back for anyone, it's for me."

"And the rest of the Elementals," Cyril added. "If I'm not mistaken, we're the reason he's here in the first place. To kill us for what our ancestors did to his lover."

"Incredibly foolish for a deity, if you ask me." Elena noted, sliding the now empty champagne flute across the table. "One dumb royal kid made a bad move centuries ago and he's willing to punish every house for it."

"The kid was Air House, Elena. *Your* House. And the bad move you're talking about is murder. The murder of someone he loved and the mother of his child. How would you react to that?" Her hands clenched into fists under the table, and she could feel the tips of her fingers tingle as black fog started to seep out of them.

"Careful, Ruby. It almost sounds like you agree with him."

"I don't agree with any of it," she said, quickly shaking off the fog. "I'm just saying that he's had all this time to let it go but instead he's channeled it into some twisted version of a war, a justice only he can dish out. He loved and he lost, being a deity only means his wrath is that much greater than the rest of ours."

The room fell silent for a few brief moments while the elders took in her point of view. She had hoped they could understand that if the murder was somehow his doing, if he was really back, there could be no plan for his return. He was angry enough to level the entire planet if he wanted to. Especially if he wasn't returning alone. A thought Ruby tried incredibly hard to erase from her mind for now.

Liam shifted in his seat, drawing attention to himself and diverting the elders' glares. "So, do we know if Demas would have some connection to ash of any kind? Or fire even?"

"All we've seen so far is his connection to shadow," she answered, relieved for the change to a more pragmatic subject matter. "I haven't seen anything either here or in the Aether Plane that would imply he can control fire."

"You can control all the Elemental powers. Is it possible he can too?"

"Not at all." Harvey answered for her, "Ruby is an AetherBorn. Made of all the Houses. That's what allows her to channel all of our powers. Demas could only control the powers of his own rights. From everything I've read on Tartarus, his strength lies in the darkness which would explain his connection to the shadows of our planet."

"Do you think it's possible I can harness some of those powers?" She asked.

"Of course. You're in his lineage so I think it's safe to assume that. Though I haven't seen anything to imply that an AetherBorn was able to do so before."

"But there haven't been any AetherBorns that have answered the sword calling in quite some time." Myriam offered, "So anything is possible."

"Or any that pulled the Aether Plane outward." Liam added, "In fact, until you Rue, no one at this table even knew that the plane existed. I'm willing to bet that if there are any unknown powers out there, you're the only one that can bring them out."

He flashed her a smile that was supposed to give her strength, like his pride was somehow a catalyst for her own inner peace. Instead, all she felt was more pressure. She didn't want to be different. Being different brought attention, and she was having a hard enough time sticking to the shadows as it was. "Let's just handle one thing at a time here. We'll cross that bridge if we ever get to it."

"Sure. But how cool would that be! If you could tap into the powers of a deity? You would literally be the strongest person on the planet!"

"Liam," she said, shooting a sideways glance that told him he needed to stop speaking.

His brow furrowed but he let it go. "So, do we think we can all agree to see how the rest of this case in Dalhurst unfolds but not jump to conclusions just yet?" Liam's eyes glossed over the table, waiting for someone to interject but when the rest of the elders stayed silent, he raised himself to stand in relief. "Good! Now we can go eat!"

Ruby watched them shuffle out of the room, starting to make her way to the door where she was sure Liam was already waiting on her when a hand grazed her shoulder. She turned around to find Cyril standing behind her, his wolf's smile filling half of his face in a menacing certainty.

"Do you think we can chat real quick?" He asked, gesturing back to the table.

Her head darted between him and the door, looking for any excuse not to accept his request. To this day she had trouble trusting him entirely, even after he fought by her side in Lakeside. She was also getting quite hungry and her stomach was singing like it was auditioning for reality television. Still, Cyril was an elder and she owed him the respect that position was due. Even if she did want to deck him right in the nose every time he spoke.

"Sure," she said hesitantly and followed him back into the library, "Let's talk."

CHAPTER 5
FORGIVE ME

Cyril's face was caught somewhere between a smirk and a frown and no matter how much she tried to read him; she couldn't quite get a grip on why he needed to speak with her. Ruby wanted to trust him. Having this aching feeling in her gut every time she was near him made it difficult for her to remain neutral, and if she could just push that feeling away, the elder meetings would go much smoother. But something about him never sat right with her. People didn't change, at least not the core of them and in his core, Cyril was the same person that blindly held control over the Fire and Earth Elementals for all those years. The same person that killed her boyfriend without any remorse. She couldn't imagine how someone like that could be anything but a villain.

She rested on the edge of the seat, waiting for him to

say something, ready to run out of the room as soon as this conversation was over. "So, what did you want to talk about?" She finally said when there was no sign of him starting the exchange.

"The Dalhurst murder, I wanted to speak to you about what you really thought of it."

Of course, she thought. The bastard couldn't fathom that she might have actually meant every word she said before.

"I think I made it pretty clear what I think of it." She uttered bluntly.

"You really don't believe we have anything to worry about there?"

"Why don't you tell me why you're worried. You seem to be pretty adamant that it wasn't just a coincidence."

"I'm worried because it was a body surrounded by ash. That can't be coincidental."

"It's just ash, Cyril."

"Nothing is just anything anymore."

Ruby turned the words over in her mind, trying to make sense of them. "What do you mean?"

"Well, the sword thefts were just thefts at first. Then they were–" He paused and looked her over, "Catastrophic."

That was a light way of putting it. The thefts of the sword pieces brought Demas out of hiding. A devil they never knew existed until it was too late. Someone who had been sulking around with nothing but time on his hands, plotting their demise. If she could just trust Cyril, they could have a real discussion about this. "This isn't the same." She said instead.

"Are you sure about that? Sure, enough to risk lives on it?"

"We're not risking any lives. Don't be melodramatic please. We're just not jumping to conclusions. The last thing we need is mass chaos in the center right now. Especially with the AetherBorns still adjusting."

"How is that taking shape by the way?"

"It's fine."

"Most of them don't leave the center. Not even to walk around the block."

"And?"

"And they're scared, Rue."

Her eyes turned feral and the heat of fire rose between her fingers, sparks of it burning into the marble of the table. "It's Ruby." She hissed from between clenched teeth. "No one calls me Rue unless they're family."

"Sorry," he cringed, quickly realizing his mistake, "I just thought since Jake and you–"

"Jake and I have been friends since we were kids. He's family. You are an elder, and it is best that we keep things strictly professional between us."

"Professional enough that you might actually forgive me for what happened before the treaty?" He asked, his eyes piercing through the armor she was trying hard to build.

"I *have* forgiven you."

"We both know that's not true, Ruby." He blurted, placing an unnecessary emphasis on her name. "We can't have a conversation without you discarding my ideas to the side like leftovers."

He wasn't wrong, even Liam had asked her to soften her approach when it came to him. She wasn't sure he'd feel the same way if she had told him what Cyril did. Although knowing Liam, he would find a way to be diplomatic about it, always trying to see the best in people. "I am not discarding anything. I'm simply saying that there is a different dynamic in the center, and I would prefer it if we didn't make everyone panic based on our own fears."

"So, you admit there's something to fear?"

"Please don't twist my words, Cyril." She said, "There is always something to fear. Until we rid ourselves of Demas or live long enough without his presence, we will never be truly unafraid. And even then, who knows? But right now, that murder in Dalhurst is just a coincidence. A sad and torturous coincidence that led to a young boy's death but nothing more than that. We can't go jumping to conclusions every time someone on the news has a story. Demas has no reason to kill humans and we need to keep that in mind. If you were hoping otherwise, then you're better off swapping conspiracy theories with Shay."

"She is quite good with those, isn't she?"

The tone in his voice was almost endearing and Ruby wondered if he had grown fond of her best friend. After all, Jake was still dating her, and she was sure that Cyril had met the woman his son was involved with. In fact, she wouldn't put it past him to run a background check on her.

"Yeah, she's a little detective in her own right I suppose."

"Maybe–" Cyril started to say and froze.

"What?"

"Nothing. It's probably not something you're interested in."

"What is it, Cyril? If you want honesty from me, you'll need to learn to return the favor."

"I was thinking maybe we could all sit down for dinner some time. The four of you, and me and Rhea. It might be nice to spend some time outside of this center. I'm sure Shaylah would appreciate the gesture."

Was he out of his mind? There was nothing she wanted to do less than spend time with him outside of her obligation to the Elementals. She wanted to knock his teeth out just for suggesting it.

"I did say you wouldn't be interested," He sneered, and her blood ran cold at his smile.

"Actually," she surprised herself with the words, "It might be fun."

What the hell, Ruby? She cursed in her head. *What is wrong with you?*

She pushed the thought out of her mind. She knew very well what was wrong with her and the best way for her to get over this innate hatred of him was to force it. She was never great at following directions until it was shoved down her throat. Maybe in this case, if she did the shoving, her brain would actually start to see him in a different light. Besides, if she was right and Cyril really hadn't changed one bit she would need to prove it to everyone else in the elder seats. This could be her way of finally getting rid of him for good.

"I'll talk to Liam and Jake and let you know. But looking forward to it!" She lied and walked to the door before he could say any more. At least she managed to get out before she burned him to a crisp. A big win before lunch time.

LIAM WAS CROUCHED on the floor outside of the library, playing a game on his phone, when she emerged. His green eyes peered up at her, melting away every negative thought that flooded her body just seconds ago. "What was that about?" He asked.

"Wait 'till you hear this!" She exclaimed, genuinely

excited to tell him about the conversation, "But let's eat first. I'm starving!"

"You're always starving." He teased.

"Come on! Less sass and more food! I have to train this afternoon!"

Ruby snaked her arm through his and dragged him down the hall towards the cafeteria. For the first time all morning, she wasn't thinking about murders or Demas. All she had on her mind was a meatball sandwich and some mild flirting with her boyfriend.

She was so entranced in her own thoughts that she didn't even notice Jake rounding the corner in front of them.

"Not even a hello?" He yelled out, making her dig her heels into the ground to look at him.

"Oh my God! Hi! I'm just so hungry I can't even see straight!" She laughed.

"That or you're completely brainwashed by this one," he nodded in Liam's direction and rolled his eyes. Liam pretended not to hear, choosing to take the high ground which made her smile with admiration. At least one of them was acting like an adult.

"Why don't you join us for lunch?" She asked even though she already knew the answer.

"Sorry, can't."

"Let me guess, you have somewhere you're supposed to be."

"Not really. Just not hungry," he added, his feet backing up to get away from them.

"Next time, then?"

"Yeah. Sure, whatever." He yelled back and rushed down the hall.

Liam grimaced, tightening his grip around her arm. "You know, one of these days I'm going to pummel that kid into the ground."

"Come on, he's not that bad."

"Not that bad? He's acting like a spoiled brat who got his favorite toy taken away."

"I'm sorry, am I the 'toy' in this equation?" Her eyebrows arched and she raised a threatening fist in his direction.

"That's not what I meant. But there really is no one else I'd rather play with." He smirked.

Ruby rolled her eyes and pulled him behind her. "Alright, let's go! I am literally about to chew my own arm off over here!"

She skipped in the direction of the cafeteria, dragging an annoyed Liam behind her. Whatever Jake's problem was; it would have to wait for another day.

CHAPTER 6
MANIFEST A DRAGON

Leah's arms stretched over her head, barely moving while she ripped cracks in the concrete ceiling. A few more pulls and she would tumble half of the city block on their heads.

She didn't.

Her eyes twinkled and she smiled, reaching her hands to either side instead. Her powers intensified and, still smiling, she manipulated the fast-growing vines on either side of the room. They flew at Ruby's arms and legs, gaining speed and thickening as they reached her.

Ruby swatted at the vine on her right but was too late, the second vine Leah pulled was faster than her. Its ragged grasp looped around her arm and pinned her in place while a third vine did the same to her mid-section. She shook and kicked, desperately trying to get free. It was useless. She was tired, thirsty and hungry. She raised her one free hand in defeat and breathed out in relief when Leah lowered her hands and the vines loosened their grip on her, scurrying back to the plants they had grown from.

They had been training for over an hour and sweat was pooling in every crevice of Ruby's body. She pulled off her soaked tee and tossed it on the floor before grabbing a few bottles of water for her and Leah.

"How are you not exhausted?" she asked, studying Leah's calm breathing. Her short, red hair was barely wet and if not for her flushed cheeks, Ruby would never be able to tell that they had battled just minutes prior. "I actually want to pass out right now."

"I don't know," Leah noted, slouching on the floor next to her, "Maybe I didn't push that hard today."

"Are you kidding? You kicked my ass!"

Leah's humble demeanor was almost infuriating. Unlike her brother, she never bothered to gloat about the strength of her powers despite the fact that she was likely the most capable Earth Elemental in the center. No matter how many times she tried, Ruby was not able to knock her down. Each shot she threw in her direction seemed to ricochet off Leah like a speck of dust. She was intrinsically in tune with her abilities and Ruby had often wondered how much more the girl had up her sleeve that she might not be using in training. "Have you been practicing on your own or something?"

"Not really. I guess kind of, but not like on purpose

or anything." Leah smiled, her freckled cheeks getting rounder than usual. "Remember that dog outside the pawn shop?"

"The one that barks nonstop?"

"Yeah. Cujo."

"You know that's not his name, right?"

"I know. But it's fitting." She laughed at her own terrible joke. "Anyway, the other day he was going nuts at something across the street and I think I talked to him."

"You what?"

"Talked to him. Like not out loud but I thought about having a conversation with him and, well, I kind of did."

Ruby was shocked. The ability to communicate with animals was one of the powers Earth Elementals were known to possess but no one in the center has been able to tap into them yet. The elders themselves could only tap into the emotions of larger animals and even then, they required to pull energy from large pieces of emerald to do so. For anyone to actually communicate with another species would be miraculous.

"How did that work exactly?" she asked, curious about the exchange. "How did you understand it?"

"It was super weird actually. It wasn't like we were talking, at least not in words. But I could feel his thoughts or something. I can't really explain it. He was pretty pissed, but I asked him to calm down and he did. Crazy, right?"

"Leah, this is huge! Did you tell Zag yet?"

"God no! Knowing him, he'll be out there all day and night trying to chat with a squirrel or something. You know how competitive he can be."

Ruby burst out laughing at the image of Zag chasing squirrels in the park. "Was he always like that?"

"Not really. If you can believe it, he used to be a pretty relaxed dude. At least when we were younger. He still is I guess but when it comes to powers, it's like he has to be the best or something." She took a gulp of water, letting some of it escape from her mouth and down her chin. "After our parents were in that car accident, he kind of had to step up. With me, I mean. The resistance didn't help either. It's like he wanted to prove himself to everyone."

"That must have been really tough. I can't imagine growing up with it being just you two." Ruby's heart broke a little thinking of her two friends being alone in the world. It was people like them that made the center such an important place, a place where everyone could find family even if it wasn't by blood.

"That's the whole thing though, it wasn't just us two. We had so many people around us that took us in. Hell, Myriam and Harvey basically raised me. But for him, it was like when they died, he thought he needed to be mom and dad. Always taking care of me." She rolled her eyes, "Even when I didn't need him. Which is like a lot of the time."

"I'm sure he means well."

"He does. Just like, get a grip, dude. You know?" She giggled, "I'm not a kid anymore. Haven't been in a while."

"I get it. Liam is kind of like that with me. It's annoying."

"Well, at least you can kick his ass if he gets to be too much. Zag would pout for days if I gave him a beat down."

"You know; at some point you'll have to show him how much your powers have grown. It might make him relax a little, knowing you can take care of yourself."

"Yeah, I know. I will. Just not yet."

"You gonna wait until you can manifest a dragon or something?" Ruby laughed.

Leah's small hand formed a fist and she pummeled her shoulder with a few hard knocks. "If I do, I'm sending it straight for you, smartass!"

Her breathing was almost back to normal and she was feeling the strength return to her body. Ever since she came back from the Aether Plane, Ruby had been able to recharge her energy much quicker no matter how many hours she spent training. She was about to get back to her attempts at out-maneuvering Leah when the door creaked halfway open and a pile of red, knotted hair peeked through.

"You guys decent?" Zag's voice boomed on the other side.

"No. We're just about to have a pillow fight. Idiot." Leah hissed, waving her brother in. "What the heck do you think we do here?"

"I don't know, girl. Whatever it is, it has to wait. I got something that Ruby needs to hear."

Leah's face scrunched and she looked over to Ruby with a half-smile. "Told you. Always a drama queen!"

CHAPTER 7
REN BARBA'S BROTHER

"**W**hat is so freakin' urgent that it can't wait?" Leah exclaimed, her arms up in the air.

"Dude, it's important. And why aren't you in class anyway? Didn't your semester start this week?"

"I don't have class on Tuesdays. But also, like, none of your business."

"So, what's going on, Zag?" Ruby interrupted hoping to put an end to their sibling rivalry. "What did you find?"

Zag pushed a few dreads of hair from his eyes and walked closer to her. His beard was even more scruffy than it had been a few days ago which made her wonder if he had even bothered to shower in that time. The circles under his hazel eyes told her that he hadn't slept much, and it immediately made her nervous about the news he was about to share.

"I know you told the elders not to worry too much about the Dalhurst murder but I of course, had to do at least some research on it."

"Of course," she sighed. Being overly involved was one of Zag's most frustrating qualities, though she could not deny that if there was anything to be dug up, he was the man for the job. "And?"

"And the kid that got killed is Ren Barba's brother!"

A silence coated the room as Ruby and Leah exchanged glances. "You going to tell us who that is, bro?" Leah asked after a few uncomfortable seconds.

"Right. Sorry, got ahead of myself." He scratched at the hairs in his beard before continuing, "So you know how we have the center here in Westerlake?"

"Uh huh," Ruby said, trying desperately to connect the dots of his story.

"Well, because of the sword and just how this all worked out, the elders and a lot of the Elementals gravitated to our city."

"And?" she asked.

"So basically, we have all the cool kids here. But that doesn't mean there aren't other Elementals all over the world. That just wouldn't make sense."

Ruby thought about his comment for a minute. She felt almost foolish now because it hadn't occurred to her that there were more of them out there. She was so preoccupied with the center that she didn't even bother with other cities. The guilt of it instantly consumed her. This was what they should have been discussing at the elder meetings, what she should have been pushing towards. This entire time she was obsessing over the AetherBorns and the Elementals in Westerlake, never once thinking about everyone else outside of the safe cocoon she created. What if they also needed help and she was too obsessed with her own problems to offer it?

She felt a hand squeeze her arm and turned around to see Leah's warm smile beaming in her direction. "They're all fine," she whispered as if in response to Ruby's inner turmoil.

"And this Ren is... what exactly?"

"An Air Elemental and a pretty strong one at that. It took me a while to connect him to the murder though. But obvi I'm magic so–" He laughed in the self-assured way that she was certain made Leah's blood boil. "I kept digging into the case, and when I found out that it was his brother that got killed, I had to come tell you!"

"So, the kid was an Elemental? But that means that–" she stopped, afraid to utter the words out loud.

"There's a pretty good chance it wasn't just a random case," Leah spewed the words for her, "Demas could be back."

Her world shattered into a million pieces. Each one cutting her soul into shreds as she made sense of what she just heard. There was no doubt in her mind that if an Elemental was dead, Demas was somehow behind this. Cyril was right and she had refused to listen to him. She wasn't sure what she hated more, him for calling it or herself for letting her distaste for him rule her decisions. If Demas was truly back, there was no telling what he might do next. They needed to act fast, she would be damned if she let her doubt get in the way again. "Do we know anything else about this kid?"

"Not from what I could find. But I have a pretty good idea of who might."

"Who?"

"We should probably talk to Elena."

"Elena? Why? She's not even from Dalhurst."

Zag snatched Leah's bottle of water and took a giant gulp from it before meeting her eyes again. "Because Ren and his brother were her nephews." He said and fell silent, letting the information sink in.

If Demas was behind this, he was making a point. One Ruby would not let go unpunished.

CHAPTER 8
BET MY LIFE ON IT

Her eyes ran over the swirling lines of the Artex ceiling in their living room. Shaylah was finally out for the evening on a date with Jake, and they had the apartment to themselves. On any other night, she would be full of energy and excitement to have this time alone with Liam, but tonight, her mind was miles away from the cozy warmth of the living room couch and his arm around her shoulders.

"Is it possible we finally found a movie that even *you* don't like?" Liam asked, pointing to the blaring television. The movie had been on for almost an hour now and she had no idea what it was about.

"Sorry, I'm just really out of it right now."

"Because of Dalhurst?" he asked.

"That obvious, huh?"

"I'm a Fire Elemental, remember? I'm pretty good at

reading people's emotions," he nudged a thumb under her chin, "But yours are all over your face so it's not even that hard."

"I know, I'm sorry. It's just that I really thought that this was over with. After last time, I don't think I can face him again."

"Demas?"

"Yeah. It's too much, Liam. I want to hide in this apartment forever. I don't want to deal with it all anymore." She crossed her legs and faced him, "And what's worse is that Cyril was right. I should have listened. I'm such an idiot."

"Hey! You're not an idiot," Liam grabbed her legs and pulled her closer to him, "Look, I don't know what's going on with you and Cyril but whether he was right or not does not change anything. The Dalhurst kid is still dead. So, what if you thought Cyril was wrong?"

"Because what if I do the same thing next time? What if something happens and he gives me advice that could help, and I just walk away because I hate him? I can't let my feelings get in the way anymore. I'm supposed to be impartial."

"That's not fair, Rue. You can't be a robot all of a sudden. Just because you're an AetherBorn, doesn't mean that you can push all your feelings away."

"Actually, that's exactly what I should be doing."

"So what? You can't get upset anymore? Can't be

happy? Can't love?" He asked, placing emphasis on the last sentence.

"I don't know. I just have to be–" she looked for the word to describe her thoughts, "More. I have to be more."

"Why is this affecting you this much? I mean, we always knew that there was a chance Demas might come back. Last I remember, we agreed to take it one step at a time if that happened."

"Because, it isn't just that he's back, Liam! Don't you see it? He's back for a hot minute and he's already killed an Elemental. And not just any Elemental. One of Elena's nephews. He's trying to send a message."

"So, he's a prick. Okay."

"Then there's the ash."

"What about the ash?"

"It has to mean something. I know it in my gut. I can't explain it, but I know it's not just a coincidence. I've never seen him wield fire so if it's not from him, then who?"

"You think he didn't come back alone?"

"I'm willing to bet my life on it. If he came back to finish this, he's got help."

"Is it possible that he has another AetherBorn army somewhere?"

Her legs wrapped around his waist and she leaned in closer, afraid to say the words out loud. "I think it might be so much worse this time."

"The other deities?" he asked, watching her nod in agreement. "But why would they even come back? I thought he told you that they've been locked away somewhere in the Aether Plane, living their best life and whatever. Why would they bother coming here?"

"I don't know. Maybe he convinced them to help somehow, to join his pathetic attempt at revenge."

"Didn't they banish him to the underworld? After the whole thing with Eirene?"

"After she was killed by an Elemental and their daughter was lost to Demas forever, you mean?"

"Yeah. After that."

"Who knows. We don't even know if any of that is true. When I was in the Aether Plane, I could feel them you know. It was like they wanted to get out. Besides," she sighed, "disagreements or not, they're still a family of sorts. And they've had how many centuries together? Wouldn't you help your family no matter what?"

"I'm not an all-powerful being from another realm, Rue. I don't think we can compare them to us. At least not when it comes to feelings."

"Well, maybe he threatened them or something. Or they're just bored. Either way, I don't think Demas would go around murdering Elementals without a plan in place. I just want to be prepared this time."

"So, what do you think we should do?" His cupped his palms behind her neck, heating up the tense muscles in it. "And I'm asking as your boyfriend here, not an elder." He added with a teasing smirk.

"I think we need to go to the source. I want to go to Dalhurst as soon as we can. And I want to talk to Ren about his brother. But right now," she said, reaching for the remote and shoving a fistful of popcorn into her mouth, "I want to watch this movie. I am personally insulted that you would think there is actually a movie out there that I wouldn't like." She turned around and nestled her back into his broad chest. "So, what's this about?"

"Killer ants."

"Sounds like an Oscar nominee to me!" She exclaimed, feeling his pecks vibrate from laughter. "Let's get this show on the road! No more shop talk for the rest of the night. And that's an order!"

CHAPTER 9
HARD TO GET TO KNOW

S haylah's mouth grimaced as she swirled a spoon in her coffee cup in an attempt to fish out a loose strand of hair. "Well that's hella gross," she noted when she was finally able to free the hair from its watery grave. "I need a trim. Like asap."

"How can you even tell?" Ruby laughed, flicking a full strand of curls of her friend's hair.

"Very funny. You know, not all of us were blessed with perfectly behaving hair. Get off your high horse, lady!" Shaylah's laugh boomed through the apartment, "But like seriously, how long is boy toy gonna shower? I need to get this tamed. Jake is almost here and I'm definitely not rolling out of the house like this." Her arm waved over her own body as if to point out some disastrous specimen.

"You look fine," Ruby noted, "maybe lose the slippers though."

Within seconds, her friend was already kicking off the fur lined slippers and tossing them into the living room. The first one made a proper descent by the couch but the second faltered mid-air, landing squarely in the center of the coffee table.

"Much better," she laughed and took a large sip of her coffee. "So where are you guys off to today?"

"Don't know. I think we're meeting his mom for lunch or something," Shaylah offered, rolling her eyes dramatically. "Supes boring, huh?"

"I'm sure it won't be that bad. You like his mom, right?"

"Rhea? Yeah, she's pretty awesome! But it's never just us anymore. Maybe I'm overreacting."

"I get it. If Liam's parents were around all the time, I'd probably lose it." She said, lowering her voice to make sure it didn't make its way to the bathroom.

"You're so lucky they ran off to Italy again! I would kill for Jake's parents to go away for a bit. Like even a weekend would be super!" Shaylah exclaimed in excitement at the thought, "How's Liam doing with it though?"

"Them leaving? He's okay, I think. It's weird you know; they don't act like parents around him. More like business partners or something. I don't get it."

"Probably 'cause your folks are cool as shit. Not everyone is that lucky."

Ruby took in her friend's comment, realizing how much truth it held. With the center being her top priority, she had been neglecting spending time with them. Not because she didn't want to see them but to keep them at arm's length from her life there. Neither of them had powers to protect themselves with if something happened. As much as she loved having them close by, she wished they had never made the move into the city. They thought they were helping her somehow; but instead, they just caused more worry. No matter how many times she hinted for them to move back, they refused to budge. At least she knew where her stubbornness came from.

"So, how are things with Jake other than that?" She asked, switching the subject before the worry over her parents took its toll on the rest of her day.

"They're okay, I guess. He's kind of hard to get to know."

"You've known him for years though."

"I know. I mean like *that*. He keeps to himself a lot and I know there's stuff he's not sharing with me. It's annoying sometimes. Maybe it's some Elemental thing?"

"Probably," Ruby said, "I'm sure he's stressed like the rest of us. Just give it time, he'll come around."

She hated lying to her friend but telling her how she really felt would not help right now. Jake hadn't kept anything to himself in the entire time she'd known him. In fact, he was more likely to overshare than hold back. If he was keeping things from Shaylah, there must be a reason for it. Ever since they started dating, their interactions seemed strange to Ruby. It was as if they were putting on a show, faking a relationship as opposed to being in one. She knew how her friend felt about Jake but whether those feelings were returned was still a mystery to her. One thing she was sure about, if he hurt Shaylah, he'd have to answer to her.

Ruby was still mid-thought when a wet hand gripped her shoulder, causing her to whip around defiantly to find Liam standing next to her. Dressed only in a towel, beads of water ran from his messy, wet hair and down his chest. The droplets curved over each heavy muscle and she found herself looking away quickly before her flushed cheeks could give away every thought.

"About time, Romeo!" Shaylah chuckled, giving her an insinuating wink. "Some of us need to get in there too you know."

"Sorry, Shay. I lost track of time, I guess." He slid unto the chair next to her, "Is there more coffee?"

"We don't have maid service here," Shaylah remarked, sarcasm coating every word. "This ain't your mom's house."

Liam slid off the chair and before her friend could block him, shook his wet hair all over her. The water ricocheted off her face and bounced in Ruby's direction, covering her in cold wetness. Her eyes met Shaylah's, offering a nod as they grabbed two apples from the fruit bowl and chucked them at Liam, hitting him square in the chest. Laughter exploded from all three of them as they watched the apples roll away on the floor. They were still catching their breath when the front door creaked open.

"Am I interrupting something?" Jake asked, his eyes moving from Shaylah to Ruby and finally settling on Liam's half naked body.

"Just Liam being a jackass as usual," Shaylah remarked. Her hand reached for Jake's, but he pulled away, tucking his fists into his blazer pockets.

Ruby pretended not to notice the hurt on her friend's face. When she got a chance, she'd have to make sure to tell Jake exactly what she thought about his behavior. She hated how he treated Liam, but he could handle himself. Shaylah had nothing to do with it, and she deserved someone who would treat her like royalty.

"So, you ready to go?" he asked, standing with his back to Liam like he was putting up a defensive wall between them.

"Almost, just need to fix my hair real quick. Fish, can you help with the back?"

Ruby followed her friend into the bathroom watching as Jake made his way into the living room without acknowledging Liam's presence. Her gaze caught Liam's, offering a shake of her head to let him know that she was on his side. She would make sure to speak with Jake this week. If they were going to stay in each other's lives, he needed to stop acting like a child.

"Oh! Did you hear they found out who that kid is in Dalhurst?" Shaylah asked, her eyes sparkling with excitement.

"Yeah. About that—"

"Don't tell me, I was right, it's some Elemental bull, isn't it?"

"Is it ever not?" Ruby laughed and continued to whip strands of auburn hair around as she filled her friend in on Zag's discovery.

CHAPTER 10
UNPREPARED

"I'm going to Dalhurst." Ruby stated before any of the elders had a chance to start the meeting. She was nervous about letting them know what her plan was and blurting out the words seemed like a good idea at the time. As she looked around the table at their confused faces, she wished she was more diplomatic in her delivery. *Here we go,* she thought while waiting for the objections to come in. She was surprised that Elena was the first to speak up.

"Why exactly?" she asked, pushing herself up slightly until her backside was barely grazing the chair. "What do you hope to find there?"

"In all honesty, I don't have the slightest idea. But it has to be better than sitting here and doing nothing."

"And what could you possibly do there? What if this

is some scheme to lure you out there?" Her words made Liam tense, and he rearranged himself in his chair so that his shoulder was flush against her own.

"That's what I'm counting on. If this was Demas, then it wasn't just some random show of power. It was calculated, everything he does is." She locked eyes with the mayor, "He was your nephew, Elena. Your family. I'm not going to hide here and let him have his way with Elementals just because they're not protected by the center. If Demas is in Dalhurst, no one there is safe."

"That is exactly my point. If he did this to lure you away from the center, how do we know he's not going to attack while you're gone?"

"He won't."

"And you know this how?" Cyril asked.

"Because it's too easy. He did this to get my attention, he knew that once we connected the dots to who the victim was, I wouldn't stay away. If he wants me in Dalhurst, I will be there. I need to play along. Besides, we can't very well know how to find him from here. We know he was in Dalhurst and there might be clues to where he might be hiding out and if—" she paused.

"If what?"

"If he's alone. We need to find out if he's alone or not, so we know how to attack."

Elena's face twitched, "you're planning to attack him?"

"I don't think we have much of a choice. He won't stop until *we* stop him."

"And if you're right and he didn't come back on his own?"

"Then we figure it out. I just know that staying here and waiting is not going to do us any good," Ruby took a deep breath in and let it out slowly as if to calm her own nerves. "Look, I don't want to put anyone in danger. And Elena, I understand if you'd prefer not to go considering what happened."

"What happened is exactly why I will be going with you. If you are truly set on seeking this monster out, I will help you. I haven't seen Ren since he was a child, I'm sure he needs family right now. But we are not going unprepared."

She was surprised Elena decided to join. When they broke the news to her about the victim in Dalhurst being her nephew, she wanted nothing to do with the situation. From what Ruby could gather, Elena and her brother had a falling out when she was chosen to take the elder seat, and he had moved his family across the country to get away from her. She was forbidden to contact her nephews, and they grew up with very little knowledge of their elder aunt. Ruby wondered what the reunion might look like and almost resented the idea that she would be caught in the middle of yet another Elemental family drama. Her run-ins with Liam's parents painted a good visual of what it could entail, and she was not looking forward to it in the least.

"Okay. Thank you," she said, trying to sound as grateful as she could, "Liam suggested we take the knights, at least some of them."

"We will join as well," Cyril added.

"We?"

"Jake and I. He is still a knight, is he not?"

She could sense Liam tense as his mouth barely parted. "Great."

"Yes, of course," Ruby nodded, remembering the conversation she had with Cyril before they stormed the old library in Lakeside. "I thought you might prefer if he stayed behind. To keep him safe that is."

"I think he'll be plenty safe there," his gaze shifted to her and she understood immediately what he meant. He had asked her before to keep his son out of harm's way, and she gave her word to do so. Leaving Jake behind meant she couldn't watch out for him. It seemed that despite her lack of trust in Cyril, he would not entrust his safety to anyone but her. The added pressure was not something she wanted but she had to admit that he wasn't wrong, if they had to fight, Jake's best chance was by her side. "And I'm certain that Elena could use some support in this time of need," he added, giving the mayor a tight squeeze of the hand.

Elena's eyes met Cyril's and she whispered a quiet *thank you* in return. The years of ruling together side by side had formed a bond between them that Ruby could not begin to understand. She used to think it was romantic somehow, that there was a love there that neither of them could act on, but this was something much more than that. Whatever her own feelings were when it came to Cyril, she had no doubt that he would die for Elena and that the mayor would do the same for him. If she could only get them to extend that bond to the rest of the elders.

"Well, if it's going to be a jolly field trip, Zag and Leah should tag along. Earth House should have a representative in tow." Myriam chimed in to break the silence. "And they would hate to be left behind."

"At least Zag would," Harvey added with a chuckle.

"I'd like to bring Nola as well," Ruby added. "It would be good to have another AetherBorn with us."

"Are you sure she'll be up to it?" Liam asked, finally able to get a word in.

"Nola? Are you kidding? She's probably readier than the rest of us! Between her and Leah, we have some serious fighting power on our side."

"And you. Obviously," he smiled.

"Right. Which reminds me, I need to go see Zag before we leave. I have an idea for the sword that might make it a little less–" she fished for the right word, "glaring."

"So, it's settled then? We're going to Dalhurst?" Cyril asked.

She moved her gaze over each one of them, making sure there was unanimity in their eyes. When she was confident that they agreed with her decision to go, she pushed herself off the chair to signal the end of the meeting. "We leave in the morning." She said and turned to the door, walking out before any of them had a chance to back out.

CHAPTER 11

WE MIGHT DIE

The stones in the hilt of the sword reflected the overhead lights, teasing their rainbow reflections across the walls as Ruby turned the blade in her hands.

"You wanna do what?" Zag asked in disbelief.

"Make it smaller. I want to make it more portable."

"Okay," he sang, dragging out the word. "But, like, how exactly?"

She sat the sword down on the metal table and the clang of iron on steel echoed down the hall like wind passing through a seashell. "I was hoping you could help with that," she finally said.

"Huh? How?"

"Remember when we broke the sword apart? Into the five pieces?"

"Girl, you gone bats or something? I wasn't there."

"I know," she sighed, "pay attention please. The way we did it the first time was to have me take all of the sword power into myself, until it was nothing but metal. Metal I melted until it snapped into parts. Then, I used the earth as a conduit to redirect the energy back into the sword pieces."

"Like a super creeptastic recycling program?"

"Kind of. I guess."

"So, you're thinking, what? That you could heat the sword enough to melt it?"

"Yeah. But then what?"

"I can create a mold for you to melt the sword into again. Like a dagger or something?"

"Could you? Without compromising it as a weapon?"

"Well, yeah! But why can't you just ask Harry or Myriam?"

She bit her lower lip, eyes to the ground before looking back up to meet his gaze. "I'm afraid they won't like the idea of tampering with the sword again. I doubt any of the elders would. But honestly, this thing is huge and way too obvious to carry around with me."

"And you need it with you? In Dalhurst?"

"Maybe not but it would be good to have the upper hand just in case. And I'm not really comfortable leaving it unattended."

"Can I ask you something?" He said, waiting until she nodded in agreement before continuing. "How come you didn't just keep the swords power? Why put it back?"

"It wasn't mine to keep. I don't even know how to explain it really. It's like I can borrow it, same as I can lend it but never for good."

"A symbiosis."

"Yeah." *Exactly like that,* "So can you do it?"

Zag rolled up his hemp shirt sleeves and saluted her. "I can do anything, madam! This is no biggie. I'll have the molds ready in an hour, just need to run some numbers first. Make sure we don't mess this baby up!" He ran a finger over the blade carefully, "Hey, so you nervous at all?"

"About what?"

"Dalhurst."

"Because of Demas? Because he might be there? With other deities? Because we might die?" She counted off the questions until she had no breath left to speak. The fire in her fingers danced and she could see embers begin to jump off her. Her eyes met his, trying to appear calm but she knew the sweat on her brow was betraying her.

"Girl, calm down. I meant because you'll be meeting new Elementals again."

"Oh."

"Yeah, you're tense, dude. Maybe get some rest before you blow up like this in Dalhurst. Ren is pretty chill but from what I know, Elijah gets his back up pretty quickly."

"How long have you known them?" She asked, trying to change the subject away from her own shortcomings.

"Ren and E? I don't even know. Like forever. I met Ren way back in the day, in school. Didn't even know he was an Air until he told me he was ditching town with his folks. He hated the elders, you know, wanted to help with the resistance. I think his parents found out and got him the hell outta here before Elena could make sense of it. I feel bad for her. I don't think she ever knew why her family left her out of the blue like that."

"Parents do weird things to be with their kids," she said, thinking of her own parents and everything they had done to stay close to her.

"I guess. It's too bad too. She would have gotten along great with Sam, he was just as gung-ho about power as–" Zag stopped himself, his hazel eyes filling with water at the memory of Ren's murdered brother. "Well, don't much matter now, does it?"

Ruby wanted to reach over and hug him, to offer some form of encouragement but thought better of it. Zag was much too prideful to accept condolences or to admit any sort of defeat and to let her hold him, help him in any way, would mean that he could not do something on his own. *Stupid, stupid man,* she yelled in her head but kept her hands in her pockets and her words buried in her throat. The best way to help Zag right now was to keep him talking.

"So, Ren and Elijah. How long have they been a thing?"

"I think literally since Ren came out. We didn't keep in touch that much, but I kept tabs on social. It'll be pretty sweet to meet him in person!"

"Not stalking him from afar like a complete psycho, you mean?" She laughed.

"Shut up," he chuckled and pumped his fist on her shoulder.

"Come on, don't lie. Do you know their blood types? Where they live?" Ruby continued to tease, "shoe size?"

"Girl, you best be trippin'. Queen or not, you better stop that nonsense, or you can give cosmetic surgery to the blade on your own."

She lifted her arms in defeat, still smiling. "Okay, okay. You made your point. I'm going to go get a snack and come back later."

Running a finger over the Onyx in the swords handle, Ruby pulled a small bit of power from the sword before letting it go. She let it swirl in her body, encircling every molecule and blood muscle until she could feel her heart race a few beats faster. Being near the sword was better than any energy drink she'd ever had, and she was hoping that what her and Zag were about to do would not take that away. "I'm really glad you're coming with us." She added as she started to make her way out.

"Me too," Zag said in almost a whisper. "And Ruby?" He called after her as she was halfway out the door.

"Yeah?"

"I do know where they live, for security purposes, of course." He winked, sending her laughing down the hallway.

CHAPTER 12
PRETTY EASY

The line rang several times before her dad finally picked up the phone. This was her fourth attempt at trying to reach them, and she was both relieved and nervous when his gruff voice huffed on the other end. "Dad?"

"Oh, hey, Rue! What's going on?"

"Nothing. I tried to call you a bunch of times already. Where were you guys?"

"Just out in the yard. Your mom got some new blueberry bushes, and well, you know how that goes."

She had no idea how it would go; Ruby had never planted anything in her life and with her powers she could grow whatever she wanted without even so much as a ray of sunshine.

"Right. So, mom's home too?"

"Yes, of course. Rue, are you sure everything is alright?"

"Everything is fine. I just wanted to let you know that I'll be out of town for a bit."

"Out of town? What for? With Liam?"

She took a deep breath in, steadying herself to start the conversation. "Yeah. And the elders. And some other people."

"I think I should get your mom on the phone too; this doesn't sound like nothing."

"No, dad, wait! It's really not a huge deal. We're just going to Dalhurst for a few days."

"Dalhurst? That's pretty damn far. Isn't that where that kid died; the one that's been all over the news?"

"Yeah. It's why we're going actually. That kid was an Elemental. Elena's nephew actually. We think it might be–" she sighed heavily, "Demas."

"Demas? That's it, I'm getting your mom. Layla!"

She could hear her dad's slippers shuffle across the floor as he quickly made his way to the backyard. "Dad. Seriously. Please don't put mom on. We're leaving tomorrow and I just wanted you to know so you wouldn't worry."

"If you don't want us to worry then you won't go."

"That's not really an option, dad."

"And why not? Why is it that you're the one that always has to be dragged into this?"

"You know why."

"AetherBorn or not, it shouldn't just be you in danger all the time. Why are you chasing this Demas person anyhow? Just leave it alone and keep yourself safe," he whispered almost in a prayer. "I need to call Liam and speak with him. This is ridiculous."

"Dad! Liam doesn't control me. And I have obligations. To the Elementals, to the other AetherBorns, even to grandma! I am not arguing over this. We leave tomorrow, I will text to check in. That's the end of it."

"What about school, Rue? Your classes?"

Time to rip the Band-Aid off.

"So, that's the other thing. I'm kind of going to take some time off from school. Just until things settle down at the center."

"Oh, for goodness sake! Layla! Where are you?" He yelled on the other end.

"Jesus, dad, calm down. It's not forever."

"Not forever? This whole AetherBorn thing is ruining your life, Rue! How can you not see that?"

"What would be better? If I pretended I was never chosen for this? If I walked away from the sword? Like grandma? Maybe killed myself like her too?" She was fuming. She didn't expect this to go over smoothly, but she was hoping for at least a bit more support. Her dad had always been in her corner, and she was starting to feel hurt that he wasn't this time when it truly mattered. "Would that be a better life; do you think?"

"That's not what I'm saying at all. I just don't understand how, in such a short time, my daughter could go from having the time of her life and studying to be a photographer to some Queen of the Elementals. It's like something out of a movie, Rue."

"I know. It's a lot. I get it. But dad, this is my life now. I was chosen for this. More than that, I want it! I am really good at this and I want to see it through. I can help so many people! And I can't leave Liam, you know that too."

"He's just a boy, darling."

"Would you leave mom?"

Silence on the other end of the phone told her she had won this round. They could circle back to it another time but her best bet at the moment was to get off the phone before her mom joined to go for round two. "Hey dad?"

"Yeah, kiddo?"

"If this was a movie, who do you think would play me?" she smiled, hoping he could hear it on his end.

"Someone very foolish." Her dad laughed. "Great! Your mom just walked in; I'm going to put her on."

"Sorry! Gotta go! I'll talk to her later, okay?" Ruby yelled into the phone, hanging it up before her mother even said a word. She rubbed her forehead with the back of her palm, drenching it in the sweat that had pooled in the crease of her brows. Going back and forth with her dad left her more drained than any physical fight she might have coming her way.

Kicking Demas' ass is starting to look pretty easy right about now.

CHAPTER 13

A HAPPY ENDING OF SORTS

Ruby trailed behind Liam through the crowd, trying her best to keep up with him until she was almost sprinting down the train platform. She had regretted not taking a backpack with her as soon as they got their tickets and was now dragging the spinning wheels of her carry-on across the poorly tiled floor like a dead body. *I'm going to kill Shay,* she thought, cursing her friend's name for making her doubt how many outfit changes she would need for the trip.

She dodged a group of teenagers in a quick spin of her heels, but her suitcase was not quite as agile, groaning at the turn and knocking her to the side until she almost fell onto the train tracks.

"Goddammit!" She cursed at her luggage, kicking it lightly with her foot.

"You okay?" Liam yelled out, well ahead of her at this point.

"I'm fine! Be right there!"

The sign in front of her hummed with electricity, whispering the information to the crowd below it. Dalhurst, Platform 9. Her lips formed the words as she drudged closer to the center of the platform where the rest of the group was already settled on the benches. Tossing her suitcase on top of Liam's, she crumpled onto the concrete bench and let her arms slouch at her sides. It was another hour or so until the train came through, and she relished the thought of relaxing for a few moments.

Ruby tossed her head back to rest on the bench rail and looked up at the glass domed ceiling of the station. The morning light poured in heavy beams, brightening sections of the station and its occupants like a prison flood light. She felt trapped. In this station. In her role. In her entire life, really. Sitting in a prison of her own creation, waiting for a runaway train that might never show. Maybe her dad was right, and she should just walk away before it was too late.

"Shouldn't be long now," Nola elbowed her in the side, shooting a jolt of energy through her. "You might want to be less of a bore on the train, though. It's a long enough ride as it is."

"Right. Sorry, just tired I guess." She straightened up and hugged her knees into her chest, her right hand lightly holding the bulge in her pant leg that disguised the dagger holster. Zag's mold worked like magic and despite its new size, she could feel the immense power of the sword in the dagger she now carried. *Small but deadly,* he told her when he handed her their creation. He wasn't kidding, she could do a lot more damage with this blade now that she could use it discreetly.

"Didn't sleep much?" Leah slid next to her on the bench, her eyebrows dancing while she pointed to Liam. "Long night, huh?"

"Maybe we should separate them for the rest of the trip? Make sure they get their beauty sleep." Nola laughed.

"You two are idiots," she scolded them and got up.

Ruby walked closer to the edge of the platform, her attention settling on the tracks below. Shifting her gaze across their metal and breathing deeply in and out. They seemed to go on forever, all the way out of the station and to the end of the world. She wished she could hop over the edge and follow them to wherever they might lead. Another life maybe. One where she didn't have to wake up in cold sweats worrying about someone else's safety. A life that didn't include Demas or his beastly vengeance. Where she could spend her days worrying about classes and fighting with Liam about foolish little things like what to eat for dinner or who did the dishes last. A happy ending of sorts.

Her fingers traced around the scars on her arm, the

memory of them pushing its way from her stomach, to her throat. Choking her from the inside. She hated them. She hated them and the man who gave them to her. The demon who stood in the way of the life she so hopelessly craved. *The bastard. Filthy, disgusting prick.*

Heat caressed her veins, tingling to jump out and burn everything around her into ashes. The same ashes they found around Sam's body. The ashes she would make sure surrounded Demas when she finally dealt with him. The color in her fingers started to turn to a maddening, fiery red. She was burning, here in front of everyone, and she didn't care. She was over all of it. As the fire within her intensified, threatening to expose her, she felt a different heat wrap around her waist. Ruby leaned back as strong arms tightened themselves around her.

"I got you," Liam whispered into her ear from behind. His breath as quiet and as sweet as she remembered. "You're okay."

She let him rock her back and forth until the flames were nothing but small puffs of smoke, barely visible to anyone but them. They must have looked like two lovers on a trip. Rocking like fools to a non-existent song that played only for them. *Maybe we have no happy ending,* she thought and rested her head on his shoulder. *Maybe all we get is this.*

The blaring horn of the train coming into the station

intensified the rushing of passengers on the platform and as the tracks disappeared beneath its shadow, she closed her eyes. Whatever ending she was meant to have; she was glad it was with him.

CHAPTER 14

FIGHT

"Oh my God, what is that?" Nola chirped, gawking at Leah's full plate of food.

Ruby had joined them in the dining car a few hours after they left Westerlake in hopes of getting rid of the claustrophobic feeling circling her chest. The new surroundings did not do much to calm her, offering instead a dimly lit, Dineresque lunchroom packed to the brim with passengers. She scooted closer to Leah on the faux-leather bench seat in order to avoid the three kids running up and down the aisle. The space was only big enough to fit two rows of booths on either end, and every time one of the children ran through, they hit Ruby's elbow with a loud, unapologetic thud. She usually liked children but, in this case, she found herself wondering if she should dare stick her leg out on their next round.

"Lemon-pepper cod, mushroom lasagna, and a sugar free Jell-O." Leah answered with a tone resembling that of a butler from the movies. "What?" Her arms flailed up in question.

"Nothing," Nola's face scrunched, "looks like a hot mess, is all."

Leah's face was stern at first but moments later her mouth twirled upward, and a loud giggle filled the car. She scraped the fork across the top layer of the lasagna with a disturbed look, "It was literally the only three things that looked like actual food. I feel like I'm eating on the set of The Martian or something."

"I'm pretty sure they didn't have lasagna on Mars," Ruby teased, finishing the last bite of her chicken salad sandwich. "Why didn't you just get the pizza?"

"Oh, you know. When in Rome."

"Leah, what the hell does that even mean in this case?" Nola's voice pierced through the dining car.

"I'm just saying, it's on the menu for a reason. Geez. Are you always this hostile?"

Nola rolled her eyes and turned to stare out the window, her face holding the usual stern expression she wore when she wanted to tell someone off but thought better of it. "Keep pushing me and you'll find out."

"Okay, let's just calm down," Ruby said. "Save that for when we get to Dalhurst." She waited until the kids made another pass by them before grabbing her plate and sliding out of the booth. "I'm going to walk around, stretch my legs a little. You two behave, please?"

She didn't bother looking back to see if Leah and Nola had started speaking again, dumping her plate in the cleaning dock at the back and rushing into the next car. As she walked down the cramped hall of the train she wondered if Liam was still sleeping. When Leah came to get her earlier, he was out cold. In fact, if Ruby hadn't seen his chest move up and down occasionally, she would have been worried enough to check for breathing.

Her footsteps slowed the further she got from the noise of the dining car and she marched forward with a calm intensity, spying bits and pieces of life outside of the train windows as she passed them. Blurred, rapid shapes that came into view one second only to be gone the next. Walking down the train hallway, Ruby felt like she was walking through a memory, trying to grasp onto parts to puzzle it together but being too slow to make sense of the entire picture.

"You feeling trapped too?" A familiar voice rang from the right, and she turned around to see Jake reclining in the seat of his cabin, the door wide open for anyone to come in. His golden hair sparkled from the passing light of the world in the window behind him, making him look like a cat playing with its food. "Wanna keep me company?" He purred and patted the seat beside him.

Ruby shrugged her shoulders, walking into the cabin and positioning herself onto the seat across from him instead. No point giving him the wrong idea.

"It's really stuffy in here, huh?" She smiled, "I know we spend a lot of time underground at the center, but this is like, next level."

"Yeah, I know. I can't wait to get to Dalhurst."

Her face twisted at the name.

"I take it you're not?" Jake asked, picking up on it instantly.

"Just wish I knew what to expect."

He quieted for a moment, shifting his gaze to the door as if someone was going to walk in any minute. "Dad says Elena is pretty upset. She won't show it, of course. But still, she's devastated."

"I wish I could help her somehow. Make it all better. I mean, she hasn't seen them in how many years? I don't even know. And for such a dumb reason."

"It wasn't a dumb reason before. Even you were willing to give up everything for it." He watched her with the intensity of a well-trained sniper, and she knew immediately what he meant. When she was willing to give him up to save the Elementals.

"Regardless, family should stick together."

"Well, with that I actually agree," he smirked and reached into his blazer pocket. He pulled out a long vape pen that looked like a mix between a ballpoint pen and a rocket ship and brought it to his mouth, taking a deep inhale. The smoke that puffed from his lips filled the cabin until only his blue eyes were shining across from her. Two sapphires in a room full of smoke.

"You know you can get fined for smoking that crap in here, right?"

"I doubt that's our biggest problem right now." He said, gesturing at the bulge from the dagger in her pant leg.

Ruby rearranged her legs across the seat, instinctively wanting to be closer to the sword strapped to her. "You think we'll have to fight? At Dalhurst, I mean."

"I doubt it. If it really is Demas, we both know he's not that much of an idiot."

"So, you think he has something bigger planned?"

"Doesn't he always?"

"And what does Cyril think?" she asked, genuinely interested in the answer.

"I'm not sure. I think he thinks that he has to help you no matter what. To make up for things, I guess. I told him it won't be that easy!" He laughed, "Once you have your mind made up, it'd take a miracle for someone to change it."

She tipped her head to rest on her own shoulder, sighing deeply. "I'm trying, you know. To get over it."

"I know. I still don't know why you're so upset with it though. My dad, I mean. It wasn't just him who had the sword before. Elena was there too. And a lot of others."

"It's hard to explain," she lied, knowing full well why it was Cyril she despised so deeply. "Maybe because I've known him so long."

"You've known me just as long. Do you hate me too?"

"Don't be an idiot. You're my best friend. There's no changing that." Ruby shoved the sole of her shoe forward, nudging his knee playfully. "Besides, if I hated either of you, you think I'd let you tag along at a time like this?"

"So, I take it you *do* think we'll have to fight?"

Her brain swirled the words around, swooshing each syllable over the cells until she made sense of it. She reached for the vape pen, ripping it from Jake's hand before he could object. "I honestly have no idea." She said, breathing in the chocolaty flavored smoke into her lungs. The smoke coated her throat in an intoxicating grip, holding her until she was ready to let it go. She watched the smoke that left her mouth rise around them and felt nothing but emptiness.

"You can get fined for that you know," Jake teased, waving his hand around to flush out the remnants of the smoke.

"Let 'em try," she said smiling and handed him back the machine.

Her gaze turned to the window as Jake blew out

another cloud of smoke that lingered for a moment before disappearing. She watched the landscape outside roll by, her eyes unable to focus on any distinct detail. *Let them try,* she repeated to herself. *Let them all just try.*

CHAPTER 15
DALHURST

Dalhurst Central Inn was a sight to take in. Ruby's mouth salivated as soon as they unloaded the cab and stepped foot in the front foyer. The grand entrance was even larger than her old theories classroom and that place was big enough to fit almost five hundred students. Everything in the hotel screamed luxury and she felt awkward chugging through it in her ripped jeans and rock tee. The hotel customers were no different, dressed to the nines and covered in jewels and designer labels. She caught sight of herself in one of the oversized, golden mirrors near the check in counter and immediately regretted not waiting outside while Elena checked them in. With her hair a braided mess, she was an ugly duckling in a sea of swans. The rest of their party was as wide jawed as her, and she was relieved that out of all of them, only Elena and Cyril looked like that belonged here. Even Jake paled in color as he slouched on a leather two-seater in the inn's grand reception room.

When Elena finally signed the paperwork and handed her their room keys, she almost sprinted to the elevator, eager to hide from the inquisitive and judging eyes of the staff.

Their rooms were spread randomly across the hotel's fourteen floors with hers and Liam's being on the top floor, facing the pond. *Of course, there's a freaking pond here. What would we do without a pond?* She thought and clunked her bag on the king-sized bed, pushing one of the ten pillows unto the floor in the process.

She star-fished herself diagonally on the bed, letting out a tired and defeated sigh.

"Well, this place is something, huh?" Liam asked and hopped on the bed next to her. "I bet we can both stretch out and still not touch each other in this bed. It's huge!"

Ruby pounced on top of him so quickly that he had no time to react. She pushed her bag off the bed with her leg and pinned his hands to his side. "Wanna bet?" she teased, wiggling her eyebrows.

Without answering, Liam spun them around until her back was flat on the mattress and she was pinned beneath him. She wriggled her hips to get out from under him, but it was no use and the motion only made his grin wider. When she realized that there was no escape, she stopped and stared into his playful green eyes, leveling her body to face him straight on. "Oh, don't stop trying to get away," he hummed, "I was enjoying that."

"Maybe I'll just fall asleep right here. Just to piss you off then," she teased.

His lips reached for her neck and she arched her back at the touch. He kissed the indent between her neck and shoulder so slowly, running the tip of his tongue across the arch, that she couldn't help but let a low moan escape her lips. He moved down her arm, kissing every inch of exposed skin until his lips were on the inside of her palm. "Still sleepy?" He whispered into her hand. His other hand lifted her shirt slightly as he moved on to gently kiss the top of her abdomen, slipping dangerously lower to where the zipper of her jeans was screaming to get undone. "How about now?"

Ruby waited until he let go of her other arm and twisted her legs tightly around him. Using all of the strength in her legs she twisted him to the side, landing herself back on top to straddle him.

"Let's see how you like being teased," she said in a commanding tone and ripped the snaps of his plaid shirt to expose his upper body. Her hands traced the contours of his muscled chest. Suddenly her breath grew shallow and she felt like someone had sucked the air out of the room. She reached a hand to the mattress to steady herself, hoping to steady the waves in her stomach.

THE ROOM SPUN AROUND HER, *darkening with every passing turn. The darker it became, the more she was able to see the black fog surrounding her. It coated the room and seeped into each crevice until everything was pitch black under its weight. Ruby trained her gaze on the wall across from her, the painting that was above the bed just seconds ago was gone, replaced now by fog that oozed down in thick drips.* Not fog, plasma, *she thought, and looked down to the bed at Liam.*

A gasp escaped her lips as she realized that he was no longer beneath her. She was completely alone. She turned her head around the room, studying it with disbelief but the more she looked, the faster she realized that she was no longer in the inn. This was somewhere else entirely. Somewhere darker.

The intricately wallpapered hotel walls were replaced by rocky edges. Black plasma oozed down their sides all the way to the fogged floor below. There was no light, no windows. Just a solid darkness that made Ruby feel like she was about to be swallowed whole by it.

"Aether Plane?" she whispered, knowing full well that there was no one there to answer her.

Something was wrong here. This wasn't the Aether Plane. It may have had some of the same characteristics, the same plasma and shadows, but there was a darkness here that was unlike anything she had felt before. A consuming power that trickled from the ceiling, to the walls, all the way into her bones.

Ruby reached down to her pant leg. Nothing. The sword wasn't there. Dagger! Whatever. *If the dagger wasn't with her then this couldn't be real. She must be having a vision. But of what? And why now? Why this place?*

She threw her legs off the bed, splashing something beneath with her boots. When she was fully upright, she gathered the nerve to look down, afraid her vision had her planted in a pool of blood or something just as hideous. Her eyes slowly focused in the dark, looking below herself, then forward. There was no blood, no hideousness. Just water. Dark, still water stretched from her feet all the way to the door at the end of the room. She took one step forward, slowly and carefully. Even if this was a vision, there was no telling what would happen next. But her steps were solid, as solid as if she was walking on the ground.

I'm walking on water here and literally no one is around to see it! *She yelled in her head and rolled her eyes.*

Her steps quickened and she was at the door in moments, reaching a trembling hand for the handle and twisting it to open. The door creaked and swooshed the dark liquid beneath it as it slowly revealed the other side of the room.

Ruby's face fell, her lips widening and her eyes growing in size. The oozing rock walls stretched down a never-ending tunnel in front of her with a dark river running through it. She tried to make out where the tunnel ended but her attention drifted to a thudding sound to the left. Her head spun to a small boat rocking at the edge of the tunnel, its hull hitting the rocks of the wall. Beckoning her to take a journey.

"Rue! Rue, wake up!"

Ruby opened her eyes groggily, lifting herself off the bed slightly to look at Liam. His face was drenched in fear, and he was still shaking her even though she was very much awake.

"I'm good," she said and held her palm up to motion him to stop, "what happened?"

"You passed out. You were on top of me and then you just passed out. You've been out for ten minutes! I was about to call an ambulance!"

"It was just a vision. I'm okay." She sat up quickly but the spinning in her head had not quite receded yet, and she reached for a pillow to help balance her out. Liam moved fast, propping her up on two more pillows and handing her a glass of water from the bedside table.

"A random vision? Now? What did you see?" He asked.

Ruby took a giant gulp of water, swirling it in her mouth before swallowing. "I seriously don't even know."

CHAPTER 16
WITH ALL MY LOVE

The vision still lingered in Ruby's mind when they arrived in the back alley where Sam's body was found.

She followed closely behind Cyril, Jake and Liam with Zag, Leah and two knights a few feet back. Dominik and Silas crept behind them slowly, constantly checking their backs for a possible imposter. The two Fire brothers were the first to volunteer for the trip, leaving the remainder of the knighthood at the center in case of an attack. Ruby was glad to have them nearby. While the two looked like complete opposites of each other– Dominik the tall, brooding brother with sleeve tattoos while Silas was shorter and stockier, resembling a small refrigerator in his build– they had one thing in common; Ruby trusted them with her life.

The dimly lit, crawl space of the alleyway was so

narrow that they could only fit through single file, and even then, Ruby could touch each one of the brick walls if she stretched out her hands. She was happy they decided to split up, the place could not hold more than a few of them at one time. *It was smart to leave the body here. Hidden away from large crowds but still controlled enough if a quick escape was needed.* The thought made her even more convinced that Demas was behind it. *Clever bastard.*

When they managed to squeeze through about thirty feet between the two buildings, the alley gave way, opening its mouth to a gaping hole that reeked of street garbage. Ruby looked around the space, trying to figure out where they were now in relation to the main street they entered from. If she was right, they were sandwiched somewhere in the center of the block, in a courtyard of sorts. There were a few windows on the buildings that sat around the yard, but they had all either been blocked off or bricked over. She doubted anyone had used this space in the last few decades.

Ruby joined the group that was now huddled close to one of the walls where the body was found. They were pushing rocks around carefully, trying to uncover any small clues that might be helpful. Jake leaned down to pick up a garbage bag, eyeing it before tossing it to the side and hitting Liam square in the chest.

"Watch it!"

"Oh, sorry," Jake smirked, "didn't see you there."

"Are you serious right now?"

She hurried over, putting herself between the two of them. "You guys know that if there's anything to see here you won't find it like that, right?" She smiled, changing the subject, and was about to start coating the space in black fog when two figures appeared in the small entrance they had used to get in.

Ruby twisted on her feet and pulled her energy inward, landing in a crouch to face the entrance with her palms outstretched. The energy twisted from her and pushed its way from her hands, shooting towards the figures opposite them. It shaped and formed itself as it flew. Shifting from smoke to fog to plasma until it was nothing but a sharp mass barreling forward at an unthinkable speed.

The figure on the left lifted an arm in defence and a shield of thick ice formed in front of him just seconds before the plasma spear hit. The spear cut into the ice, shattering it into pieces before dropping to the ground. Shards of ice coated in plasma melted beneath the feet of the impostors. It looked like someone had chopped a dirty snowman into pieces.

"Well, that is definitely quite the hello!" the figure on the left exclaimed. As he moved toward her, she tried to make sense of his familiar dark hair and black eyes, something about him made her feel like they had met before. She quickly looked behind him to the other man he came with, her eyes drifting over his shaved hairline down to his light skinned sharp face. Before Ruby could realize who she was looking at, Zag pushed his way past her and ran to them.

"Ren! Elijah! Dudes!" He ran over, pulling them into a massive bear hug.

"Been a while, brother." Ren said trying to wiggle his way out of the embrace. His bald head ducked under Zag's arm and he was free in under a second, leaving Elijah trapped. Ren patted Zag's shoulder to let him know to ease up, and she was baffled by how quickly he obliged. The last time she asked Zag to do something, it took him weeks just to get started. He must have really liked these guys.

Elijah jumped at the chance and took a step forward and away from Zag as soon as he let him go. "And who are these lovely people?" He asked, his black eyes rolling over the group and landing on Ruby.

"Yeah, dudes, sorry! Let me introduce you guys." Zag shuffled over, naming each person one by one until her got to her, "and this is Ruby. Our little queen bee. Obvi." He motioned to her with a swirling hand and an over-exaggerated bow.

"Great to meet you!" Ren offered excitedly and elbowed Elijah who only managed to get out a quick nod of the head.

Ruby watched the pair interact and wondered how they managed to be so effortless together. Everything about Ren and Elijah pointed to them being a couple.

From the way they stood next to each other, always touching lightly in some way. Their playfulness with one another when they spoke. Even the way they looked complemented the other's appearance. Elijah's bronze skin and bushy dark hair was an intricate balance to Ren's paleness and piercing narrow eyes. It was as if they were formed to fit into a mold together, intertwined somehow until both bodies filled the space in their own way. She wondered if Liam and her had a similar outward appearance. After all, Elijah towered over Ren in the same way Liam did her but somehow, she doubted they looked as flawless. One glance back at Liam had her almost laughing as she watched him motion forward with his head, his eyes wide, beckoning her to snap out of her daydream and be social. *I guess we fit a different mold,* she thought and waved a hand. "You too!" she yelled back, looking at Liam again with a quiet thank you.

"Dudes, we are so glad you're here! You can show us around! What's the best place to chill out at night? Oh, how about dancing? Tell me everything!" Zag hopped around the couple like a puppy waiting to go for a walk.

"Can you cool it down on the man-crushing?" Leah interrupted, pulling her brother back by the scruff of his hemp shirt. "They literally just got here and we're not really here to socialize."

"It's not a problem at all. We'll be happy to show you all around later tonight," Elijah smiled, the first smile Ruby has seen on his face thus far. Her attempt to kill them earlier likely had something to do with that.

"Yes, that would be lovely gentleman. We should all meet tonight for some food and drinks. In the meantime, would you mind helping us look around?" Cyril noted to her relief. She was more than eager to get back to work. "Ruby here was just about to fog the place and see if anything pops up."

"Oh right!" Ren exclaimed, "I heard you can see symbols and stuff!"

"Not always," she admitted, "only when someone leaves them for me."

"You think someone would? Why?"

A memory of Cyril's safe room covered in symbols flashed before her. Demas left the symbols for her then and she missed their meaning, not realizing the danger they were truly in. By the time she'd figured it out, it was too late. If she had just paid more attention maybe Alice would still be alive. She wouldn't make that mistake again.

Ruby clenched her teeth. "If it's who I think it is, then he's toying with us. Using this as a way to drag us out here, like some sick game."

"You're telling me that Sam could have died because of some game?"

Her eyes widened as she looked over Ren's slumped body. She felt so foolish and embarrassed. She hadn't even thought about what this must be doing to him, to be in the same place his brother's body had been found.

First you try to kill them and now you're acting like an insensitive tool. Great first impression.

"I'm sorry. I didn't mean it that way. It's just I wouldn't put it past Demas to do something like this is all. I'm really sorry for your loss." She wanted to run over and wrap her arms around Ren for comfort but doubted her affection could help him in any way right then.

Elijah gripped his boyfriend's hand and squeezed it lightly before walking closer to her side of the courtyard, "Well, let's see if we got something then, shall we?"

She nodded. Relief coated her heart with a grateful sigh, letting her get back to what she was actually good at. Her eyes darkened, not quite the pitch black they were in the Aether Plane but a deeper, fogged shade than the brown they normally possessed She moved her hands from her sides, to her heart, then back down to her hips. As she started to push the fog away from her fingertips, readying herself to coat the small yard with her power something caught her eye. A piece of paper tucked behind one of the bricks in the wall opposite her. Ruby let go of her power immediately, her eyes lightening, and her hands returning to their usual clammy state.

Her steps quickened as she almost ran towards the wall.

"Rue! What's up?" Liam yelled behind her, but she

was already at the wall, clawing at the brick to pull it out.

"There's something here! Come help me!"

He rushed to her side, followed by the rest of the group on his heels. His hands were stronger than hers and it took him only a few seconds to wiggle to brick out. It had definitely been taken out before, there was no debris or cement to hold it in place, but it was carefully positioned so that it wouldn't look out of place compared to the rest of the wall.

Ruby reached a shaking hand into the brick-sized opening and pulled out the paper. An envelope sealed and hidden for her to find.

"Demas," she whispered as she turned the envelope over in her hands.

"Rue, we don't know that. It could be anything. Some kid playing around from when this place was still in use. Or a random note someone left behind. Don't jump to conclusions."

"It's for me. And it's from him."

"How can you be sure?"

"Because my name is on it." She said and lifted the envelope up to face him. The intricately scribbled words looked like they had been etched by an artist. Every letter was perfectly sized as if it was typed by a computer.

"To my dearest Ruby. With all my love. Demas."

CHAPTER 17

ONE MORE TIME

"Read me the note again," Liam urged when they were back in their room, "Maybe we missed something."

"We didn't miss anything."

"Please?" He tilted his head to the side and made a begging motion with his hands that made Ruby want to chuck a pillow at him. "Pretty please?"

"Ugh! Fine. Just stop whatever it is you're doing," she laughed and unfolded the note. "I don't see what you think you'll find here all of a sudden but here goes.

"*My darling Ruby.*

It's been some time and I cannot help but wonder how you've been getting on. I must admit, I truly hated how we last parted. Such gloom! But I am glad to know that we shall see each other soon and this time I'll make sure to make it a memorable event for you.

I do hope you enjoy the little gift I left for you, I thought it might pique your interest. He was a tad bit more of a whiner than expected, and I imagine even you would have found the silence when it was all done pleasurable. A most needed relief after hours of screaming. Like laying in bed after a hard day of work.

Here's hoping that this note finds you well.

We'll talk soon my little queen and don't forget, you chose this.

Best wishes,

Demas

PS. Please send my regards to Elena."

"WHAT A PIECE OF SHIT!" Liam yelled when she was done reading. His hands rolled into fists and before she could try to stop him, he ran one right through the lampshade on the bedside table causing it to topple to the carpet below.

"Liam! What the hell! Calm down."

"I'm sorry. I just don't understand how someone can be so vile. If he has a problem with us, then take it out on us. Why some innocent kid? And why make you the center of his psychotic obsession?"

"I think psychotic is the key word here. He's insane. Demas let his anger dictate who he became, now it's all he has. As far as he's concerned, every Elemental deserves a death like his Eirene. He's crazy. I just happen to be the first one in his lineage that stood up to him, he must hate that!"

"How did you even know to look there?"

"In the wall? Not sure, just caught my eye. I think he knew I'd look at the walls, after the symbols he left when he stole the sword pieces, the walls are the first place we'd check that no one else would. Makes sense to hide it there."

"Weird there were no symbols though."

She thought back to the emptiness she revealed after she dusted the courtyard in fog. The darkness just hovered in the air around them and dissipated as if it itself gave up on finding clues. "There's still that ash. Did you see how much of it there was all over the floor? Like someone swept a chimney in there."

"Yeah, I thought that was odd too. Just not sure how it relates to anything."

"It might not, but I think we should check with some of the Elementals here for anything they might know on the other deities. If the ash isn't from Demas, it might be from someone else that got out of the Room of Mirrors."

"So, you're convinced he had help?"

"I would if I was him. But it's just a hunch. Maybe we can ask Ren's family to help gather information from the Dalhurst Elementals. I'm sure that if we—"

"Rue, that's not a good idea." Liam stopped her

before she could finish the sentence, "I know you want to find Demas, but I doubt Ren's parents are in any condition to be helping right now. And besides, Elena hasn't even spoken to them since we came, it's probably not the best idea to push them together like that."

Her eyes started to pool. "I'm an asshole," she said, thinking about how insensitive she must have been this entire time. "Have you talked to her? Since we got here?"

"A bit. Not much. I think she was glad to stay back today but she did say she's coming out tonight. I think she really misses Ren."

"Speaking of, what's with Zag around those two?"

"Ah! The Bewitched you mean?"

Ruby let out a high-pitched laugh, slapping her palms on her thighs before falling over onto the bed in a giggle. "He really is quite into them, isn't he?"

"Zag has been wanting to find friends that get us outside of Westerlake for years. Those poor boys have no clue what they're stuck with now."

"Well, I think it's sweet. And if you're not careful, they'll snatch your best friend right out from under your nose," she bopped the tip of his nose with her finger.

Liam's hand reached over to her, using the belt buckle of her jeans to pull her closer as his other hand grabbed for the note and tossed it on the nightstand. "Oh, is that what you think, huh?" he purred as pulled her into his chest.

"I think I need to get ready for tonight unless you want to show up with this unwashed mess on your arm!" She howled in response and jumped away from him.

As Ruby walked past the nightstand, she quickly scooped up the note and folded it carefully into her pocket, blowing a kiss to Liam before she ducked into the bathroom. When she was certain the door was locked behind her, she sat down on the bathroom floor and unfolded the note. Her eyes narrowed as she whispered the words into the lonely air one more time.

"My darling Ruby. It's been some time..."

CHAPTER 18
LIVE DOWN A HEARTACHE

Ren wasn't kidding when he described Dalhurst as being a stereotypical surfer town. The walk along the beach front to the bar they were meeting at was a cacophony of shops, cafes and hangouts that tailored specifically to the scantily clad beach residents. Ruby felt overdressed in her t-shirt dress and platforms. The last time she put on a bathing suit was years ago, and she wasn't about to start sporting one now.

They passed a group of girls wearing brightly colored string bikinis and Ruby immediately felt like she disappeared in comparison. She glanced over at Liam to gauge his reaction, but he was more preoccupied with teasing Zag and seemed not to notice the posse of sirens next to him. Feeling foolish for checking in on him, she tried to avoid looking around for the rest of the walk and spent the time wandering over to the small shops to pick out knickknacks for Shaylah. Her best friend was quite upset about not being asked to come along; it took Ruby hours to convince her that it wasn't a vacation. Although she was quite certain that it wasn't her that Shaylah was eager to spend time with.

The Tiki bar they were meeting Ren and Elijah in was an over the top, loud, and dimly lit shack that was filled to the brim with locals from the beach. Ruby squeezed close to Liam as he led the way and continued to look back at Zag and Leah to make sure they weren't lost in the crowd. Not that Zag would have any trouble fitting in, this was exactly the type of joint Ruby could picture him spending all of his time in. It was no wonder he was so intrigued by Dalhurst, it fit his personality much better than Westerlake ever could.

When they finally managed to bounce through the sweat covered, globs of people, she could see that the rest of their party was already seated in a straw-roofed booth. Jake and Nola were laughing hysterically over something Elijah had said; and she felt awkward sliding in next to them, as though she was late to a performance and had to move people out of the way to get to her seat. Jake's eyes met hers, lingering for a moment before he caught a glimpse of Liam at her side and frowned.

"Well, look who finally decided to show up!" Nola yelled over the table, "We're two drinks in already.

Better catch up!" She raised her glass in the air and took a sip of whatever red concoction was filling the cup.

Ruby tried to deny her but the AetherBorn was already ordering another round for everyone who had just come in, and she knew there was no arguing with Nola when it came to having a good time. "Where are Ren and Elena?" She asked, leaning over the table.

"They're by the bar," Jake said and pointed in their direction, "Been there for a while now. My dad just went to see if they're making their way back a minute ago. Maybe your Fire bodyguard can lend him a hand." He let out a low cackle which she chose to ignore.

Ruby moved her slim body from side to side trying to see them over the bobbing heads in front of her. Spying on Ren was an easy task, his shaved head gleamed under the pot lights, and the black mesh shirt he wore stood out amongst the loose tanks and board shorts like a sore thumb. When she turned to Elijah, she realized the two of them were the only ones not dressed like the rest of the locals. Elijah's cuffed shirt and tie were something she'd be used to seeing in Cyril's office, not at a casual dinner by the beach.

"We don't come out here much," Elijah leaned over as if reading her thoughts, "Ren just thought it would be a nice change from Westerlake for all of you."

"Right. It is! I'm just not used to so many people."

"Of course. Jake filled me in a bit about your entire situation back home."

"Situation?"

"The AetherBorns," he whispered the word as if she might take offense to it, "and the center and such. Can't be easy."

"Well, it's no ocean waves and sunshine that's for sure. But we make it work. At least we're trying." She looked over toward Ren and Elena again, "How's it going? The meeting, I mean."

"Honestly, not that bad. A little awkward at first but for two people that haven't seen each other in years, they're getting along quite well." He shifted his gaze from her to the bar, "Elena is kind of great, actually."

"You sound surprised?"

"I am a little. Ren's parents always painted her out to be some kind of monster but now that we've met her–"

Ruby thought back to when she first met the mayor. She could see why Ren's parents would not want her around their children, especially since they were against the elders and their iron fist ruling. But she had to admit that Elena has come a long way since then, adapting to the peace treaty almost immediately. Ruby couldn't help but wonder if her eagerness to unite the houses stemmed from wanting to reconnect with her family. Whatever the reason was, she couldn't help but agree with Elijah now. *This* Elena *was* in fact kind of great. "Now that you've met her, you see how awesome she is." She completed his sentence.

"Bingo. And Ren is almost giddy with having her here so that makes her good in my books." He flashed a protective grin that reminded her of Liam.

"So, how did you two meet?"

"Me and Ren? Oh geez. It was so long ago I barely even remember. Some bar I think." He shifted in his seat, raking his bronze fingers through his thick head of hair as he tried to recall the story. "It was probably a place like this one. Or some other crazy scene. Ren was big on the party scene back then."

"And you?"

"I was getting over an ex. You know us Waters, we don't live down a heartache easy."

She glanced at Jake who was having a discussion with Liam opposite them and hoped that his heartache was long gone by now. "Ren helped? With the heart I mean?"

"Oh yes! He was a wonderful distraction! So wonderful I stuck around for another ten years," he winked and laughed.

"Ten years? Holy crap. That's like–"

"About the lifetime of some small animals actually."

Her drink nudged itself deep in her throat when she laughed, causing her to cough up the entire contents of her mouth onto the table. She was still trying to wipe it down when she heard a pop at the other side of the table followed by a rackety clang on the floor. She looked up to see Liam's stool lying sideways, his hair a mess and his eyes on fire. His fists were shaking, and he would not take his gaze off Jake, who was smirking in front of him. Liam's fists raised and she could see smoke begin to trail off him. She needed to calm him down right away or everyone in this bar was in trouble.

"Guys! What is going on?" she ran over to him, placing her own hands over his fists and lowering them to his side. "What just happened?" Her eyes darted to Nola who only shrugged implying she was just as in the dark as the rest of them.

"Nothing. We were just chatting, and your boy here couldn't take a joke, I guess." Jake said, a self-assured smile on his face.

"What joke?"

"It was nothing." Liam answered quickly.

"Clearly, it wasn't nothing. You almost blew up in here."

"Rue, it was nothing. Not important. He's a dumb kid that needs to watch his mouth but that's all it was."

"Who are you calling a kid? Tough guy now that your bodyguard is here?" Jake teased.

"Jake, cut the shit. You're not helping." She raised her palm in front of him in warning, "Will someone please tell me what's going on here?"

"Nothing is going on. We've been cutting this kid too much slack because of his little crush on you but he's taking it too far. I don't care who your dad is, next time you say anything like that again, I'll kick your ass!" Liam was almost yelling, and it made her afraid for what he might do if she couldn't relax the situation. *What the hell did Jake say?*

She turned around to scold him for whatever foolishness he started but when her eyes locked on his she could see tears begin to drown them. Jake's eyes were blue pools of wet when he finally spoke again. "You told him? About all of it?"

Great. Now he was pissed at her, just what she needed at the moment. "Jake, look, it's just–"

"Forget it. Forget all of you."

He turned on his heels and started to walk towards the exit when his dad caught his shoulder, spinning him back around towards the group. Cyril lightly dragged his son back to the table, his cellphone clutched in one hand. He gestured for Elena and Ren to rejoin them with a quick wave of the arm. "We need to get back to the hotel right away. That was Harvey on the phone. Another Elemental has been killed in Sherfield."

CHAPTER 19
BREADCRUMBS

The water swirled in the glass, picking up speed and shooting droplets on the table as Ruby moved her hand in circles over it. She has been toying with the cup for almost an hour while the lull of the train rushed by her ears, calming her senses like a meditative soundtrack. Her brain was on fire. Rushing through emotions and solutions until she felt like she was short circuiting.

"Yo! Earth to Ruby," Nola sang from across from her, "You gonna drink that or is it just display water?"

She finally managed to lift her head and lift the corner of her lips, but the smile barely reached her eyes. "Sorry, just thinking."

"Care to share?"

"I'm pissed."

"Because of the murder?"

"No. I mean, yes but no."

Nola's face wrinkled as she stared at her, "Sorry, what?"

"It's just that we got no information in Dalhurst and while we were off getting wasted like a bunch of fools, someone died. An innocent Elemental that had nothing to do with this."

"Whoa, whoa, whoa! Slow down. You know that's not your fault, right? And we don't know when she was killed so let's not play the blame game here. We're allowed to take a night off."

"No, we're not! People are dying. We don't get nights off until we catch that son of a bitch and put an end to it!" She bellowed, her fists slamming against the train seat. "This girl was almost our age. She was probably just some student and he butchered her. For what? We still have no clue!"

"Look, I'm going to say this one time only and I really need you to listen. You're spinning. You're taking this way too personally and it's going to screw you over."

Ruby raised her legs and crossed them beneath her, rocking a little from side to side to shift her weight. "How should I take this then if not personally?"

"Like a leader. There's no point wallowing in self-pity right now. You need to get ahead of him, and if there's one thing I learned from the years I spent with Demas is that everything means something. You're saying you didn't find anything last time? Bullshit. You got a note from him. Then there's the ash."

"There was literally nothing in the note that mattered."

"You sure about that? He wouldn't write it if every single word didn't mean something."

"I went through it a million times already!"

"So, go through it again," Nola leaned in, "everything means something."

"What about this kill? What did she mean?"

"Maybe it wasn't about her at all. Have you even considered that?"

"Well, we know it was Demas. She was an Earth and then there was the ash again. But why cut her? Cyril's guy on the force said there were almost twenty cuts all over her body. Sam's body had nothing on it. It was like he just fell asleep and didn't wake up."

"Yeah, but Sam's family was looking for him, right?"

"Uh huh–" Ruby nodded, trying to follow Nola's reasoning. She could see her mind going through every scenario and was grateful to have another opinion since she was getting nowhere herself.

"And this girl was some student that wasn't even from Sherfield."

"Yeah, and?"

"So, if he didn't draw attention to killing her, she might not even have been found. No cuts, no news. And if there's no news–"

"Then we wouldn't know about it." Ruby added, "he's leaving breadcrumbs."

"Ding! Ding! Ding!" Nola sang.

She sank deeper into the seat and let the rumble of the train hitting the tracks settle her into a more comfortable position. "That's actually a pretty good point."

"I know. I'm not just a pretty face. Kind of brilliant here!"

"Okay, let's get over ourselves a bit, huh?"

"Hey, I'm not the one sitting around powering up water jugs like some emo magician!"

"I get it, alright. Geez."

"Just sayin', don't be lame." Nola smiled and dipped her finger into the glass, "We need you." She said and flicked drops of water at Ruby's face.

"Oh, you're in for it now!" Ruby yelled, grabbing the glass from her hand. She got up from the seat, ready to pounce on Nola when the ceiling speakers hissed, and an automated voice vibrated through the train car.

"Next stop: Sherfield! Please make sure you have all your belongings before exiting the train. Thank you for riding Union Rail and have a great day!"

Their gaze met when the speakers settled back into silence.

"Here we go again," Nola rolled her eyes and got up, reaching for her bag in the compartment above the seats.

"Hey, Nola?" She said before grabbing her own luggage.

"What's up?"

"I'm really glad you're here."

"Yeah, me too. Even though you are kind of a pain in the ass sometimes." Nola laughed and shoved her down on the seat before running out the door. "Better get your act together for this one, princess!"

Ruby watched her disappear down the hall, her white hair bobbing like a water buoy.

Easier said than done.

CHAPTER 20
SHERFIELD

T hey waited until the crowd of people getting off the train was mostly gone before making their way down the Sherfield railway platform to the exit. Even though they were still inside, Ruby could already feel the cold air seeping into her bones. She couldn't believe what a change a two day's ride north could make and eagerly zipped up her leather jacket, wishing she had packed a warmer coat for this trip. Unlike Dalhurst, Sherfield was a freezer almost all year round with the exception of a few weeks deep into the summer when the sun managed to defrost the barren lands. Her hands turned blue as soon as they exited the train station, and the cold air hit her face like a sucker punch in a boxing match.

"I think the van is just around the corner!" Cyril beckoned, tucking his jacket collar up to warm his face.

Despite not wanting to be petty, she was glad that he was suffering alongside her.

Liam unzipped his coat and slipped one side of it over her shoulder, the heat off his chest warming her instantly as she buried herself in his body. The perks of having a Fire boyfriend and the mobile furnace he offered. She couldn't wait to get into their room and take full advantage of his burning flesh. Luckily, there were no five-star accommodations in town, and they were staying in a small motel that suited Ruby much better. She didn't need the added pressure of feeling out of place on top of everything they already had to deal with.

Everyone in their group shivered as they galloped down the street to the pickup point Cyril had arranged for them. Everyone except Elena who had managed to change into appropriate attire on the train and was casually strolling behind them in a red, down puffer with a fur lining and a massive hood. She looked like a drop of blood against the blank landscape of Sherfield.

"Remind me again why we couldn't just fly in?" Elena asked, her eyes casting an indifferent gaze towards Ruby.

She didn't bother answering but simply lifted up her pant leg slightly to let the silver of the dagger's hilt catch the light. No one was letting them on a plane with a weapon.

"Right," Elena nodded, not entirely satisfied with her answer.

They turned the corner and spotted the black van parked across the street, awaiting their arrival. The sign in front read 'Okenos' and Cyril eagerly waved to the driver who looked like he had been asleep for the last few hours.

Ruby's face turned white when she caught sight of the van.

There, in the middle of a Sherfield street, leaning against their rented van stood Ray. Her purple locks hung in pieces around her face, framing its paleness. She looked up when she heard them turn the corner, her eyes beading under her bangs as she smirked. "About time you showed up. I'm freakin' freezing out here!"

Ruby dropped her suitcase to the ground and pushed herself away from Liam. She ran across the street, her hands palming together as she got closer. Fire burst between them. It anchored itself to her fingers. Swallowing the anger in her and turning it into a weapon. She was going to burn this girl down where she stood.

Her steps were faster now, running in Ray's direction. Ready to strike her. Ready to kill her if needed. Her hands shifted to fists, each one holding a ball of fire. She was almost in front of Ray when an arm reached around from behind, clutching her waist and pulling her away. Heat warmed her back. Not her own, someone else's. Liam's. "Not here," he whispered in her ear and continued to hold her steady, "too many eyes." He nudged her ear with his nose, and she turned in the direction of his eyes to a row of taxis lining the street.

Goddammit!

"Jake, can you grab Dominik and make sure she doesn't go anywhere?" Liam asked, pointing his free hand at Ray.

To Ruby's surprise, Jake didn't bother shooting back a sarcastic remark but motioned for the tall knight to join him. The shock of seeing Ray in Sherfield overpowered any other emotions they had before. Jake and the knight walked carefully over until they were on either side of Ray, each grasping one of her arms.

"No, thanks boys. I'm not really looking to date right now." She mocked, but their hold only strengthened.

"You're coming with us. Now get in the van." Ruby said and rested a cold glare on Ray's face.

"Well, obviously. That's why I came here."

Ray rolled her eyes and shook the knight's hold off her, climbing into the van and plopping herself comfortably on one of the seats. She lifted one of her legs and rested her boot against the seat back in front of her, tossing a cat-like grin in Ruby's direction. Before climbing in behind her, Ruby reached down and pulled the dagger out of the holster, pressing the tip into the back of Ray's neck. If she had to spend a van ride with a traitor, she was going to make sure it wasn't a comfortable one.

CHAPTER 21

YOU'RE GOING TO KILL HER

R ay was flush against the hotel room wall, her hands outstretched on either side and held in place by ropes of black plasma. The room had quickly filled with the smell of burning flesh as the plasma ate its way through her wrists. Her purple hair was plastered in patches across her sweaty face, and she was breathing faster than an Olympic runner.

"Let me go! I'm trying to help you!" she screamed but Ruby did not budge.

Instead, she buried her feet into the floor and shot two more plasmic ropes to wrap around Ray's ankles. The hit was instantaneous, making Ray yelp out in pain as the plasma penetrated her skin. "You think I'm going to believe you? You think any of us will believe you?" She yelled, tightening her fist and twisting it as it pulled out the air from Ray's lungs. Her breaths were desperate now, shallow and full of begging. "Tell me where he is!"

"I–" Ray tried to speak but could not get the words out, "I–"

Ruby let go of the hold on her lungs, "Speak."

"I don't know. I'm here to help you. Are you actually that big of an idiot?" Ray shouted.

"Wrong answer," Ruby said and twisted her fist once again, feeling her power intensify as she grabbed hold of Ray's lungs.

"Enough!" Zag yelled from behind her, rushing to help Ray. His hands moved quickly, reaching toward an overgrown bush outside the window next to them. He intensified his power and pulled the shrub into the room, stretching it until it surrounded him and Ray. "You're going to kill her if you don't stop!"

Ruby's eyes changed to a deep black until they were nothing but darkness, devoid of any emotion. She could feel the dagger pulsate against her palm. With a single breath she flipped it in her hand and charged the wall Zag erected. It shrank away with every cut she made as if out of fear. Leaves fell to the ground in an avalanche of green. She was going to make Ray pay no matter what. She made quick progress, ripping a big enough hole to reach through.

"Rue! What are you doing?" Liam screamed, running into the room, Jake on his heels. "And why the hell are you guys not stopping this?" His attention shifted to Dominik and Silas behind him, "You were supposed to help while we got the bags!"

He reached Ruby right before she sent another shot of black plasma, this one aimed at Ray's heart. Grabbing one arm, he twisted her away, motioning for the knights and Jake to hold her other hand. She struggled, kicking at the ground as they carried her to an armchair at the other end of the room. Her body hit the chair like a sack of potatoes, knocking the dagger out of her hand. The sharp banging sound of the metal hitting the ground jarred her attention back to the room. Her eyes settled back into their usual brown shade when she finally looked up at Liam. "Goddammit, Liam! She's a traitor!"

"Maybe. But you're not a killer," he knelt in front of her, "or are you trying to be one now?"

She huffed and put her trembling hands in his. He was right, she wasn't a killer. But why did she want to end Ray so badly? She looked over Liam's shoulder, Zag had brought the rest of the wall down and was helping clean the plasma off Ray. She could see the welts form on her wrists and ankles where it melted into her skin, disgusted by the small amount of joy it brought her. "Is she okay?" She asked, not entirely sure if she meant it.

"She'll be fine. No thanks to you, girl." Zag said and helped Ray stumble to the bed.

Ruby watched her sit down carefully, rubbing at her wrists and yelping from the pain as she touched them.

"Don't rub it. It'll heal faster on its own," she

offered. "AetherBorns recover pretty fast from plasma but you have to leave it alone."

"I know that!" Ray snapped back, "I'd recover even quicker if you didn't try to kill me at all."

"Do you blame me?"

Ray didn't answer, rolling her eyes, and turning back to face Zag who was almost done removing the plasma from her ankles. His apologetic eyes met hers, as if it was him who did the damage.

"What the hell happened here?" Nola screeched from the doorway, Leah following close behind her. She pointed to the piles of shrubs on the floor. "Someone filming Jurassic Park in this joint, or what?"

"Our little queen had a meltdown," Zag offered, handing Ray a bottle of water from his bag. "Almost killed this one."

"Yeah, well, lucky you were there, Zag. If I was her, I wouldn't have stopped."

Ruby's gaze met Nola's, suddenly understanding the anger she must feel all the time. Every AetherBorn she met must remind her of the time she had spent under Demas' influence. She was surprised Nola didn't kill Ray right when they first found her. If *she* wanted to hurt her so deeply, Nola must want to cause a lot more damage considering Ray spent all that time helping the monster that enslaved her and her mother. She never asked Nola about it, but she was pretty certain that her hatred for Demas would not be healed until he was gone. After all, he had fathered many daughters during his time on Earth in an attempt to grow his army and almost all of them wanted him dead after Ruby freed them. If she was in Nola's place, she would have ripped Ray's head off there and then. In fact, she would have if it wasn't for Liam and Zag.

"Hey, Noles?" Leah placed her small palm on the AetherBorn's shoulder, "Why don't we go for a walk or something? They have a killer movie collection in the lobby! Come check it out with me?"

Nola ripped her eyes away from Ray and followed Leah out the door. "They better have drinks in the lobby!" She added and walked away.

When they were gone, Jake gestured for the two knights to leave the room. He walked over to the bed where Zag sat next to Ray, quietly watching her. His feet planted firmly as he towered over them. "Why don't you fill us in on why you're here." He said calmly.

"You sure that psycho won't try to kill me again?"

"I'd watch what I say," he added, crossing his arms.

"Ugh, fine." Ray sighed and jumped further onto the bed, leaning her back against the wicker headboard. "Like I already said, I came to help."

"Why should we believe you?"

"Because why the hell would I come here otherwise? It's not like I didn't know you'd try to kill me. I'm not an idiot."

"Could have fooled me," Ruby whispered under her breath.

"Huh?" Ray jerked her head in Ruby's direction, "You want me to tell you how I can help, or what?"

She rolled her eyes but let Ray continue. No point arguing with her now.

"Anyways," Ray continued, "I think I can help you find him."

"Why would you want to help us? You were a pretty diligent soldier for him before."

"Not to mention running off after Ruby came back from the plane," Liam added.

"Yeah, well, let's just say I had some time to think about it. And I'm pretty sure he wasn't going to fulfill his end of the bargain even if I stuck around. Turns out Demas was kind of a liar."

"You think?" Jake sneered, "what did he promise you anyway?"

Ray thought about the question as if wondering whether to answer it truthfully or not. Her expression shifted with each thought and Ruby realized how young Ray really was. Just a scared kid with no one to turn to. She wondered if she would have been as afraid and naive if she hasn't stumbled on Liam and the Elementals.

"Just that he would make sure I had power and whatever. That I wouldn't be alone. Like ever," she sighed, "as if anyone could really promise that."

"So, what made you change your mind?"

"Well, because where the heck is he, right? I mean, you kicked his ass, I get it. But I've been looking for him this whole time, and he hasn't so much as tried to come for me. Now I find out he's got his little fam helping him out. Just tossed me out for a new pony. The asshole."

"Wait," Ruby got up and started to walk towards the bed, she stopped and backed away when she noticed Ray tense up. "You're sure his family is here?"

"Obvi."

"How can you be sure of that?"

"You saw the ash, right?"

"Uh huh..."

"Well, that's Nyx's signature. Always a trace of ash after a kill. Everyone knows that." Ray looked at their blank expressions, "or I guess not everyone."

"Nyx? As in the Night Deity?" Zag asked.

"The one and only. And if she's here, Hemera must be with her. From what Demas told me, she would never leave her mom on her own," she paused. "Let me guess? You don't know who *she* is either."

Ruby shook her head. Her knowledge of the deities was minimal at best and right now, she wished she had spent more time going through the mythology books in the library instead of daydreaming about killing Demas.

"The Deity of Day. Her and Nyx are as close as they can get. Talk about an unhealthy mother-daughter relationship. I mean, geez. Cut the cord lady!" Ray's lips twirled up into the first smile Ruby had seen on her.

"Is that it?"

"For the fam reunion? No clue. I'm hoping so. Otherwise, we're screwed."

The way she said the word 'we' made Ruby feel uneasy. They hadn't agreed to work with her yet and she wasn't even certain that she could be trusted. "So why get involved at all? If it's this dangerous, why don't you just hide out until it's over?"

"You kidding me, right?" Ray raised an eyebrow, "The prick left me alone. He promised me a bunch of crap then just ghosted me! I am not gonna let that slide. Besides, I've literally never walked away from a fight."

"Except when you ran off last time you mean?" Liam smirked.

"Yeah, well, that was different."

"Right. You weren't on our side then." Jake said, rolling his eyes.

Ray finished off the water and tossed the empty bottle on the floor. "Look, you can trust or me not. It's your call. But if you don't, get ready for a wild goose chase. You'll never get to him in time."

"And how exactly can you help with that?"

"Because, bozo," she laughed, "they're using the Aether Plane to get around."

"And?"

"And I know how it works. Demas showed me. So, if

you want to track them, I'm your best bet. Just need to get me to the last place you know they were."

She looked at Ray's self-assured smile and sighed in frustration. If she wanted to get to Demas, she would have to work with this brat.

Just when things couldn't get worse, she thought and sank back into the armchair.

CHAPTER 22
BROTHER

Frozen solid was not even close to describing how Ruby felt walking from the van to the wooded area where the Sherfield police discovered the body just a few days ago. If Cyril's contact hadn't given them a copy of the crime scene report, she would have guessed the poor girl died of exposure to the cold. She couldn't fathom how people could live here year-round. They'd been in Sherfield less than a day, and she was already homesick and desperate to replace the empty, small-town landscape with skyscrapers and sunshine that actually provided heat. She could see sun rays hit the tops of the evergreens, but it was as if the town was protected by an invisible dome that stopped anything other than snow and wind from getting through. Ruby released another quick shudder and scooted closer to Liam in hopes of warming up.

One quick look around the group and she could see they were just as miserable as she was. Shivering like pigeons huddled on top of a street grate. Even Elena was starting to turn blue despite her gear.

The only one that seemed completely unaffected by the temperature drop was Ray. Prancing along next to Zag, trying to make small talk. He didn't seem to mind her company but every glimpse of purple hair out of the corner of her eye made Ruby anxious. How was she so relaxed right now?

I guess you can't be chilly when your heart is made of ice.

The road behind disappeared as they strayed off the path and into the tree line. The evergreens were a massive layout of indistinguishable patterns, growing in random patches and intertwining their lush branches above their heads. She felt like she was entering another land and had to glance back every now and then to make sure they still had the road in sight. The last thing she wanted was to get lost in a forest in this temperature. Comforted by the sight of the van, she reached for Liam's hand, startling him enough to jump.

"I guess everyone is on edge right now," she smiled and squeezed his warm palm.

"Yep. Especially Leah." His head nodded to the left where Leah crept carefully behind Nola, her eyes a wide pool of fear.

"Do you blame her? The amount of crime TV she

watches, I'm surprised she leaves the house at all!" Ruby joked but her heart felt a touch of sadness, wishing she could take her friend's fears away.

The trees ahead got denser, and they had to squeeze together until they were marching single file into the abandoned wilderness. It was like someone was funneling them in. The entire scene reminded Ruby of war tactics and her stomach twisted and turned from the nerves. She brushed the thought out of her mind and walked on, listening to the chatter in front of her until they reached a small opening between two trees and could finally see a sliver of light shining through.

She watched as their group passed through one by one, Jake leading the way. If they were correct in mapping it out, the body would have been dumped just on the other side of these trees. An odd place from Ruby's perspective but according to Zag, the small open area in the woods is a big draw for teen parties and gets patrolled often by police. Another smart move from Demas.

Half of the group was already on the other side, their silence suddenly deafening.

Ruby held out her arm, stopping Liam in his tracks. Zag, Nola, Leah and Ray paused abruptly behind them, following her lead. "Something is wrong. It's too quiet," she noted, reaching down to unstrap the dagger from her leg. She tightened her grip on the handle, feeling its weight begin to circulate the power within her. One step at a time, she pushed her way to the other side of the trees.

Heat. Unbearable heat rolled off her as she made her way into the clearing. To her right stood the rest of their party, frozen in place and afraid to move. Her eyes followed their stares and gaping mouths to the center of the clearing. There, in the middle of the ash covered, frozen grass stood Demas. His black curls whipping madly in the wind, matching the ebbing flow of his long leather jacket. Dark, hateful eyes narrowing as he spoke.

"How wonderful. A reunion!" He exclaimed, his thin lips parting into a devilish grin. "Eros, look! Your little toys are here!"

Her attention shifted to Ray who mouthed a quiet *shit*, her way of letting Ruby know they were in trouble. She had a pretty good idea who this Deity was but as far as she knew from her limited studies in high school, Eros was the Deity of Love. What could they possibly have to be scared off? Though Demas would not have chosen a puppy dog to help him in his plans, so whatever this Eros had to offer, it couldn't be good for the rest of them.

There was a rustle in the trees a few feet away from Demas and within seconds, a strapping hunk of a man stepped into the clearing. His broad shoulders knocked through the branches like they were puffs of dust and Ruby had a hard time figuring out if she was afraid or attracted to this creature. *He's helping Demas*, she had to recite in her head almost like a mantra while Eros shook his shoulder-length blonde curls with an enticing grin. As if on cue, Liam put pressure on her hand and she straightened her back, holding the dagger in front of her.

"Oh, my goodness! Is that the sword?" Demas laughed, "I told you brother, these things ruin everything they touch. They're absolutely useless."

Eros took a few steps forward, the muscles in his thick legs tensing through his slacks as he walked. "I don't know about that," he purred, "this one seems like she could have a use or two." He sneered, licking his bottom lip.

"Back off!" Liam commanded, stepping in front of her. With a silent call, Jake and the knights followed suit and were at her side in moments while Cyril and Elena protected the others.

"Look what you did, you made lover boy mad," Demas teased and puckered his bottom lip. "Now he'll get all hot and bothered and burn the forest down."

"I wouldn't do that if I were you," Eros laughed, trailing the echo of his voice across the field, "I know a thing or two about the fire of love. Are you sure she's worth it?"

Without words, Liam balled his fists and set them ablaze.

"Well, excuse me, Romeo!" Eros lifted his arms in dramatic defeat, "I guess I was wrong. Good for you, kid!"

To her left, Ruby heard a slight commotion followed by small steps in the grass. The crunch of the ice covering the clearing amplified as it got closer until Ray's back was in front of them, facing Demas head on. "What the hell are you doing here?"

"Miss Carolina Raymond! There you are! Where have you been this whole time?" Demas exclaimed.

Carolina? Seriously? Not so tough now, is she?

"Where have *I* been? Where have *I* been?" Ray yelled, "Where the hell have *you* been? Coward."

"It's not nice to call people names, Carolina."

"Oh, and it's nice to kill them?" she huffed, "And it's Ray."

"That's quite the accusation, and I don't see a body here," he sang. "Do you, Eros?"

"No body, no crime." His brother offered in return, his blue eyes wildly dancing over the rest of the group.

"There's ash everywhere! We know Nyx did this!"

"Well, aren't you a clever little traitor?" Demas smirked, "Running around spilling our secrets to anyone who would listen?"

"I'm not the traitor here," Ray started. "You're the one that–"

"That's enough." Ruby said and pushed through Liam and Jake to get closer to the brothers. The dagger's hilt glistened, amplifying the bright colors of the gems set in it. "What do you want, Demas? You want me? You got me. Here I am! Was it really necessary to kill these people? Haven't you heard of a phone?" She yelled.

"Necessary? Of course not. But most things that are fun aren't necessary."

"You're disgusting," she spat back.

"As for what I want, well, I don't really need to share that with you, do I? Last time we bonded I really thought you'd be more helpful, but you were just a thorn in my side. And you took things away from me;" he gave a side wave to Nola who looked like she was going to walk over and slap him right across the face, "there's a price to pay for that."

"You're seriously psychotic," Jake said from behind her.

"I see you brought both of your pups out to play today," he smirked, disregarding Jake's presence with a slight twirl of the hand.

Ruby widened her stance, holding the dagger in front of her with both hands. Her body tensed as she swirled its energy into her, inch by inch through every finger until it was pouring into her like an open faucet. She let it consume her until she could feel every blood cell in her body morph into something else. Something stronger. A being made of blood and black plasma. An AetherBorn in her true right.

She let the energy seep back out, encasing the dagger and her palms in a deep, dark fog.

"No one is playing today."

CHAPTER 23
ONE BY ONE

The dagger shook as black plasma shot from the blade and hurled through the air towards Demas. His head craned to the side allowing the plasma to miss his face by a fraction, grazing one of his dark curls and singing its ends. "Straight to business I see," he grinned, ripping his hands upwards and shooting a bolt of darkness back at Ruby. She tried to swerve out of the way, but the bolt moved as if it were magnetized to her body, hitting her in the stomach and knocking her back until she toppled to the ground.

"Rue!" Liam yelled from behind her.

"I'm fine," she returned, hopping back on her feet, ready to attack again.

She gestured for Nola, who ran in her direction immediately, positioning herself to the right of the dagger. To her surprise, Ray jogged closer to them as well, attempting to help in the fight.

Ruby's hands moved in circles, collecting energy into a ball between them. She met Nola's gaze with a side glance. Intuitively, Nola repeated the motion and gestured for Ray to do the same. They continued to move, picking up speed with each pass as black fog formed in the winds their palms were creating. Ruby closed her eyes. Her thoughts emptied; the only thing left was the power of the dagger surging through her. She connected herself to it, urging it to feed on the AetherBorns next to her, to demand their strength for itself. The dagger obliged, sucking in the fog winds Nola and Ray were creating, powering her up as she stole their powers for herself.

When the black fog in her hands was too heavy to hold, she forced her palms forward, catapulting it at Demas' grinning face in front of them.

This should knock him down, she thought as the ball of fog transformed into a rock of plasma mid-flight.

She waited for the hit. For the agonizing scream as the plasma burnt into his flesh but there was nothing of the sort. Nothing but a whispering bang as the plasmic rock collided with the shadow wall that Demas had formed around him.

"He's got a shield!" Liam yelled out, shooting a ball of fire at the shadow wall to demonstrate. The ball

AETHERBLOOD

flashed on the shadow wall, hit, and disappeared as if it never existed. "We need more force!"

His cry alerted Elena and she was working within seconds. Her eyes closed, hands moving quickly to rip deathly winds through the shadow wall.

Nothing worked.

She watched as Demas laughed behind the wall, mocking them. The shadows crept around his legs, crawling up his thighs until he was completely encased in it. The wall fell with one quick swoosh, revealing only a darkness in the air where Demas just was.

"Elena! We need to see him!" She yelled.

Elena's arms outstretched, blowing more wind in his direction. The air breathed its life through the shadows and dispersed them upon impact. Her eyes darted around trying to find Demas. He was gone. He was just there and now he was gone. Ruby felt like she was in a bad magic show. Her legs started to turn to survey the clearing when a sharp pain hit the curve of her back.

Her teeth clattered together, and she bit down on her tongue hard enough to draw blood. She could feel its iron taste swirling in her mouth. The pain in her back intensified, growing as it moved up her shoulders and down her thighs. It felts like a thousand hot irons were being pressed against her, pushing her to the ground. She wanted to cry out, but all she was able to do was kneel before hitting the ground stomach first.

There were screams all around her. From her

ground level sightline, she could see Liam turn his heels, shuffling, likely shooting Demas who had somehow managed to creep up behind them and attack. She couldn't turn her head to see but she was sure that Elena, Nola and Ray were doing the same. One by one she heard a thud on the ground next to her, cries of pain. Nola and Ray's cries. Whatever he hit her with, they were paying the same price.

In the distance, Jake, Cyril and the knights had Eros cornered. Zag and Leah had built a wall around him, containing him in a cage of earth.

Get him! Kill him!

Cyril had formed a grip of ice around his legs while Jake flushed a current of water into his open mouth.

They're trying to drown him!

Eros coughed, blowing air out of his lungs and pushing his hands in front of his face to keep the current out. His legs tightened and every muscle in them screamed as he ripped the ice shackles away. The shards of ice flew back at Cyril and Jake, shattering their flesh to pieces with small, ragged cuts. They rubbed their eyes, trying to regain a line of sight with no success.

With his friends on the ground, Zag circled around the barrier of earth and rock and stretched an arm in each direction. His face was as red as blood, covered in sweat as he pulled the trees from around the field towards Eros. Their branches flying in like sharpened knives.

Before the first branch could make contact, Eros ducked. Rolling away from the center of the attack. His arm reached back and when he turned to face Zag, he was pointing a ready to fire bow at his heart. Eros stretched back the bowstring with self-assured ease, cocking his head to the side and winking before letting go of an arrow. A plasmic arrow. An arrow of pure death.

"No!" Leah yelled out, dropped her hold on the wall she was maintaining and reached for the trees instead. Her body shook but she managed to pull one of the branches in fast enough to knock Zag out of the way.

The dirt sloshed between Ruby's fingers while she tried to get herself back up. She was halfway lifted on her forearms, her back screaming in pain with each move. Next to her, another thud sounded. Heavier this time. Not Elena. Someone with more weight.

"Liam!" She finally shouted, watching his body fall next to her. His entire front side covered in shadow. A shadow that seemed to be burning him from the inside out. Her hand reached for him, wrapping around his fingers to let him know it would be alright. But she couldn't promise that, not right now.

Ruby tightened her grasp on the dagger and pushed the blade into the ground, using it to help her steady herself until she was on her knees. Her gaze fell to Eros and she was about to raise her legs to stand when she suddenly couldn't move. It was like everything around her froze. The knife still breathed life into her while she tried to figure out why her body would not respond. She was staring right at Eros when it happened, his hands twitched and then...

The bastard can stop time!

This wasn't anything like what she did the night of the peace treaty. When Ruby turned back time, she had almost lost herself to the sword's energy. Eros seemed to be able to control it with just a wave of the hand. She wanted to be strong like him, to have the power over time that he possessed, but she didn't even know how she controlled it in the first place let alone how to summon the power that easily.

Each second that passed she fought within herself. Something about the dagger kept her mind intact and functioning throughout but even her breathing was suspended. All she could do was kneel and watch.

Watch as Eros shook the debris out of his beachy hair.

Watch as his hand drew a large circle in the air, revealing a glowing light that shimmered with the Aether Plane air.

Watch as Demas walked by her kneeling body and leaned down to kiss her on the cheek moments before jumping in through the portal after his brother.

When the portal closed, she fell forward, using the palms of her hands to break her fall. Her breaths were quick and shallow even though she knew she wasn't really suffocating. She looked around at the rest of the group. Some were still unconscious, and some were slowly getting up, trying to make sense of what had just happened. Her own back was starting to heal, and she crawled towards Liam, lifting his head up to rest on her lap.

"What happened? Where did they go?" He asked as his eyes searched through the clearing.

She didn't answer. She just held him and stared into the empty spot in the field where the portal was moments ago, feeling for the first time that they might not have a fighting chance.

CHAPTER 24
NEVER-ENDING TRAIN OF CROW FEATHERS

A small pool of blood started to form on the bathroom tile floor from the soaked shirt Ruby discarded. She stared at it, mesmerized by the movement of the deep red liquid before grabbing a towel to wipe up the mess. The shredded skin on her back and legs had already started to heal, and the pink flesh made it look more like she had fallen asleep in the sun than been seared by a bolt of other worldly darkness.

She reached down to the bath to test the temperature before turning the faucet off. Leg by leg, she lowered herself into the calm of the water, her blood tinting it a dirty shade of orange. Splashing her palm on the surface, Ruby let her shoulders finally relax as she sank deeper into the bath. Her thoughts were jumbled, a tightly woven throw stitched with memories of the fight and her own anger.

A light knock on the door rippled through the air.

"You okay?" Liam said on the other side of the door in an almost whisper.

She closed her eyes and rolled her head back over the edge of the tub. "I'm fine," she responded, letting sleep roll over her until the world she knew was well beyond her reach.

RUBY'S LEG *draped over the tub, landing on the slick floor. She looked down, seeing only black and her own reflection. Wherever she was, it wasn't in the hotel bathroom. Hopping over the edge, she landed on the dark water, standing atop it just as she had in her previous vision.*

Here? Again?

Her eyes searched the space for something to cover herself with but there was not a sheet of fabric in sight. Instinctively, her hands grasped to shield herself despite knowing that nothing she experienced here was real.

She took one step forward. Then another. Stopping short when she felt something graze her toes.

The black water swirled beneath her, rising higher and higher up her legs. Teasing her with its touch as it scaled her body until it was just above her breasts. She swatted at the murky liquid, trying to wipe it off but it wouldn't budge. Instead, it mutated around her. Water that grew frills and lace. She watched in awe as the liquid dressed her in itself. First a deep cut corset, then black lace sleeves, all the way down to a never-ending train of crow feathers.

Ruby's mouth gaped, twirling to see the full details of the gown. It was exquisite.

She ran her hands down the bodice which felt like it was made of thousands of small needles. Her breath caught suddenly. The corset was shrinking, tightening with each breath she tried to take. The dress was killing her.

Her hands tried to rip at the fabric, but each grasp only made it worse. She toppled to her knees, gasping for air.

Feeling her heartbeat slow, she rolled to her side, letting the waters envelop her in their cocoon. She sank. Deeper and deeper until there was nothing of her left on the surface.

RUBY JERKED out of the bath, gasping to breathe. Her hair was soaked from sinking to the bottom of the tub. Her lungs felt like they were on fire and she coughed up bath water as she draped herself over the edge of the tub. Tears and mucous covered her face. Tears and mucous and fear.

Grabbing the nearest towel, she dried herself off, ringing out the water from her hair before gathering her bloodied clothes. She was about to throw them into the sink for a scrubbing when her hand grazed an odd shape in her jean pocket. Discarding the rest of the pile, she reached in to see what she was feeling.

Eyes as wide as a four-lane highway, she traced the blood-stained paper with her fingers. This was no vision; she was sure of it.

Demas had left another note.

CHAPTER 25
WISHFUL THINKING

R uby unfolded the paper like she was waiting for a booby trap. A fold at a time, careful not to rush through it. A part of her wanted to tear it to shreds and erase the memory of Demas and his horrid letters but she knew she had to read it. Whatever performance he was putting on; she was the only one in the audience. The only one invited to the show.

With an unsure hand, she traced the words with her fingers, hoping that it might incite a vision of his whereabouts or at least some clue to his next move. Her last few visions were entirely useless. Some queen she was. Wasn't the sword supposed to offer her the power of sight? What point was it to have any visions at all if they weren't helping her when she most needed them?

She sat, balanced on the edge of the tub, and urged herself to read.

. . .

"MY DARLING RUBY,

I am certain that you are full of the predictable self-loathing you crown yourself with as you're reading this.

Why kill this girl?

Why torture her?

Why— well, you know the rest.

Would it surprise you to know that I used to find myself asking the same questions? Not about this worthless Elemental, of course, but of my dear Eirene. Did you get a chance to find out more about her?

You really should. She was extraordinary. Taken too soon, but exceptional just as well.

I am hopeful that by the time this letter finds its way to you, I will be on to the next adventure. It's shocking how many Elementals I've been able to uncover outside of your little center; it seems my job to rid the world of them will be a bigger project than I thought. Lucky I always enjoyed a good project.

You strike me as someone who would enjoy that as well. It's a shame your grandmother was not more loyal to our family tree; I have a feeling that the two of us would have gotten along quite well under different circumstances.

Oh, well. Wishful thinking, I suppose.

Before we part, I'd love to offer you a word of advice if I may. Don't be too hard on yourself, my darling. There *is nothing you can do to stop what's coming. Enjoy the time you have left with the Fire elder. Smell the roses and so on.*

Until we meet again.
The best of wishes,
Demas"

A TEAR DROPPED on the page, smearing his name until the letters were barely legible. She crumpled the piece of paper and tossed it into the wastebasket. Her eyes bloodshot from the tears and almost drowning earlier.

This was madness. Why was he leaving her these notes? To torture her? To confuse her? Perhaps to throw them off his tracks? Whatever his reasoning was, she needed to get one step ahead of him. She hated how little they knew of his plans, and that to figure them out, she needed to think like him. But, how could she? How could she possibly find a way to relate to this monster? This heartless creature that wanted nothing more than revenge for something that these people were not even responsible for. She hated him. With every cell in her body, she hated him.

There was one thing they knew now that might prove to be useful. He most definitely wasn't alone. Eros, his brother as it turned out, was going to be a problem. He was much stronger than she anticipated a deity to be. The bow alone could take out dozens of them in a heartbeat. Not to mention his ability to manipulate time or to open that portal. With him by Demas' side, they could go anywhere within seconds. It would be nearly impossible to keep up.

Nearly.

Ruby considered what Ray had said about her knowledge of the Aether Plane. If she really knew how the plane functioned and its layout, they could use it to track Demas and his family. Find out where they're planning to go next. Get ahead. The only issue was that she would have to trust Ray. Trust her enough to follow her into the plane, blindly and without any proof. Possibly into a trap that could lead to catastrophe.

Zag seemed to have no problem falling for her little act. Swooning over her and defying Ruby to protect her. But she wasn't him. She wasn't so foolish and easy to trust. She'd lost too much to allow that.

Tightening the knot on her robe, she walked to the wastebasket and pulled the crumpled note back out, straightening the paper and folding it again into her pocket.

She needed help, all the help she could get to make this decision. Everyone who was here with her now was risking their lives based on her idea to follow Demas around the country. The least she could do was lean on them for support.

"Babe?" She called out, pulling her wet hair out of her face. "You think everyone might be up for a drink?"

CHAPTER 26
WE'RE JUST TOYS

The bar next door to the motel complex had just opened for the evening when their large group arrived. The eager look on the hostess' face spoke volumes as she led them to the large banquet table next to the kitchen. Ruby doubted this place had a steady volume of foot traffic, making the eight of them the highlight of the night for the staff. She fought the urge to ask for privacy while everyone on shift rushed around them– adding place settings, detailing the specials and attempting to make small-talk about their visit to Sherfield. Instead, she settled into her seat and grinned while Cyril made up a story about a non-existent cousin's wedding. When they finally managed to place their orders, she pushed a napkin into her lap, pinching the corners of it to calm her nerves.

"Sorry to drag everyone out," she said, "I thought it might be good to get a change of scenery for the night."

"I don't know about you guys, but I could sure use a drink after today!" Zag boasted, rubbing the side of his neck where the hints of a fresh bruise were starting to form. "Anyone else feel like they were run over by a car a few times?"

Nola and Jake sighed in unison, their faces covered in puffy scratches, making them both look like they had fought a clowder of cats and lost. "More like a bus. That was on fire," Nola added.

"Any ideas on what we're dealing with?" Liam asked no one in particular.

Their attention shifted to Ray who was particularly quiet while sipping a diet coke. Her silence made Ruby uneasy, either the kid was afraid, or she was trying to act like the rest of them to gain her trust. She hated not knowing which one was true. More so, she hated that she needed Ray's insight to move forward.

"Did you know about Eros?" She asked her, hiding her emotions beneath an icy glare, "When you told us about Nyx and Hemera. Did you know he might be involved?"

Ray shook her head violently, widening her eyes. "Of course not! I wasn't even sure about the other two. I mean, I kind of had a feeling but I didn't know. If Eros is here, we're in shit."

"Why?"

"Because he's almost unbeatable," Zag answered for her. "If what the books in the library say are true, he's stronger than most of the other deities. Crazy strong! Girlfriend here is right, we're in shit."

Ruby took note of his use of the word 'girlfriend', the tone of it softer than when he threw it around on other occasions.

"What I don't understand is why they're helping him. And why he wants their help." Elena said.

"How so?" Cyril asked.

"From everything Ruby has told us, these are the same people that locked him away in the underworld. Why would they help him now? And doesn't he despise his family for creating all of us in the first place?"

"It's not that black and white for him," Nola spoke up, "He's a slimy bastard but he's not an idiot. He knows he can't get rid of every Elemental on his own. Especially now that Ruby ripped apart his AetherBorn army. He needs help."

"He was always planning on bringing them here. The other deities, I mean," Ruby added and ran her fingers across the raised scars on her arms. "I didn't know why he'd care but I guess this is it. Army or not, he always needed their powers to wipe us all out."

"Yeah, well, do you blame him? That Eros isn't just a pretty face! They almost killed us today and that was just the two of them. If Ray's right and there's two more, I don't know about you peeps, but I do not want to find out how that plays out!" Zag exclaimed.

Ruby's gaze shifted from him to Leah, whose face was knotted with thought. "What do you think?"

"Who? Me?" Leah asked, startled by the attention. "I just keep thinking about the Aether Plane. If Eros, Nyx and Hemera have been there this whole time with God knows who else, why leave? It just doesn't make sense."

"It does if you think about who you're dealing with here," Ray said bluntly.

"Meaning?"

"You're all way off. You're trying to put yourself in his shoes, right?"

"Of course," Ruby said.

"Yeah, well, that's dumb. No offense," Ray smiled apologetically, but it seemed to come off more mocking than she had aimed for, "You'll never get anywhere that way."

"So, what's your solution?"

"Try to think like the most powerful beings in the freaking universe. That would be a better start. These aren't just some randoms that you're dealing with. They're deities! The originals! They don't have feelings like we do. And they definitely don't have feelings for us. From all the stories you've heard, Demas is the only deity that hooked up with someone on this planet. What does that tell you?"

They stared at her quietly, eyes blinking fast. Not a single answer around the table.

"That he's the least of your worries, that's what! You think he's bad? We're just toys to the rest of them. Him wanting to kill all you people is the good part. Eros and Nyx just want to play! They've been chillin' in the Aether Plane forever and are probably bored as hell! Demas was the perfect excuse for them to come out of hiding. And trust me, if we can't figure this crap out and end it, you'll be praying for him to kill you by the time the other two are done with you."

The seven of them were silenced entirely. There was not so much as a breath escaping their lips as they took in her words. There was a rapid shuffle of legs next to their table that sounded more like a herd of elephants than the server delivering their second round of drinks.

"Let's see here. We got one gin tonic, three rapid fires, a pint of light and–" she ran off the order as she placed the glasses in front of them, "looks like I'm missing the diet coke. Sorry about that folks! I'll be right back with it!"

She tossed the tray under her arm and bounced away towards the bar in the back giving everyone time to readjust in their seats. Nola took as sip of her drink, barely flinching at the double shot of gin in her glass.

"She's right," she said and met Ruby's gaze. "Demas

is garbage but these deities, they're something else entirely."

"So, what? We just sit back and wait to be taken one by one?" Jake asked, his face turning an angry shade of red that Ruby has not seen before. He took his glasses off, cleaning them with a napkin on the table before continuing, "We need a plan. You hear me, Rue? What do we do now?"

"I–" she stammered. "I don't know."

Liam shoved his elbow in front of her on the table as if he was protecting her from an attack. "You have any ideas yourself or are you just going to put this all on her?"

"I want to know what she thinks we should do. Pretty sure I'm not the only one," Jake fired back. He motioned around the table, but no one spoke up. "See?"

Her hand rubbed the stone on her necklace, tracing the finely shaped edges of it in a circular motion. She seized Liam's leg with her other hand, feeling his thigh tense then relax under her grip. Jake wasn't wrong. They needed a plan and she needed to give it to them. Especially after dragging them out on this goose chase across the country and almost getting them killed today. Her thoughts rushed to think of the next steps or at least some semblance of an idea.

She was tired, she was jaded, and she was afraid.

Forcing the defeat from her eyes, she let her hands rest on the table, silencing the slow burn of power that was building in them. "We can't get ahead of someone that does not have a rational plan," she said finally.

"Girl, you need to work on your delivery. That's not really reassuring," Zag scrunched up his face, flipping a red lock of hair from his face.

"We can't get ahead of his family," she continued, disregarding the interruption, "but Demas isn't like them. At least not entirely from what we've seen. Nola, you said it yourself, he is nothing if not calculating. Everything he does has a reason, a well thought out reason. We don't need to figure out how to fight off Eros and Nyx. At least not yet. What we need to do right now is figure out where Demas is going to hit next and be there before him. If we can surprise them, maybe we'll actually stand a chance."

"And how do we do that exactly? Call him up and ask?" Jake smirked.

Her head turned away from him to the opposite end of the bar table. "We use what Ray knows about the Aether Plane."

"Oh, look at that! Suddenly I'm not so bad, huh?" She hissed from behind her purple bangs.

"You said you know how the plane is laid out. Does that mean there are entrances and exits in it?"

"Sort of. It's not like a hallway or something."

"What is it like then?"

"The plane isn't a place. You need to stop thinking of it that way. It's everywhere."

Jake laughed. "Another incredibly helpful explanation. Is this an AetherBorn thing?"

"Shut it, pretty boy! Or I'll make you eat that sweater vest!" she barked. "Anyway, the plane isn't a solid place. It's more of an energy field of sorts. Something that exists outside of the physical place we live in but is dependent on it."

"Like an in between layer?"

"Exactly like that!"

"Uhm, in between what?" Leah asked.

Ray grinned at Ruby, happy that at least someone in the group was catching on. "In between where we are and where the deities are. Think of it like a train station. Some parts of our world are closer to it, making it easier for those of us with ties to it to get in."

"Anchor points," Ruby whispered to herself.

"See? Your queen bee is getting it!" Ray's eyes twinkled mischievously while she spoke, "Circling back to our little lesson here. There are no entrances and exits. But there are places where it's easier to get through to the plane."

"The old library in Lakeside?" Zag asked.

"Yep."

Ruby's mind ignited, a plan burrowing its way to the surface. "And probably everywhere the bodies have been dumped so far," her eyes shifted to Elena apologetically. She knew how careless that must have sounded considering her nephew's death but they could not afford to be sentimental right now. "Judging by the portal Eros opened in that clearing, I'm willing to bet that he is also constricted to these anchor points. And if that's true–"

"Then I can give you a list of the places I remember from when I travelled in the plane with Demas to cross reference with Elemental populations."

"That's what I'm hoping for anyway. If we can narrow down the locations, they're able to go to by using the plane, we can maybe find out where they're planning to go next," she sighed. She knew it was a long shot, but they had nothing else they could try right now. She needed to give them some hope at least. "Zag, you think you can work with Ray to map this thing out? Maybe Elena and Cyril could help with the breakdown of Elementals?" she asked, knowing that if anyone had the knowledge on where every Elemental in the country lived it would be the two elders that used to lord it over them.

"What about the rest of us?" Jake asked.

"The rest of us are going to figure out what we should expect from the deities. If we have to fight again, I don't want to be unprepared like we were today."

"Here's the diet coke folks!" The server chimed at the edge of the table. The bar had a few more patrons now, and Ruby didn't even hear her creep up next to them. She used the interruption to pull Leah aside without anyone noticing.

"Can you do me a favor?" she asked quietly.

"What's wrong? Why are we whispering?"

"I just don't want this to be a huge deal in case it doesn't work."

"In case what doesn't work?"

"I was hoping you could maybe try something."

Leah wrinkled her nose to show her confusion. "Okay..."

"Do you think it would be possible for you to try that thing with the animals? Talking to them, I mean."

"Uhm, okay. Why?"

"This is probably a long shot, but I thought you might be able to use it to check the clearing again. See if there is anything–" she paused. "Never mind, it's probably a stupid idea."

"Are you kidding? It's not stupid at all! I'll go back tomorrow, see if I can find any wildlife. No guarantees it'll work though."

"I know. Thanks for trying anyway. Every small thing helps, you know."

"For sure. Oh, and Ruby?" Leah smiled shyly, "I don't actually talk to them. You know that, right?"

"Yeah. But it sounds way cooler the way I said it," she laughed and made her way back to her seat.

The group seemed to have moved on from the grim situation they were in and were already yelling over each other, filling the long table with multiple conversations. She pulled out the stool next to Liam and squeezed in close to him. His eyes trailed over her face, questioning if she was alright without any words. She nodded and reached up to run her fingers through his messy hair.

We'll be fine, she told herself. Almost believing it.

CHAPTER 27
NO OPINIONS

L iam kissed her forehead and offered a sly wink before leaving the bar. He was careful not to show too much affection around Jake and she appreciated his effort to keep the seas calm for the time being. The group had decided to split up for the evening when Dominik suggested target practice in the woods, leaving only Elena, Leah, Nola and herself at the bar. With the exception of Ray who stuck to Zag like a wet Band-Aid, this was the closest to a girl's night Ruby had had since they left Westerlake. The realization made her miss Shaylah instantly and she made a quick mental note to call her in the morning.

Their stomachs were growling beasts by the time the chipper server dropped off their meals; and Ruby ripped into her pizza, swallowing the cheesy crust with minimal chewing. "Hopefully the guys keep their powers to a minimum in case they're still patrolling the woods," she said, wiping the oil off the side of her mouth.

"I'm sure they're clever enough to figure that out," Elena said reassuringly.

"Not all of them," Nola added under her breath and shoved a French fry in her mouth. She pushed the basket over to the center of the table, but Ruby was unsure if it was her cue to share or if she'd simply had enough of the meal. "I'd check in if I was you. Just in case."

Leah's small hand reached into the basket, swiping a few fries for her own plate. "They'll be fine. It's nice to have a break away from them."

"You mean from your brother, right?"

"Who else? He's too much sometimes!"

"Well, definitely not from Dominik," Nola raised her eyebrows devilishly.

"What does that mean?"

"Oh, please! You're crushing hard. It's so obvious!"

"Shut up, Nola! I am not," Leah's cheeks burned, and her face was starting to resemble a freshly plucked tomato. "Rue, tell her she's crazy."

"I mean—" she hesitated. "It's a little obvious."

Leah crossed her arms and puffed out a breath of air. Her body slumped in the chair and she looked down at the table, still a solid shade of red.

"But it's good!" Ruby sang, "This way he'll definitely catch on. And he'd be an idiot not to like you. So good play!"

"You think so?" Leah raised her eyes slowly, like a timid child.

"Of course! You'll see."

"I don't know. Maybe."

"Elena will settle this!" Nola yelled, fixing her dark eyes on the mayor. "Think our girl has a chance or what?"

Elena's mind seemed to have been drifting elsewhere, deep in thought and concentration. She was twirling the edge of her fork mindlessly in the bowl of spaghetti in front of her, barely noticing Nola's gaze on her. "I'm sorry, what were you saying?" She asked, quickly rearranging herself to show interest in the group.

"Leah and Dominik. What are the chances do you think?" Nola repeated the question with a slightly annoyed tone. The lack of respect for the elders that she projected always took Ruby by surprise, and she found that when it came to Nola, she had to constantly remind herself that she did not have the same relationship with the Elementals. Until quite recently, they were people that she was raised to hate. She couldn't very well expect her to start bowing down to the elders as though the first part of her life with Demas never took place.

"Oh! I had no idea you were interested in him, Leah!" she blurted.

"See? It's not that obvious," Leah smirked and stuck her tongue out at the two of them.

"But if you are interested, I can tell you the same thing I would tell my daughters if they were your age. Go for it! Life's too short so have fun while you can!"

"Ha!" Nola laughed boldly, "It's not always fun you know. Just ask Demas."

"Geez, Nola! Way to make everything super gruesome!" Leah said and tapped a light punch in her friend's ribs.

"Yeah, Noles. That was a touch harsh," Ruby added.

"Are you defending him? You're kidding, right?"

"I'm not defending anyone. Just saying that despite who he is now, the guy lost the only person he cared about. That's pretty rough. I don't know what I would do if someone did that to Liam."

"Well, you probably wouldn't go on a murder spree. That's for sure. And he's not a guy. He's a deity. You're giving him way too much credit. Don't compare him to us."

She focused her gaze on Nola whose posture was completely rigid. Quickly realizing her mistake, she refilled the AetherBorn's water glass and pushed it closer to her. "I'm sorry. I didn't mean for it to sound like I was defending him. What he's done isn't okay. The way he made you live isn't okay."

"It wasn't all bad," Nola said, drooping her shoulders a little. "I had my mom and some of the other

AetherBorns that weren't too into the crap he was spewing. When he wasn't using us to suck our powers dry it really was just like anywhere else. Just with more chicks." She laughed at some distant memory that only she was privy to.

"You didn't feel trapped at all?" Elena asked.

"Not really. I mean, I knew I couldn't leave. Mom made that pretty clear from day one but it's not like it was some cult or something. More like a homeschooling situation. Don't get me wrong, I definitely wanted to get the hell out of there a lot of times!"

"How come you didn't?"

"And leave my mom? And the rest of the girls? No way!" She smiled stiffly, dipping two fingers in the water glass and running them through her platinum locks. "Like I said, it wasn't all bad. It's girls like Ray I actually feel bad for."

"Why? What's wrong with her?" Leah's ears perked at the name. "Other than the obvious."

"Well, she was screwed right from the start. No family, no friends. Total loner. Her little hacking stints didn't exactly pay the bills, so she was basically living on the street when Demas found her. Brought her to us like a wounded bird."

"She seemed to have fit in just fine with him," Ruby added, furrowing her brow in disgust.

"I doubt she had a choice. He wrapped his evil fingers around her and squeezed until she had no opinions other than the ones he was feeding her. I'm sure she just saw it as a way out of whatever hell she was living in before him. I mean, I hate her guts and all. But you know."

"Still not an excuse."

"Maybe not, sweetie," Elena flicked her long hair over her shoulder, revealing a neckline that exposed more of her chest than Ruby was comfortable with, "but it is understandable."

"How she acted?"

"More the choices she made. She's quite young and it sounds like he was the first authority figure she had. I'm certain he did everything he could to brainwash the poor girl into following his orders."

"Did he ever!" Nola yelped, "That prick made sure that girls like her lived and breathed by his theories of hatred. Everyone he pulled off the streets pretty much salivated at the mouth from all his promises."

"Not everyone," Ruby said, thinking of her own grandmother.

"True. But most did. Happy even to give him their powers willingly. The rest of us that were born into it hated those days, but the street girls... Not them. They all but lined up outside his doors offering themselves up like sacrificial lambs. It was disgusting."

Leah pushed the basket of fries she had completely annihilated back towards Nola. "It sounds pretty nasty," she added, watching her pick up a dried-out fry to eat.

"Meh. It is what it is," Nola brushed it off, "just saying cut the kid some slack or something."

"You mean me, right?" Ruby asked.

There was no answer to her question. Nola simply raised her eyebrows, giving her a look that implied that there was no one else at the table that she could be referring to.

"It's not that easy, you know. I can't just trust random kids that show up. Especially her and especially after everything she did last time. She's the reason we all almost died. She's the reason Alice died!" She yelled. "I can't trust her. I can't trust anyone anymore. It's suffocating to live like this. Always afraid of the next day." Her breath quivered and she placed her palms on the table, trying to pull air into her lungs. She felt like her heart was going to explode from her chest. Sweat started to form at the edge of her hairline. Her eyes concentrated on the mixed drink in front of her that was about to shatter from the waves she had created in it.

"Ruby, sweetheart. It's alright." Elena rubbed a palm on her back, trying to calm her down. "You don't have to be afraid. It's not all on you. Please don't ever think that you have to do this alone."

"But I do have to do this alone. Everyone keeps asking me for plans and what I think of this or that. I don't think anything. I think I don't want to die, and I think that I don't want that bastard to kill all of you. That's all I got right now!"

"Oh, honey! I wish I had known you were putting this much pressure on yourself. You're not going to die. None of us are. We'll figure it out. Together."

"Okay. I'm okay." She lied, shaking her back slightly to get Elena's palm off. She didn't want them worried about her. The last thing she needed was for them to be thinking about her well-being instead of concentrating on the fight ahead of them. What she needed even less was for this to get back to Liam somehow.

She wasn't okay. She knew that for certain. No matter what Elena might have said, she couldn't count on them to make the decisions that she knew would need to be made. She most definitely couldn't strap them with the fallout of those decisions. The guilt that choosing to end a life might bring. The comfort of Elena's words was fleeting. Death was coming and she would have to be the one to bring it.

She needed to kill Demas and everyone who stood in her way before everything she loved got ripped away from her.

CHAPTER 28
THE MAIL NEVER RESTS

The light of the moon sparkled brilliantly against the metal benches lining the garden walkway on Ruby's way back to her room. Feeling suddenly exhausted, she left the rest of the girls at the bar for the comfort of a good night's sleep. She was hoping Liam would be back by the time she got in and rushed down the winding trail, almost tripping over her own feet several times.

"Crap!" she cursed as her foot caught a loose stone, making her lose her balance once more and knocking the room key out of her hand.

Her head buzzed as soon as she bent down to reach for it, the nights festivities already rearing their ugly head. Drinking had never sat well with her and she was regretting staying for as long as she did. *I'll definitely pay for this in the morning.*

A light tap sounded behind her.

"Excuse me?" a female voice echoed, "are you Ruby? Ruby Black?"

Ruby whipped her head around, taking in the sight of the stranger behind her. She was still on the ground and had to crane her neck to be able to see the tall woman fully. Her sharp features lay in complete contrast to her accentuated curves, making her look like a replica of an old pin up model. "Maybe I have the wrong person," the woman said, flipping her wavy blonde hair over her left shoulder.

"No, no. That's me." Ruby said and raised herself to stand. Even with the added height, she still had to arch her back slightly to meet the stranger's eyes.

"Oh, wonderful! I'm sorry if I startled you."

"Do I know you?"

The woman crinkled her small nose and slapped her palm against her forehead, "I am such a fool, I must be really scaring you right now."

Ruby waited for her to start talking again but the woman just blinked rapidly and tilted her head to the side. "Uhm, kind of," Ruby said, crossing her arms.

"Well, I won't keep you. I was supposed to deliver something to you."

A courier. That makes more sense. Ruby thought, relieved enough to relax her shoulders.

The woman reached around and flipped a golden

toned cross body bag to her hips. With a quick motion, she pulled out an envelope and handed it to Ruby.

"You guys deliver this late?" she asked as she took the envelope from the courier.

"Oh, you know, the mail never rests!" The woman sang and skipped down the walkway towards the street. "You have yourself a great night, Ruby!"

Well, that was weird. She thought and brushed a hand over the dirt on her jeans.

She looked down to her hands holding a standard white envelope, the type she'd seen her mom use to send out Christmas cards. There was no sender information, in fact, there was no writing anywhere on the envelope other than Ruby's own name on the front. Her finger slid under the flap, tearing the glue away in a swift glide. Her hands squeezed the paper inside on either side, forming indents that were beginning to rip at the edges. She wanted to scream. Loud enough for everyone in the motel to hear her. Loud enough to shatter glass. Instead, she sat on the edge of one of the benches and read.

"My darling Ruby,

I'm glad you're finally getting to spend some time with the ladies. I was beginning to worry you don't get out enough.

To a lovely night,
Demas

PS. How was the pizza? It looked divine! I must try it the next time I'm in town."

THE HAIRS on the back of her neck were at attention and sweat started to pool at the base of her neck, running down her back until her shirt was soaked, even in the cold of the evening. He was there. He saw them tonight at the bar. What else had he seen? Did he watch Liam and the rest of the group leave? Did he know where they were? Were they in danger?

Her brain was a battlefield of questions. She pushed herself up, her head still dizzy, and turned to run back into the bar. Her hands shot up in front of her a moment before Ray appeared in her peripheral. There was no stopping the collision. She met Ray's forehead with her own, causing a dull pain to spark between her temples and knocking her backside to the ground.

The moon still glistened as the two stared at one another. One in shock and one in fear. Both rubbing the red bumps growing on their foreheads.

CHAPTER 29
ONE OF US

"Ow!" she yelled and shook her head. "Watch where you're going, will ya?"

"Uhm, *you're* the one that ran into *me!*" Ray scoffed back, angling her hips to the side and crossing her arms.

Ruby slowly got herself up from the ground. Her hip was already starting to hurt, and she was sure she'd be completely bruised tomorrow. *Great! Just freakin' great!*

"Hey, what's that?" Ray asked, pointing at the note in her hands.

She quickly crumbled the page, shoving it in her pocket before Ray could glimpse any of the writing. "Nothing. It's not important. What are you doing out here anyway?"

"Going to my room. Obviously. What else would I be doing out here?"

"I don't know. Where are the others?"

"Still in that dumb forest. I got bored so I figured I might as well get some sleep."

The forest? Why were they there so late? What if Demas attacked while they were there? If he kept an eye on her then he might be doing the same with them. She needed to get there right away. The wooded area was only a ten-minute drive from the motel. Or a half hour jog. If she started now, she could get there fairly quick but still not quick enough if there was an attack coming their way. She squeezed her fists tight enough to indent her nails into the skin of her palms. She could text Liam to warn him and check on the girls instead. But what if she was wrong and they were perfectly safe? She'd look like a paranoid lunatic. "It's kind of late, no?" She said quietly, not sure if Ray could pick up on her anxiousness.

"Relax. They're leaving soon. Zag texted me when I got here saying Leah and them already went home and that they were heading back too." Her eyes moved up and down Ruby's face, "you need to chill out more, you know. Maybe get some sleep or something. You look like crap."

"Wow. Thanks."

"Just sayin'," Ray shrugged.

"Well, don't."

"Okay, geez. Don't bite my head off," she raised her arms defensively, "I'll keep my concern to myself."

"So, you and Zag are pretty friendly," Ruby sneered, trying to change the topic.

"What? Why? He's just being nice. More than I can say for the rest of you. You know, you should be more appreciative of someone trying to help you."

Here we go! More 'tude from this kid! She thought and scowled, "Look, Ray, no offense but you'll never be one of us. You will always be the kid that faked her own death to spy on us to report back to Demas. No matter how nice Zag is."

Ray's face dropped, her once self-assured expression was nothing but a shattered and hopeless void. Was she actually showing some sort of emotion? Maybe she was being too harsh on her. After all, it was possible that Ray truly had changed and wanted to help them. Ruby started to feel bad for the girl. Standing there in the middle of the night, her purple hair making her features look even more melancholy than they usually were, she could almost relate to her. That is until Ray kicked a pebble with her shoe into the bushes and pushed her way past her with a huff. "No wonder you have no friends!" She wailed before stomping away.

Her fingers traced the edges of the note still tucked in her pocket when she finally breathed out, relieved to be free of Ray for the night. If she knew it was that easy to get rid of her, she would have put her in her place

long ago. The street lamps in the garden passage flick-
ered a few times before returning to their golden glare,
awakening the miniature trees around her. Everyone
was safe. There was no attack. It felt like she had won a
lottery: the gift of a worry-free night and some sleep.
With a smile, Ruby turned around to trek back to her
room, her fingers dancing quietly at her side, calling on
the plants around her to rustle and bend as she passed.

CHAPTER 30
IT'S MY JOB TO PROTECT

L iam lounged in the motel bed, using his right arm to prop up his head and drew lazy circles with his finger across her stomach. The sheets were neatly draped over him, revealing every curve of his chest which she was certain he had done on purpose to tease her. Not that she minded the view one bit. They had been quiet for quite some time, trying to acclimate to the day after making a mess of each other upon waking.

Raising herself halfway up, she rested her elbows on the pillow behind her and sighed loudly, "I am really not into getting up right now."

"We can stay here for a bit longer," Liam said with a sly wink. "I'm in no rush to get up."

His hand started to travel down towards her navel, twirling in circles as it inched further down. The grin on his face told Ruby that unless she wanted to lose another hour of her day, she had better start getting dressed. She swatted at his fingers with her palm, laughing when he jerked his hand away and cursed under his breath.

"We need to get up."

"What's the hurry?" he asked but she was already halfway to the bathroom.

Ruby almost gasped when she met her own gaze in the mirror. It was as if she was staring at a stranger. The girl standing in front of her was nothing like who she remembered herself to be. She wasn't meek and eerily skinny with a fear in her eyes that dressed her entire face. This girl, this woman really, was strong and confident. She was shapely, with strong muscles protruding from limbs Ruby felt could not be her own. She ran a finger over her bicep, feeling the pounding strength within it. Her attention holding on the warrior in front of her for a few more moments before splashing cold water on her face and reaching for the toothbrush.

"Hey! Doooo huu know whahh hime everyhum hot hack laaat night?" she asked.

"What?"

She spat the toothpaste into the sink and quickly rinsed her mouth. "Sorry. I said, do you know what time everyone got back last night?" She asked again, leaning her side against the door frame.

"Oh! Not sure. Probably midnight or so. Why?"

"No reason. Just asking. I ran into Ray, and she said

you guys were still in that forest, so I was worried."

"You were worried about a bunch of Elementals with powers being on their own?" He smirked, "or just me?"

"Get a grip. It was late and we're in a place we know nothing about."

"It's Sherfield. There's probably fifty people total living here. What could happen?"

"Anything really," she said under her breath.

"Wait, you're not still worried that he'll come back, are you? Because he's gone, Rue. To wherever he's going next. You said it yourself, remember?"

"I guess. But that was before–" she stopped.

"Before what?"

"Nothing. No matter."

"Rue. Before what?"

She bit her lower lip and looked down at her toes. Counting each one to avoid making eye contact with him. "Okay. I'm going to show you something, but you have to promise not to overreact," she said and walked over to her backpack. Her hand reached into the front pocket and she sat down next to him on the bed, tossing the letters into his lap.

"What is this?"

"They're letters. From him. He sent more."

Liam unfolded each new letter and quietly read them over. When he was done, he read them again. And again. Until she could see his back and thighs grow as rigid as stone. She reached over to put her palm on his arm, but he jerked it back. "How long have you had these?"

"I don't know. Not long. A few days. He left one of them in my pocket after the last attack."

"And the one from last night? Where did you find it?"

"He had some courier drop it off for me. In the garden after the bar."

"Do you even understand what a huge deal this is?" He asked, "How could you not tell me? And why are even keeping these letters?"

"I know it's a big deal and I didn't tell you because I knew you'd freak out. Like you're doing right now."

"And?"

"And I don't know why I'm keeping them. Maybe they mean something. I mean, why would he even write them?"

"To scare you! Don't you get that? He's trying to scare you shitless so you don't follow him around." Liam slapped his hands on his thighs and sat back down next to her. He slumped his head, breathing slow and deep. "You can't hide this stuff from me. It's not your job to protect me."

"Are you kidding? It's my job to protect everyone!"

"Not me, Rue. Never me. I'm the one that has to watch out for you. If he hurt you last night, if you hid those letters and there was a threat in there that you didn't realize, and he hurt you–" he shook his head violently, "I don't know what I'd do. I'd kill him. I'd probably die trying but I would do it."

She tried to reach for him again and this time he let her. Her fingers entwined with his as she let the coolness of her Water powers collide with his Fire. Her other hand rested on his cheek, stroking it gently. "I know," she whispered, "I understand. I'm sorry." Ruby pulled him in lightly until his head was nestled in between her neck and shoulder and continued to stroke his face. Their silence enveloped them, spreading from their bodies to the bed, the floor, to every inch of the room. She held him until she was sure his body temperature returned to normal, as normal as a Fire Elemental's temperature can be. When she was certain he was no longer fuming, she elbowed his side lightly. "Wanna throw those out and have some coffee?"

"Coffee sounds amazing right now," he said, shifting his attention to the letters. "But maybe you're right, let's hang on to these. Just in case."

"You sure?"

"Not really," he smiled.

Ruby got up and headed for the coffee machine near the front door, catching a glimpse of her vibrating phone on her way. She ran to the table, catching the cellphone right before it fell on the floor.

"Oh! It's Shay!" she cheered. "I wonder what she wants!"

CHAPTER 31
DARKNESS AND PLASMA

"What the hell were you thinking?" she shouted at Jake, watching him cower in the doorway.

"Morning to you too. Wanna come in maybe?" he stepped aside and let her trample into his room, "that's quite the greeting, by the way."

"I could seriously kill you right now."

Jake grinned sheepishly and started to fumble with the buttons of his shirt. She had caught him mid-dress and he barely had time to throw clothes on when he heard her furious pounding on the door. "I take it Shay called you?"

"You think? You broke up with her in a text message? Who does that?"

"Not that it's any of your business but I can't exactly rush back to Westerlake right now to have a heart to heart with her. Not sure if you noticed but we're a little busy here."

"It is my business, Jake! You made it my business when you decided to hook up with my best friend and then treat her like dirt!"

She tried to read his expression which seemed to border between regret and gloating, unable to believe that he could be so heartless. When she finally got Shaylah to stop crying on the phone that morning the first thing she did was rush over to give him a piece of her mind. Liam was convinced it wouldn't do any good, urging her to stay out of it but there was no way she could keep quiet. Not when her best friend was falling apart on the other side of the country. She's never heard Shaylah cry, especially not over a guy. The more she thought about it the more she realized that she's never known a guy to break up with Shaylah. It was usually the other way around. When it came to men, her best friend tended to get attached fairly quickly only to leave them in the dust when the next best thing came around. It caught her completely by surprise to see this reaction to Jake's thoughtless text. Maybe it was the fact that the three of them were so close. Whatever it was, she was going to tear him to pieces for upsetting Shaylah.

"I didn't treat her like dirt. I just didn't want her getting the wrong idea."

"And what idea is that exactly?" she asked, tossing a pair of pants from the bed his way.

His face reddened and he quickly put on the slacks, turning around to pour himself a cup of coffee so as not to face her. "The idea that this thing with me and her was going somewhere."

"Maybe you should have thought of that before stringing her along all this time. Did you seriously think you could just have your fun with her and move on?"

"It's not like that. I never told her it was anything serious. Which is exactly why I had to end it. Before things got too complicated," he turned to face her, stretching out a cup in her direction. "Coffee?"

Ruby waved off his gesture, the look of disgust on her face deepening. "They already are complicated. I can't believe you'd do something like that. I feel like I don't even know you anymore."

"Yeah, well, that makes two of us."

"What the hell does that mean?" she raised an eyebrow his way.

"You know exactly what that means."

"Please, enlighten me."

"Ever since the whole peace treaty fiasco you've been a completely different person. You don't even look the same anymore."

He had her there, she had changed drastically in the last few months but she didn't think it was for the worst. And she most definitely did not know what any of it had to do with him and Shaylah. "So?"

"So just because you've changed, doesn't mean the rest of us did. It doesn't mean I did."

"Seems to me you've changed quite a bit. The Jake I knew would never do that to a friend."

"The Jake you knew was in love with you," he murmured, "he still is."

Ruby tried to find his eyes, but he refused to look at her. This wasn't an act or some heartless way to get out of the situation. He meant it. When Shaylah and him first got together, she wasn't sure how to feel about it. It was an adjustment, but she truly thought he was finally happy. Happy and over her. Seemed like she couldn't have been more wrong about him.

"So, what? You used her? To do what? Make me jealous?"

Say no. Please say no.

"Not at first. At first, I was angry, and she was there, and she cared. It just happened," he sighed, "then I saw how you reacted when you caught us, and I guess I liked knowing that you might be jealous. That you might care."

Goddammit, Jake!

"Look, I'm sorry I hurt her feelings. Honestly. I swear when we get back, I'll fix things. I'll get things back to how they were."

"With Shaylah?"

"With everything."

Her back sunk into the wall as she processed his

words. He still thought there was a chance for them. After all this time, after everything she'd said to prove otherwise, he still wasn't letting go. "Jake, things will never be how they were."

"Maybe. But they can be something different." He tried to smile but his lips barely parted, leaving his mouth half open, like he was about to swallow a gulp of air. "I will get you back, Rue. You'll see."

"Get me back? You never had me to begin with!"

She was tired of the back and forth. It was fine when it was just the two of them but now, he'd gotten Shaylah involved, and worse– broke her heart. He had to stop. Whatever delusions he had about her had to end. She wasn't his property. He didn't lose her in a bet, and he wasn't going to get her back in one. She pulled away from the wall, dropping her weight to her feet and raised her palms in front of her. The scars on her arms bulged from the blood rushing into them, dark red blood that turned black when it reached her fingertips. It coated each finger and swirled its energy around her hands, the molasses dripping from her nails all the way to the floor. Her attention drew to Jake, his eyes wide, a bead of sweat forming at the top of his brow. He was afraid. Of her, of what she could do. *Good! Let him be afraid!*

"I am not yours to get back! I am your AetherBorn! That is as far as our relationship goes!" she howled and let a bolt of plasma catapult in his direction. It hit the wall behind him just inches from his face, leaving him stunned and breathless. "If you ever hurt anyone else I care about again, you will answer to me!"

Ruby fisted her hands and shoved them in her sweatshirt pockets before turning to the door. The anger swam in her stomach, pushing the bile away to make room for something even more sordid. She took a sharp breath, settling the hatred that now filled her entire body. As she walked out of the room, leaving Jake speechless and shocked, she caught a glimpse of herself in the hall mirror.

Another girl she couldn't recognize peered back.

This one had eyes filled to the brim with darkness and plasma.

CHAPTER 32
EST. 1926

The flash of anger slowly subsided as Ruby made her way back to her room. The further away she got from Jake, the less her blood smoldered and boiled in her veins. She could feel each cell as it cooled down. The rage she felt just moments ago dissipated next to the relief that she hadn't actually hurt Jake. She had not lost herself like that since she first discovered her powers and it worried her that she was actually unable to rein herself in. What would have happened if she hadn't left? What could she have done?

"Ouch!" Ruby yelped at the sudden sharp pain on her fingertips.

It was as though she got stung by a bee, a very large bee. Her eyes drifted to her hands, hoping to find the culprit and swat it out of existence. But there was no bee on them at all, no insects of any kind. Nothing bit her.

. . .

INSTEAD, *her hands were covered in a dense mixture of blood and black plasma. She followed the trail of sluggishly flowing and burning liquid to the scars on her arms, open now as if she had just endured the cuts. The plasma curled and twisted around her finger, the burn intensifying by the second. Every twist was tighter, squeezing her finger into submission, almost breaking it right off.*

"No!" Ruby screamed, her voice catching before she could complete the word. She pulled at the bottom of her sweatshirt with her other hand, trying desperately to stop the blood that was now pooling from her wounded finger and dripping onto the cement beneath her feet. Slow drops,– the color of rust and dirt. Blood and plasma.

Her head spun.

She reached for the corridor railing, using it for balance. She was going to pass out from the pain if she didn't stop the bleeding. There had to be something around she could use. Her eyes wild, she scanned the corridor. Nothing. Not so much as a doormat. She could have sworn she passed a housekeeping cart on the way here. Where was it and where was the maid? Ruby's attention shifted from one end to the other. Where was everyone?

The corridor was lifeless. Not just lifeless but entirely void of movement or sound. Even the parking lot on the other side of the railing was half empty aside from a few cars. It felt like someone had erased half of her reality and replaced it with a stagnant version of it.

"Of course!" she exhaled and let the echo of the place carry her yelp away. This isn't real.

She looked back to her hand, expecting to see a shattered pinky, and laughed deliriously. The plasma was gone, and her hand was whole. She was whole. Stretching her fingers wide, she smiled and looked over the railing onto the lot. Except for the initial pain, this may be the calmest place she'd been to. Just as calm as—

Ruby gasped, realizing where her vision had taken her. The minimal details of the real world, the emptiness and quiet. This was the Aether Plane; she was sure of it! As soon as the realization crept into her mind the air brightened, filling with the glittery spark that she was accustomed to seeing in the plane. Her mind was filling in the details, starting with the glitter and ending with the row of doors on her left. Bravery grasped her and she walked over to the door closest to where she stood, eager to try the handle. Before she could pull it open, something on the door caught her eye. She raised her gaze to read the inscription burned into the wood.

'Welcome to Coalfell. Population: 8592. Est: 1926.'

CHAPTER 33

A FRIEND

"**P**ack it up dudes and dudettes, we're going to Coalfell!" Zag shouted, lounging a little too comfortably on their bed and leaving the rest of them standing around awkwardly in whatever small niche they could find.

"And you're sure about this, Ruby? There isn't the possibility that your vision was wrong?" Elena asked.

"When have they ever been wrong?" she scoffed and shoved Zag's feet off the bed so she could sit down. "It definitely felt like a sign. I'm sure that's where Demas is heading next. Zag, can you check which Elementals live there? It's not a big place, so maybe we can warn them on the way."

Zag fumbled to sit up and offered her a halfway decent albeit mocking salute before reaching for his phone. "I'll get Harvey to look into it back home," he noted, his fingers moving fast to type a message. "Maybe we should get some more people?"

"To meet us there? You think we can't handle it?" Jake asked.

She perked up, meeting the question with an annoyed glare. "He thinks that we almost died. Unless you're willing to go up against Demas and Eros again? Because from what I can tell, you're still limping from yesterday."

"So, Ren and Elijah should come? Cool. I'll text them." Zag said cheerfully and continued to type.

"You guys okay with that?" she asked the group in front of her. Her gaze meeting Liam's who had finally finished pacing back and forth. His restlessness since she told him about the vision was starting to make her dizzy.

No one answered. A few nodded in agreement only to look away when she saw them. She rolled her eyes, fixing her attention back on Zag. "Good to go, I guess."

"I already asked, girlfriend. They're in." He grinned and shot a wink in Ray's direction, "Ya know I got you!"

"Thanks. They'll meet us there, then?"

"Yep. Said they're bringing a friend."

"Who?" She hated getting more people involved than was necessary.

"No clue. Someone hardcore, I'm sure. Ren wouldn't mess around."

The density of fear in the room was impossible to

ignore. Ruby looked around her, trying to gauge their emotions but the only one that dared look back at her was Liam and she wished he hadn't. The concern on his face was paralyzing. Even Leah was obsessively tugging at the chipped polish on her nails and she was the cheerleader of the group.

"There's nothing to be afraid of," she said, trying to sound convincing.

Zag's eyes darted her way but lowered when they met hers. "Are you serious? There's literally everything to be afraid of."

"So, what? We run away and hide like cowards? Would you like that better?"

"Ruby, honey, there's no need to shout. No one is running away, we're just worried." Elena rested a hand on her shoulder but jerked it away quickly. She hadn't noticed that she had raised her voice let alone the fire that built up in her body in a matter of seconds.

"It sure sounds like you're too scared to fight."

"That's not fair, Rue." Liam's arm tightened around hers, oblivious to the heat. "We're all on the same page."

She lowered her gaze, stretching her palms open and closed until the blood in them ran cooler. They weren't on the same page at all; this she was sure of. Whether they admitted it or not they were scared, she was too but unlike the rest of them, she wouldn't give Demas the satisfaction of seeing it.

"So, we should pack?" she said quietly, "catch the next train if we can?"

They filed out of the room quietly, trailing mixed emotions in their wake. Ruby couldn't help but wonder what she was getting them into this time. She waited until Liam closed the door behind them and the shadows of the group's slow-moving bodies passed by the curtained window. Sinking into the pillows on the bed she let out a sigh, feeling like she could take a breath now that it was just the two of them. "Are you worried?"

"About Coalfell?" Liam sank into the mattress next to her, "A little. You?"

"A lot."

She flipped her hair to one side and sloped her head onto his shoulder. The scent of him filled the room and she inhaled his cologne, letting the spices of musk and African violet fill her nostrils.

"I'm more worried about the rest of the group. If we get there in time and it's not just Demas and Eros–" she trailed off.

"I think it might be worse if we don't get there in time."

He was right. She knew he was right but a part of her felt rigid at the implication. A very small and selfish part that wished to be too late. To arrive in Coalfell after Demas and his band of deities had already passed through. To avoid any more damage to her people, to her family. *Selfish!* She cursed herself. They couldn't be late.

Demas was using these killings to taunt her, and if they were even one step behind, more innocent Elementals would be hurt. His savage brutality was escalating with each kill and her conscience couldn't handle another vicious murder with a pathetic note at the scene.

She shot a brief glance to her finger, suddenly remembering the vision.

"Does it hurt?" Liam asked and raised his chin in the direction of her hand.

"The finger? No, not really."

"What do you think it meant?"

The tension in her hand lifted as she squeezed her fist open and closed. "I don't know if it meant anything, but it was super strange. I felt like I was hurting myself, you know? Like my blood was bad or something."

"Maybe all that time you spent in the plane is starting to affect you somehow. Ray did say that the longer you stay there, the more the effect lingers."

"Yeah, but why now? It didn't happen before, and it's not like I had black veins and eyes when I snapped out of it. Why would the effect appear in a vision?"

"Who knows, Rue. We're kind of dealing with a bunch of guesses here."

"What do you mean?"

"Well, growing up, I didn't even think AetherBorns were real and now we have a center full of them. Then we get hit by deities of all things. Stuff just keeps dropping from the sky, and we deal with it. You could tell me tomorrow that the earth is actually flat, and I'd believe you. There's no such thing as normal anymore. If this otherworldly plane you get to visit is suddenly having some weird side effect, well, as far as I can tell, that's the most normal thing to have happened so far!"

A smile sneaked its way to her lips, and she reached over to graze his stubbled cheek with it.

"What was that for?" he asked.

"For putting things in perspective."

"Ha! That's me. Perspective Liam!"

"I'd work on the nickname if I was you," she teased and dropped her head back on his shoulder allowing her eyes to close.

Even if it was just for a moment.

CHAPTER 34
COALFELL

The view from the waiting area in the Coalfell train station offered about as much interest as an empty warehouse. The flat plains stretched for miles and even though Ruby could feel the chilled breeze from the lake on her face, she couldn't squint her eyes tight enough to see the shore. This place made Sherfield feel like a metropolis, and she wondered if perhaps they got off at the wrong stop. When the announcement for the station buzzed over the speakers, they had been the only ones to leave the train car. She had hoped to find a small shop at the station to keep herself busy while they waited for Ren and Elijah to arrive from Dalhurst, but at this point, she'd be glad to settle for cell reception.

It was as if they had stepped foot in a silo. No

people. No sound. Just the eight of them and the vast-
ness of the fields outside.

She reached her hand into her backpack, finding the
edge of the dagger hilt to make sure it was still there.
Not that she couldn't feel its energy revving up when
they settled on one of the benches. It seemed the dagger
was even more on edge than she was.

"Is anyone else bored out of their skulls right now?"
Nola rolled her eyes, finally breaking the silence. "These
guys better get here fast. This is some mental torture
crap right here." She stretched her arms over her head
and yawned to prove her point. Any other day, Ruby
would have snapped back at her, but she couldn't
exactly disagree. They were all bored to tears waiting for
the train from Dalhurst to come in.

"It should be here soon," Cyril said after checking
the arrivals board behind them.

"Yeah, girl, chill!" Zag yelled out, ducking out of the
way to avoid the empty coffee cup Nola chucked at him.
"Yo, that's straight up littering." He walked off to throw
the cup in the garbage.

"And that's how you get rid of him. Good to know."
Nola chuckled and went back to reading her book.

With the exception of a few polite exchanges, the
group was quiet, and Ruby couldn't figure out if it was the
fear or the exhaustion that was making them brood. Jake
had been especially silent since they left the motel,

though out of all them, he was the only one that had a valid reason not to speak to her. She wondered if what she said had any effect on him but one glance in his direction proved otherwise. His steel blue eyes were fixed on her. Not in a possessive manner, it was the stare of someone who is longing for the impossible. Calculating how to get his hands on it. With one flick of her wrist, Ruby swirled the coffee in the paper cup he held, making it splash all over his blazer. He jumped back from the impact, trying to wipe the stain from his clothes without success.

She muffled a chuckle into her chest just as three figures appeared in the archway.

"Guys!" Zag yelled and bolted towards them, "Finally!"

He was still chatting up Ren and Elijah when she noticed the third person standing next to them. It was hard not to notice her. *This is the great fighter they brought?* Ruby thought, studying the newcomer.

The girl in front of them was one of the most beautiful girls she'd ever laid eyes on. Her blonde hair was scrunched in a beach wave that would take Ruby hours to recreate, while on her, it fell in effortless locks and framed her bright blue eyes like curtains. Eyes that pierced through the room with a glance. Ruby felt herself disappear, zipping up her leather jacket as high as it would go and tucking her head into the hood of the sweatshirt beneath it. She had no idea how this girl wasn't cold in the mini dress she was wearing and doubted the knee-high boots helped much.

Completely impractical.

Her attention shifted in Liam's direction and she ground her teeth in an attempt not to pull herself into him. He was watching the girl just as intently, trying to figure out who she was. A little too intently for Ruby's liking.

"Sorry for the wait folks. It's quite the ride from our place," Ren waved when the three of them walked over.

"Next time, we fly." Elijah added, tugging at Ren's jacket sleeve. "I don't know why you thought this would be more relaxing, sweetheart."

"Oh, don't be such a grouch!" Ren exclaimed, planting a soft kiss on the back of his hand. It was the first real sign of sensual affection that Ruby has seen from the two and she averted her eyes, feeling as though she had interrupted a private moment.

"Ahem," the girl cleared her throat next to them.

"Right! Sorry!" Ren hollered, "Everyone, this is Sealie."

The girl curled a loose strand of hair with her finger and gave a slight wave with her other hand. "Nice to meet you guys!" she sang, her voice as chipper as a fairy tale princess. She took a step forward, fixing her eyes on Liam. "Fire, right?"

"Uhm, yeah." He said reluctantly and draped his arm over Ruby's shoulder. "How did you know?"

"You have that Fire look about you," she winked, and Ruby resisted the urge to throw a punch. "Me too!" Sealie added, flipping her golden locks over her shoulder. Her hand lit a flame to prove it and she blew it out with a wave.

Liam nodded, trying to look less uncomfortable. "Zag tells us you're quite the warrior."

"Oh, goodness! What have these silly boys been telling you? I mean, I'm not terrible but I doubt I'm anywhere close to you. How can someone even compare themselves to an elder. And such a young one at that!"

It was official; Ruby hated this girl.

"Maybe you two can spar some time," Zag offered, "Wouldn't mind seeing Liam getting his ass kicked by one of his own."

"I think Ruby does enough kicking to last me a lifetime," Liam smiled and pressed himself closer to her.

She found herself smirking against her better judgment, but the disappointment evident on Sealie's face was worth it.

"But hey, if you're up for it, I'm always up for more practice," he added.

Her hand dropped his as instantly as her smile vanished. It took her a moment to regain her composure. She was being petty and childish, and it needed to stop. They had much bigger problems to deal with than her jealousy. *He doesn't mean it like that. Relax.* She let her shoulders drop and picked up her backpack. "Have Ren and Elijah briefed you on what's going on?"

"Oh, yes! Seems like you all have quite the situation on your hands!" Sealie chirped.

"*We* all." Ruby corrected her quietly.

"Of course. Yes, of course. But don't worry, between all of us, I'm sure we can handle it!"

The cheerfulness was starting to bother her. From the corner of her eye she could see Nola was just as annoyed and was already dragging her suitcase to the exit.

"I guess we should head to the hotel," Ruby motioned to Nola's disappearing figure with her head. "We can catch up more there. Zag did you get the list of Elementals?" She lowered her voice. She was so used to being discreet that even though they were the only people in the station with the exception of the ticket teller, she still felt the need to keep her voice down.

"Sure did! I have it in my bag. You wanna see it?"

"It's okay. We can all look at it when we get to the hotel."

"Perfect!" Sealie cheered, "I don't know about you guys, but I am itching to get out of these clothes!"

Ruby rolled her eyes. Less clothes seemed to be the least of Sealie's problems. Pushing the thought out of her head she followed Nola outside.

She glanced back only once, telling herself that it was to check on the group but knowing full well that she was only looking for Liam. Waiting for him to rush behind her.

The palms of her hands almost melted the suitcase handle when she saw that he was still chatting with Ren and Sealie, and she quickened her stride for a faster escape.

Well, you wanted a normal relationship. This is it. Congrats.

CHAPTER 35
EVERY SINGLE ONE I PASSED

C lothes laid in piles on the floor of the hotel's bathroom while Ruby tried to find something to change into– though she was mostly tossing her belongings from her suitcase onto whatever empty space there was around her. She picked up a dress, eyeing it carefully before throwing it on top of a pair of jeans behind her. Why did she even pack a dress? This wasn't a vacation.

"Rue? I'm gonna grab a snack from downstairs! You want anything?" Liam yelled.

"Sure. Yeah. Whatever." She mumbled, pushing the door closed with her foot.

She was still upset. Meeting Sealie and her unbearable flirtation with Liam left her feeling inadequate. Up until now, Liam's attention had been unwavering and her very limited experience with men left her unprepared for the jealousy she was currently feeling. Not just jealousy, raging anger towards Sealie. She needed to get a handle on it before she blew up on someone who was risking their life to help them. Flirting or not, Sealie came to help them and she needed to accept that. Liam loved her and she had to trust him. But first, she had to get her things off the floor.

The high-pitched creaking of the door sounded outside, and she grabbed a handful of clothes in her arms to tidy up.

"Oh, hey, Leah!" she stopped in her tracks, realizing Liam was still in the room. "You looking for Rue?" There was a mumble of words behind the door followed by light footsteps. "Babe! Leah's here!"

Ruby waited until she heard him walk away before venturing out of the bathroom.

"Hey!" she yelled out to Leah who was awkwardly picking at her nails in the doorway, "You wanna come in?"

"Uhm, yeah, sure."

Leah took a few small steps into the room and paused in front of the open bathroom door, her eyes taking in the mess on the floor. "Everything okay here?"

"What? That? Just trying to pick an outfit. All good. What's going on?" Ruby tried to sound as nonchalant as she could, hoping her poor acting skills were enough to convince Leah she was alright and not the mess of nerves she actually was.

"Nothing. Actually no, something. I guess. I don't know."

"Seriously, what's going on?" she gestured towards the bed in hopes that Leah would sit down. She didn't.

"It's probably nothing."

"If it was nothing, you wouldn't be here. So, spill. What's up?"

Leah bit her lip before blowing a lock of fiery hair from her eyes. "I've been practicing."

"Practicing what?" she was growing impatient with the back and forth. As much as she loved Leah, she wished the girl could be more open and frank with her thoughts.

"The animals. My connection to them."

"You have? That's great, Leah!"

"Yeah, it's pretty cool, I guess. After we talked, I called Myriam and she emailed me a bunch of excerpts that could help."

"Did they?"

"Sort of. There was a lot to go through, and I kind of got bored," she pulled the hem of her blouse, "and just kind of went for it. Figured the best way to nail this whole animal communication thing was to actually do it. And–" her voice cut off like she wasn't sure she should keep speaking.

Ruby tried to read her expression. Was she scared of telling her or just plain scared?

"They're afraid," Leah finally said.

"Who's afraid? The animals here?"

"Yep. Like all of them. Every single one I passed on the street was scared. Not like the way they are back home when something bad is about to happen. The ones here are terrified."

"And you think it's because of Demas?"

"What else could it be? I'm sure they're picking up the energy from him and the deities. I've never felt anything like it."

Ruby felt awful for asking Leah to even attempt this. She was so much more sensitive than the others and tapping into massive fear such as this was likely to break something in her. She never should have asked her to do this. "Are you okay?" she asked, knowing full well that there was nothing she could do if the answer was no.

"Uhm, just shaken up, I think. It was a lot."

"I'm sorry."

"Don't be. I wanted to help."

"At least we know we're in the right spot," she smiled.

There was a tap at the door, a few quick knocks followed by the twisting of the handle. "You guys good?" Liam poked his head through the door, "We need to get going."

"Where?" Leah asked, tilting her head sideways.

"They found bodies. It's all over the news." He said and walked past them to turn on the television. "We're too late. Again."

CHAPTER 36
ZAG AND HIS MAP

A photo of the couple that was found dead in their small, rural home flashed on the screen and Ruby shivered before looking away. They looked so much like her and Liam. The same age, similar features, even the way they were posed holding each other resembled their behavior. She was hoping no one else was making the same connection. One look at Liam told her he was oblivious to the hint the murder left. Only *she* seemed to understand that this was a direct warning. If they didn't back off, they were next.

"Waters," Zag said from the corner of his mouth. "Died in their sleep."

"That's what the cops think happened?" Liam asked.

"Yep. Fools. Who just stops breathing in their sleep?" He shook his head as if insulted by the thought.

"They were suffocated?" she asked.

"Nah, girl. They literally stopped breathing. Like by choice."

"Wait, what? You're telling me they went to sleep and then decided to just hold their breath until they died? Both of them?"

"Uh huh. Newscaster said something about clenched jaws and whatever."

"Well, maybe it's not Demas then. Could be a coincidence."

The video suddenly paused. In a brief moment, Ray was standing in front of the television holding the phone they were using to stream the news. "Oh, it's him alright!" She hollered, pointing at the screen towards the floor of the crime scene. "See that? Ash."

Ruby squinted her eyes and leaned closer to the screen.

"Nyx did that. They're here. The ash proves it." Ray said.

"That and the animals," Leah whispered from the corner of the room.

Zag's attention shifted to her abruptly. "What animals?"

"What? Nothing. Not important," she brushed him off, her cheeks looking wind swept. "Assuming you know where these two were found?"

"Dude, do you even need to ask? Of course, I know! I already had them tracked on our way here."

How could they let this happen again? They knew who Demas was after. Why did she let them go to the hotel in the first place? They should have gone straight to the couple's home as soon as the train touched down in Coalfell. If she wasn't so busy with her foolish jealousy, they could have gotten there in time to save them. Or at least to warn them. This was all her fault. Demas may have killed them, but she was the reason they were dead.

"I guess we should head over there?" Liam asked.

"We're not going," she said, her voice booming through the silence in the room. "It's a waste of time."

"But what if–" he started to ask but stopped, meeting her eyes instead.

She knew exactly what he was wondering. What if there's another note? She didn't care anymore. She was done playing this game with Demas. If he had anything he wanted to say to her, he'd better do it to her face.

There was another light knock at the door.

"I'll get it!" Liam yelled, already halfway to the front.

She didn't need to turn around to see who came in. Sealie's sugary voice carried through the room, making Ruby roll her eyes when it reached her. White knuckled, she kept her eyes fixed on the screen. "Zag, were you able to figure out where the portals might be?"

"We did!" Zag pulled a crumpled map from his back pocket and shot a smile in Ray's direction before flattening it out in front of Ruby. "The red marks here," he pointed at the scribbles across the map, "are where the plane is closest to us. At least from what Ray remembers," he threw another grin in the AetherBorn's direction and Ruby almost upchucked her coffee.

"That's a lot of places. All of these could be used to portal through?" she asked.

"Basically," Ray shrugged.

"So, he could be going anywhere next," she said, her face contorting.

"Not exactly," Zag smirked. "See these blue lines? That's where the Elementals we know of live."

"That doesn't exactly narrow it down too much. It looks like at least, what? Twenty or so places they could be in? Maybe there's a pattern in the type of Elementals he's after?" She tried to recall the details of the last three murders. "Liam, what do you think?" she asked but there was no answer.

Her eyes turned to the door; a bowling ball dropped in her gut as she watched Liam lean his arm above him against the door frame while Sealie giggled at something he said. Her nostrils flared at the sight. Sealie let out another laugh, and this time her hand reached over to touch Liam on the shoulder. Within seconds, Ruby was on her heels and storming towards them. Was this actually happening? Now, in the middle of everything?

"You two have got to be kidding me!" she shouted, her fists dark with plasma at her side. "We are all busting our butts trying to figure this out, and the two of you are over here giggling like fools. That's great!"

"Rue, we're just talking."

"Is it about Demas? About our impending doom? Because if it's about anything else you're wasting my time! You're wasting all of our time!" She pushed a fist into the doorframe, the force of the plasma fueled hit shattering a small part of the wood. Sealie jumped back but Liam held his ground, his eyes trained on her, beckoning her to calm down.

She pushed her way through them, not bothering to say another word and ran down the hallway to the elevator. She could hear Liam call for her which only made her run faster. Let them figure it out for themselves. He betrayed her. She needed him more than ever right now, and he would rather flirt with some Fire from Dalhurst than help. She needed to get some air, to get out of the hotel that was making her feel caged in an impossible situation.

The elevator doors slowly closed in front of her, and she waited until the numbers started flashing their descent before letting her eyes flood with tears as she collapsed on the floor.

"Rue?" Jake's voice sounded grim behind her.

She wiped the tears from her eyes quickly, trying to

hide the evidence of her breakdown before turning to face him. He was only a few feet away from her, his blonde hair tousled by the wind and slightly wet from the stray drops of water the fountain expunged. She had sat on the ledge of the fountain in the hotel driveway for quite some time, hoping the sounds of its waters would drown out her hysterical tears.

"Oh. Hey! What are you doing here?" She asked, trying to sound as cheerful as possible.

"Came out to clear my head. What's wrong?"

"Nothing. Everything's fine," she tucked her fists into her jacket pocket.

"Come on, stop bullshitting me. I've known you my whole life, remember? I know when you're upset. Spill it."

Jake sat down next to her, his hands floating awkwardly above his thighs. It was as if he was trying to decide whether to hug her or not. He stayed that way for a few moments before choosing to cross his arms instead. "So, what happened?" he asked again.

"Nothing. I just can't do this anymore."

"Do what?"

"This whole AetherBorn garbage. I'm tired. And I suck at it."

"You don't suck at it."

"Obviously, I do!" She slapped her legs dramatically, sending a tingle of heat into her thighs from the hit. "How many people have died already? What good am I if I can't stop this bastard from killing Elementals right and left whenever he feels like it? I can't even figure out where he'll go next, let alone protect everyone!"

"Whoa, whoa, whoa! Slow down please," he hesitated then placed his palm on her back. "Take a breath. A real one." He waited for her to grasp some air. "Good. What triggered this? Was there another murder?"

"Yes. They found them this morning."

"Them?"

"A couple. Water House. They were in their apartment. They stopped breathing in their sleep."

"Water, huh?"

"Yeah. Why?"

Jake twirled a finger over the pool beneath the fountain, forming small waves that followed his hand. "No reason. Just the first one of my House he killed. I was starting to think he might actually like us Waters." He shrugged, pushing the waves further down the pool.

Ruby watched the waves hit the edge of the fountain, splashing a little before settling into a natural calm. Just as they stilled, another set of waves splashed the edge, obeying Jake's insistent powers. Her red eyes widened as she watched. "Oh my God! How did I miss this?" She yelled excitedly.

"Miss what?"

"The water!"

He looked at her like she had finally lost it. His eyes

tried to follow her train of thought but hit a dead end. She grabbed his shoulders and shook him lightly, "The water is the answer! He's only been hitting places near water. He's staying coastal!"

"But why?" Jake asked.

"No clue! But I might know where he's heading now!" She grabbed his sleeve and started to drag him behind her, her feet picking up their pace the closer they got to the hotel. "Come on! We need Zag and his map."

CHAPTER 37
CHARRED TO A CRISP

She was grabbing everything she had originally dumped on the bed back into her suitcase. If her mom could see how she was packing, she'd never hear the end of it. Every piece of clothing she'd brought was balled up and crammed in between shoes and toiletries. Once they'd narrowed down the next town Demas would go to, she couldn't pack fast enough. If she was correct in her assumptions, he'd be going to Marlton next. Other than Westerlake, it was one of two other water adjacent towns and the closest to Coalfell.

She'd asked Liam to tell the others, eager to get him out of the room before she had another meltdown. She couldn't face having a conversation with him about Sealie, at least not yet.

A bead of sweat ran down her spine and hit the top of her jeans as she crammed a pair of boots into the overflowing suitcase. She pressed down on the clothes, straining to make more space where there was none. Defeated, Ruby slouched over the suitcase on the bed and exhaled with a sigh.

The air left her lips and glittered in front of her.

Ruby perked up, the sudden feeling of being watched setting her senses aglow.

"My darling, Ruby."

Her head jerked to Demas who was half leaning on the wall behind her. Without hesitation, she reached for the dagger on the bed, kicking away black fog with her legs as she leapt towards it. She turned back, holding the dagger in front of her.

"Tsk, tsk. Now, that's not how you treat a guest, is it?"

"What the hell are you doing here and why are we in the plane?" she demanded, dagger still pointing at his throat.

"I wanted to check in since I didn't get a chance to write to you this time. But what's this?" He brought a bony finger forward to the suitcase, "Leaving already?"

She said nothing, her eyes scanned the room for an exit point. His body was directly in front of the only way out. She would need to go through him to get away – not that she wanted to get away. What she wanted was to kill him right where he stood.

"I'm guessing Ray let you in on the plane's little secret? I'll have to talk to her about that later, won't I?"

He grinned, eyes flashing to the reflection of light on the blade. "Now what are you planning to do with that, dear?"

Again, she was silent. Taking a step forward she tightened her grip, flipping the blade in her hand and readying to strike. She called on its power, gathering it into herself, strengthening her approach. When she had enough power in her hands, she lunged toward him. Her hands in front, one holding the dagger and one in a fist, she shot a solid bolt of plasma at his heart. It spiralled as it flew, sharpening its edge until it was an exact copy of the dagger. The plasmic blade shattered the air, its tip almost hitting her target when Demas spun out of the way. His grin widened as he landed low after his last spin, open palms facing her. Before she could adjust to his new placement, she was hit by the liquid he sent her way. The plasma coated her left arm, burning into the scars on it. She looked down and howled as she watched hundreds of black plasmic ants burrow their way through the scars AND into her skin. Ruby tried to swat at them, only burning her palm with each ant she managed to kill. "AAAAAAH!" she yelled louder and dropped her left hand to her side. The skin on it was charred to a crisp by the plasma and even lifting it caused a senseless amount of pain.

Ruby sliced the dagger through the glitter in the air and as she completed the movement, a circle of plasma shot through. The Chakram she manifested spun its sharpened edges, picking up speed toward her opponent. Demas tried to spin away, moving to his left as quickly as he could but the Chakram was faster. The blade sliced through his arm, blood forming on the fabric of his sleeve within seconds.

"Well, that's not very nice," he tried to sound nonchalant, but she could hear the pain in his voice.

The confidence made her stand taller. She switched the dagger into her hurt hand, forming a plasmic flame with the other, and ran towards him. The fire grew as she ran, and she readied herself to burn him where he stood. Demas grinned, baring his canines at her.

There was a flick in his wrist and shadows crept quickly from beneath him, covering the entire room.

Suddenly, it was pitch black. Not even the glitter in the air could be seen.

Why did I insist on closing those goddamn blinds? She thought, stopping in her tracks and trying to reorient herself. There was a light breath over her left shoulder. She jerked to face it, her hands outstretched in front of her, feeling for something recognizable. Another breath on her right. She twirled, finding nothing again. He was taunting her. Ray did tell them that Demas preferred the darkness. *Can he see me right now?*

She backed up. A step more. Then another until her back hit a wall. Waiting.

The sound of his demonic laughter echoed through the room. She wanted to throw up. Not just from her disgust for him but from fear. She was afraid of him. No matter how much she tried to act otherwise. The shadows slowly crept away, leaving a trail of light as they dispersed. They crawled towards the center of the room, gathering themselves into a recognizable form. She watched as one by one the shadows twisted and twirled until they weren't shadows at all. Until Demas was standing in front of her. Laughing.

He didn't want to kill her. That's not what this was about. He wanted her to know that she couldn't win. That he was stronger.

Ruby raised her hand, the ball of black plasma fire still lingering in it and sent it towards his face. When it was almost in front of him, she pulled her energy inward, finding a connection to the Air powers within her. With the power at the edge of her throat, she exhaled sharply, blowing a massive wind at the barreling flame. As the air left her lungs, it darkened, taking on the characteristics of the Aether Plane. It joined the ball of fire in its flight, adding to the momentum and causing it to expand. She had him now.

The flame was right in front of Demas when his hand moved from the top of his head to his chest. From where Ruby was standing, it looked like he was playing 'now you see me, now you don't' with a baby.

Something was in front of him now, shielding him from her attack. A darkness that was almost reflective. *The shield!* She gasped, realizing he had summoned the same protection shield he had in the clearing. But it was too late.

Just as Ruby understood what had happened, the flame hit the shadow barrier he put up and exploded upon impact. The power of the flame shot in every direction, plasmic fire burning through the air, ready to destroy everything it touched. Ruby crouched, covering her face with her hands. The rest of her body screamed with pain as the flames took their claim. Her legs, her arms, her hair. Everything was on fire. She dropped to the ground, rolling to put out the flames. The smell of burning hair, clothing, and flesh was overwhelming. Ruby jerked and kicked, screaming from pain and fear. Her leg kicked the side table, knocking over a lamp that shattered when it reached the floor.

Wait, I hit the table. We're not in the plane anymore. She thought just moments before her eyes closed and the room went dark.

CHAPTER 38
YOU NEED TO HEAL

"R ue?" Liam's distorted voice swept across the back of her mind, "Rue, wake up! Wake up!"

She could feel someone shaking her shoulders. Strong, warm hands that ruffled her body with desperate shakes. Liam's hands, she was sure of it. Her brain swam as she slowly peeled her eyes open, squinting to bring the light into focus. Her ears perked when she saw him in front of her, his face a wrinkled mess of concern.

"Rue! Jesus, Rue! What happened?" He grabbed different parts of her body desperately, inspecting each wound. She winced when his hands stretched around her arms. "Sorry! I'm so sorry!" He cried, letting his mouth crash into hers. "What happened?"

She raised herself halfway, resting her weight on her forearms, immediately regretting the choice. The pain shot through her arms, crushing her bones as it moved. Ruby looked down in horror. Her throat clenched and she forced herself to grind her teeth to stop from screaming. She was covered in bleeding, burnt scabs. Black plasma embedded itself into every nook and cranny of her wounds, making it impossible for her heal. That's when she noticed it.

The smell.

Sulfur clung to her nostrils, the stench of it coating every tiny hair, making it impossible to shake off. "My... my hair," she whispered, touching a singed lock with two fingers.

Liam was quiet. He looked her over quickly and scooped her up in his arms, carrying her to the bed. It was the first time after she'd been hurt that he didn't console her in any way, didn't tell her things would be fine. Probably because she looked like a car had run her over.

"I'll go get some towels and water. Please don't move."

She watched him run to the bathroom and took the chance to inspect her body once more, cringing while she pulled the burnt fabric away from her.

"I thought I said not to move," Liam murmured and sat a bowl of water on the nightstand. He dipped one of the hand towels into it and slowly began to wash the plasma off her. She could see the palm of his hand redden when he gripped her arm, but he didn't seem to notice. He kept lapping the towel, trying to get out as much of the plasma as he could.

"Babe, careful. Your hands," she said.

"I need to get the plasma off," he answered, eyes as wild as valleys, "I need to clean this off, you need to heal."

He continued scrubbing until she placed one hand over his, applying slow and steady pressure. Ducking her head slightly, she met his eyes. "Liam. Stop."

The towel flopped against her skin. Its rigid fibers scratching the flesh that was still untouched on her arm. Liam's hand reached to pick it up again, trembling. "I–" he whispered, his voice breaking. "You weren't moving. You weren't even breathing." He grasped the edges of the towel, but his hands fell away as if its weight was too heavy to bear. "I thought you were dead."

"I'm alright. At least I will be."

"You don't look alright. I should have been here. If I hadn't been so stupid and got you mad, I would have been here. I could have stopped this. I'm such an idiot!"

"You're not an idiot. I'm the one that got jealous and stormed off."

"Rue," he met her gaze, his green eyes clouding with the onset of a storm, "there's nothing to be jealous of. I swear! Sealie, she was just being too friendly. It's not like that. You know I love you. Only you."

Ruby fought the pain and reached up to cup his face, "I know. I was dumb."

"Not at all. I'd have torn her apart if I was you." His face froze. "I'm sorry about Jake. About how I acted."

"It's okay."

"It's not though. I should have walked away instead of getting angry. If you hadn't shown up, I don't know what I would have done."

"What did he say exactly?"

"Nothing. Nothing important."

"Liam," her palm grazed his cheek, "tell me."

"What's the point? He's a dumb kid who said something he shouldn't have."

"About me?"

He nodded.

"About getting me back?"

Another nod.

"You know that's not going to happen, right?" She sat up, "Ever."

"I know. I'm just saying that I get why you pitched a fit. With Sealie, I mean. Jake says one thing and I go off. At least you didn't threaten the girl!"

"Wish I could take the win but trust me, I wanted to," she smiled.

"Well, hey! If it makes you feel better, I'm pretty sure she's more into Jake than me."

"Ha! Right now, I wouldn't wish that even on her!" she laughed.

"Oh, really? Wanna fill me in on this drama?"

Ruby sank into the pillow at her back, letting him

continue removing the remaining bits of plasma from her wounds, and started to explain her situation with Jake. She took her time, filling him in on every detail and making sure not to rush through the story. Despite what she might have been telling herself lately, they had all the time in the world. It seemed she'd finally started to believe that.

A charred lock of hair fell on the train bathroom floor joining the pile of others that Leah had cut off in an attempt to give her a semi-acceptable haircut.

"Stop fidgeting," she scolded when Ruby started to shift anxiously from side to side. "Or you'll end up looking like–" she tried to find a good comparison.

"Like someone cut my hair on a moving train?" Ruby offered with a sly smile.

"Hey! Don't diss my talents please! I used to cut Zag's hair all the time. Before he went all hippie on me and refused to come anywhere near the scissors. Trust me, I won't ruin it."

"I'm pretty sure that ship has sailed. Setting your hair on fire is as much ruined as you can get."

Leah wiggled her nose and snipped another piece

off the front. "It's really not that bad. I think short hair kinda suits you."

"Whatever, it's just hair," she lied. "It'll grow back."

"You don't have to pretend, you know. I get that this sucks."

"The haircut? I thought you said it's not bad!" Ruby laughed.

"No, Dumbo, not the haircut. Everything that came with it." Snip, snip. "How are you holding up anyway?"

"I don't even know anymore. I wish I could just feel confident about this whole thing for once. Take a page out of Nola's book."

"She's not confident! Are you kidding?" Leah exclaimed, almost chopping half her ear off. "She might come off that way, but the girl is just as scared as the rest of us."

Snip.

"So, everyone is scared?"

"I mean, not everyone."

"Name one person that isn't."

"Uhm..."

Great, she was getting further and further into this mess and they weren't even sure they could win. Why were they following her in the first place? She should tell them to go back, follow Demas on her own, and stop putting them all in danger. What if they couldn't win, and she'd just risked the last days everyone might have to spend with their families on a wild goose chase? She needed to cut them loose, stop being selfish, and let them go home. So, what if she couldn't win this without them? That didn't give her the right to string them along. Besides, she wasn't even sure if she could win this *with* them either.

"Hey," Leah said quietly, "it's not what you're thinking."

"So, I'm not just some asshole that's forcing people to follow a murderous psychopath across the country?"

"No! Well, yes. Just not the asshole part," she sighed and lowered the scissors to her side. "It would be weird if no one was scared. You're scared, right?"

"Petrified."

"But you're still following him. Still trying to end this, to make it right. That's exactly what we're all doing."

Ruby took a deep breath, her back hunching as she breathed out.

"We're not here just because you need us. I mean, we'd definitely help you. That's what friends are for. But it's not just about you. All of us have people we love back at that center. All over the world really. If we don't stop him, we're done."

"Yeah, I guess."

"Well, maybe try to remember that the next time you get all depressed." Leah snipped the scissors in front of her face and laughed.

She let her work in silence, hypnotized by the sound

of the blades and the whirl of tendrils hitting the ground. Soon, there was so much burnt hair on the floor that it looked like someone had placed a very disturbing rug in the bathroom.

"All done," Leah sang and stepped away, letting Ruby take in her new look.

Well, this is different. Her fingers ran through the short strands, turning from side to side to get a better view. She felt like she was playing a role on a stage. Between the still healing scars on her arms and legs and the jagged haircut, she couldn't even tell that this was her. Maybe that was for the best. Maybe this new girl could get a grip and step up already.

She tousled the hair again, roughing it up to look well worn.

"I love it!" she yelled and jumped up to give Leah a hug.

"You look like a totally different person," Leah said, clearly proud of her creation.

"Yeah. That's kind of the point."

THE SMALL, east coast fishing town was a welcome sight and Ruby was deliriously overjoyed to finally wrap her jacket around her waist. Sporting only a tee without getting frostbite felt like a definite win. Her and Liam led the way down the bustling main street, and she couldn't help but gallop past the small shops and restaurants. This place reminded her of Lakeside, with all its charm and perfectly arranged shop windows. Even the people who walked down the street seemed happier here. Every lunch sign they passed boasted fresh fish and varieties of seaside inspired menus. Ruby had never realized how much one could do with shellfish until she walked by yet another variation of fried tacos. Despite being near the water, Westerlake was not quite as proud of its shoreline, making places like Lakeside such a novelty for the city dwellers. Marlton, however, put Lakeside to shame. There was not one building that they passed that didn't somehow manage to grasp attention.

"We almost there?" Ray yelled out from behind them, tearing her away from the window sirens.

Ruby rolled her eyes, hoping her silence would make Ray leave her alone but within seconds she could hear tiny steps rushing to her side.

"Did you hear me? How far is this place?"

"It's just a few blocks more. Do you have no patience at all?"

"Patience? Are you kidding?" Ray scoffed. "We're literally marching to some stranger's house just because she's a Fire Elemental and lives by the water and hoping she's not dead. How do you *have* patience right now?"

"Okay. You don't need to be so morbid about it. We made good time and Demas doesn't know we figured it out," she leaned in, almost whispering his name. "She's not dead."

"Well, at least we have more peeps this time," Ray gestured behind them to the large group of Elementals following down the street, "The three from Dalhurst look like they could kick some ass. Even Barbie."

She scowled at the mention of Sealie. Even though Liam explained what happened she still cringed when she heard her name in conversation.

"What's up with her anyway? She tryin' to get in on your dude or something?"

"Mind your own business, kid." Ruby said and sped up her pace to catch up to Liam who was already well ahead of them.

"Ah! So she is. The tramp!"

"You need to back off. And don't call people names! Didn't your parents ever teach you to be polite to strangers?"

Ray shrugged and walked fast enough to be next to her again, "Didn't really have those. So, no."

"Sorry."

"For what? Never had a curfew either, or someone that told me what I should say and what I should wear. It was great!"

They turned the corner, crossing the small street towards a long line of three storied townhomes. Trees lined each side of the street and Ruby could have sworn she heard the birds sing in unison. This place was like a fairy tale.

"It's the one with the green door!" Elena noted.

"Finally!" Ray rolled her eyes and ran back to join the others.

Ruby couldn't agree with her more.

The townhome was divided into three apartments, each floor getting its own unique resident. Ruby scanned the names on the doorbells, her eyes finally finding what she was looking for. M. Sutton. *Madeline.* She started to ring the doorbell when the door opened and an older man stepped out.

"Oh, I'm so sorry!" he muttered, clumsily trying to push past the group.

"No, no. We're sorry! We're in your way!" Ruby said and painted a friendly smile on her face. "We're just here to see Madeline. I'm a friend of her family, they said I could find her here."

"Maddie? Oh, yes of course! I'm glad to see she finally has some friends over!" He flashed a toothless grin and started to hobble slowly down the street. "Oh! Can you perhaps ask her to keep that cat quiet? It's been hollering all hours of the night!" The man yelled and disappeared behind the corner.

Cyril and Elena exchanged a melancholy look when he passed which left her feeling anxious. Maybe this Maddie wasn't home? Maybe she was on vacation? That couldn't be it. People don't leave their cats alone and possibly unfed while they go on vacation. There was a growing bulbous pit in Ruby's stomach when she pushed the green door open and took the first steps up the stairs. She jogged to the second-floor apartment with the group on her heels and knocked. One knock. Then, three. Soon she was banging on the door like a madwoman until Liam seized her wrist and lowered it, twisting the handle instead. The door to the apartment slid open, sending the pit in Ruby's stomach into her throat. She all but choked on it when the small orange cat bolted out the open door down the stairs.

Liam held a hand out to stop her but she knocked it out of the way and flew into the apartment. The pit exploded, firing a thousand nails into her mouth. She tried to inhale, tried to breath, tried to look away. There was no point looking elsewhere. Her eyes followed the light movement of a girl's small feet swinging back and forth, swaying ever so slightly from the blow of the air conditioner hitting the noose. Ruby shifted from side to side, swaying with her. Her eyes filled with tears. She opened her mouth to cry out but there were no words.

Arms wrapped around her as Liam pulled her in, turning her into his chest. Away from the girl. She fought against him, pushing him away and rushing to get her down. She had to cut her loose. She could still be alive. They might not be too late.

"No! No! No! No!" she yelled, struggling to cut the rope with the dagger.

Jake and Liam ran over, holding up the body while she stabbed at the rope, ripping it to shreds until it finally gave way. The two of them lowered the young girl to the floor and Ruby pounced on her, trying her best to remember how to perform CPR. Why didn't she pay more attention in that class in high school? She was so useless! She pumped at her chest, taking small breaks and blowing air into her unmoving lungs. All the while whispering, "No! No! No!". Her hands were starting to turn red form the repeated pressure, but she couldn't stop. When Liam knelt beside her to pull her back, she pushed him away. Continuing to pump her chest. She could save her. *She's not dead. She's fine. She'll be fine.*

She felt another hand on her shoulder, cold this time, frailer than Liam's and turned to see Cyril standing over her.

"She's gone, Ruby. There's nothing we can do for her now."

Her eyes burnt, floods escaping their prison like a dam had burst. The tears rushed down her face. She grabbed his hand, tossing it away from her. "Don't touch me!" She screamed, "Don't you dare touch me!"

"I'm just trying to help. You need to let her go."

"You're trying to help? *You?*" She continued to yell, "I don't need your help! You've done quite enough!"

His face contorted as he tried to figure out what she meant. "Please, Ruby, calm down."

"Don't tell me to calm down! You murderer!" She

was angry, so angry she could burn him down right where he stood. Her hands shook. She scrambled on the floor, looking for the dagger. Where was it? She had dropped it when they got the girl down, but she couldn't see it anywhere near her.

"Rue! What the hell are you talking about?" Jake yelled from behind his father.

"Oh, he didn't tell you? Wait, that's right! He probably doesn't even know it happened! How convenient! You kill someone and don't remember you did it. Is that how you can sleep at night?" She yelled, eyes still madly searching the floor.

"Ruby, you need to calm down," Cyril took a step towards her, motioning to her arms.

She glimpsed down, catching only a peek at the black veins speedily making their way up her body. She could feel them rush through her blood until they were at her chest, encasing her heart.

Her eyes spied a light jump on the floor in her peripheral and she ran in its direction, speeding to pick up the dagger.

She raised it with a quivering hand, shaking the blade at Cyril. "I know who you are, Cyril!" She howled, "You killed Liam! You slaughtered him right in front of me! If my powers hadn't kick in, he'd be dead! You're no better than this monster! You murdered him in cold blood all over some stupid sword!"

She chucked the dagger to the floor and stood

breathless. Her blood burned with the power of the plasma, stifling every heartbeat. Claiming her very essence as its own.

A light hand grazed her shoulder and she turned to see Leah inching closer towards her. Nudging her to breathe. She obliged, her attention turning back to the room. To the group in front of her.

To Liam.

To Jake.

Then to the rest of them, standing wide eyed and open mouthed in front of her. Their eyes dancing between her and Cyril who was slouched with his head bowed in the center.

They were afraid before; Leah had told her that much at least. They were even more afraid now.

Except this time, it was her they feared.

CHAPTER 40

IT'S NOT REAL

"So, this is why you hate Cyril so much?"

Liam sat on the front steps of the townhome while the others stayed upstairs to put the crime scene back to the way they found it. Elena suggested they clear out as soon as possible before someone else saw them. It was an unanimous choice to reposition Madeline's lifeless body to the noose and Ruby was surprised that so many stayed behind for the foul task. Although, after her little melt down, she doubted anyone wanted to spend much time in her company.

"I'm sorry I didn't tell you."

"Why didn't you?"

She bit her bottom lip and slid her hip lower on the railing. "I thought it would make you upset. Or mess you up somehow."

Liam raised an eyebrow in her direction.

"I know. It messed *me* up instead. I get it."

"I'm just saying, it would have been good information to have. This whole time I thought you just carried a grudge against Cyril for no good reason."

"Yeah. I wish."

"Seriously, though, you should have told me."

"I really didn't want to hurt you."

"You think that would hurt me? Something that sort of kind of happened? Rue, it's not real. Not as far as I can tell. What's real is you driving yourself crazy carrying it around all this time." He rested his chin in his hands and sighed loudly. "And not that I'm a huge fan of Cyril or anything but you have to admit he's been solid when it comes to the Elementals."

"I guess."

His arm reached around her legs and pulled her closer until she was perched on his lap. She dropped her head on his shoulder, breathing in the musk beating off the side of his neck. The hair on his chin was already starting to grow in and she let the rough surface scratch the top of her brow; finding some comfort in the touch. Liam's hand ran through her short hair and she perched uncomfortably in his lap.

"I like this look!" He declared, almost in answer to her self-consciousness. "It's pretty sexy."

"Ha! I'm glad you think so 'cause it'll be a while until it all grows back." Ruby fired back while trying to tuck a loose strand behind her ear.

His hand reached for hers, pulling it away. He leaned in– slowly at first– then, as if struck by sudden urgency, he crushed into her, his lips claiming hers. The anger she had felt in Madeline's apartment was just a memory now; the plasma in her veins gone. The only burning she felt in her heart was her desire for him.

"You're beautiful." Liam said when their lips finally parted, "But if you keep hiding things from me, I'll call your parents. Don't think I won't do it!" He raised a mocking fist and shook it in front of her, "Please stop acting like you're alone in this."

"Wait, what did you say?" She curved her back to face him.

"Stop acting like you're alone?"

"No, before that! Parents!"

"Huh?"

"Madeline's body, he made it look like a suicide."

"So?"

"So, why?" Ruby hopped off his lap, pacing back and forth on the porch. "All the other murders were big shows that were meant to look like murders. He left them in public places, bunch of ash everywhere, hid little notes, came for me in the Aether Plane. Why not this time?"

"Maybe he was in a hurry?"

"No. That's not it. He would have made time. This was different. You heard the neighbor. She didn't have anyone over, and Zag said he couldn't find any trace of a family. This girl was all alone. No one would think twice if she had killed herself. No police. No news. It's like–"

She stopped pacing, her gaze meeting Liam's. "He knows."

"Knows what, Rue? I'm not following."

"He knows we've caught on. No more breadcrumbs, there's no need to string us along."

"So, it was just a game?"

"Not a game," she said, "a tactic. He's been baiting us this whole time. Getting us away from where we should be."

The pinching tingle at the back of her neck told her she was right.

"He's going to Westerlake."

"I think so. And we're not there to defend it."

Liam sprang from the steps, his face contorting into a mess of worried wrinkles. She could tell that he was no doubt listing out everyone that was in the center. Everyone they had left to fend for themselves. "We need to get back there immediately!" He yelled and started to make his way into the townhome. Ruby jumped in front of him, blocking him before he could get inside the door.

"Not yet. Please," she begged, "not here."

He caught her eyes as they flew up to the second-floor window.

Not after what I just did in there, she thought. Loud enough that Liam understood and sat back down. His head heavy in his hands again, waiting for the others to finish so they could get back to the hotel.

"I'M LEAVING, RUBY." Elena crossed her arms, leaning against the hotel doorway, her eyes locked on Ruby's.

"What? Why?"

Elena rubbed the side of her arm with an index finger. "Someone should get back to Westerlake as soon as possible."

"I know. We're all going there. I thought–" she trailed off. "Why really?"

"I can't stay with you. Whatever this is, it's no longer my fight."

"What are you even talking about?" Ruby's voice raised, her blood starting to boil. "It's everyone's fight! We have to defend ourselves!"

"We both know this is no longer about that."

"Oh, please enlighten me! What is it about then?" She balled her fists until the knuckles turned a pasty white. Their light shade more evident against the red of her skin, against the fire sparkling to the surface.

The mayor nodded in the direction of her hands. "It's about that."

"My powers?"

"No, Ruby. Your lack of control. This is no longer

about the Elementals. You've–" Elena rubbed her forehead, "You've changed."

"I haven't changed," she scoffed. "I'm just stronger now."

"There is a difference between strength and revenge."

"Not from where I'm standing."

"I think that is exactly the problem."

"So what? You're just leaving us?"

"No. I'm going to catch the next flight back home. I want to be there. Harv and Myriam shouldn't be the only elders in the center. Not if they're in danger."

Ruby raised her hands, the sudden movement made Elena take a step back. She pushed the hurt out of her mind, not willing to accept that the mayor might actually be afraid of her like the rest of them.

"Elena, please. We need you. I–" she lowered her eyes.

"I can't stay. I won't stay. I'm sorry."

"Is this about Cyril? About what I said?"

"The next flight is in a few hours," the mayor started to back away, ignoring the question. "I should head out now. I wanted to tell you in person. I will do what is best for everyone in the center, but I cannot do it your way."

She watched as Elena walked away. Her heart leapt until she could feel its beat pummel at her chest. She knew her loss of control might have shocked them, but this was something she didn't expect. The elders were supposed to be on her side. She was the one that united them. The one that saved them from a future of self-destruction. How could Elena walk away from her? From everything they'd been through so far?

Her hand reached to clasp the edge of the door-frame, letting the fire in her scorch the metal. She pressed her fingers tightly into the frame, feeling its weight buckle beneath her grasp. Tears flooded her eyes and she gasped for air as the realization hit her.

She was losing them.

Ruby's body shook and she tipped forward, letting the tears flow down her face and hit the floor. She missed home. She missed the comfort of her childhood bed, her mother's cooking. She wanted to run after Elena. To tell her that she was sorry and that she needed her help. That she needed her to stay.

Her eyes turned to the singed doorframe; the shape of her burning fingers embedded in it.

Ruby straightened up, brushing the palms of her hands against her stomach. Elena was right, she had changed. It was up to her now to decide what she would do with that change. She'd been scared and angry for too long and being an AetherBorn had cost her too much. She wasn't going to wait around until more people left her side.

If they were scared, let them be scared. She was their AetherBorn. She had delivered them to safety time and time again and nothing would stop her from protecting them. Elena would come back to her, perhaps not right away but she would come back.

It was Ruby's job to make sure there was something to come back to. That she was someone worthy of her return. Someone worthy of her leadership.

She was an AetherBorn and she had cowered in fear for long enough.

CHAPTER 41
DOORWAY

"Ruby! Liam! Ruby!" Zag knocked incessantly on their hotel room door. "You guys there? It's important!"

She unlocked the door, barely having enough time to tighten her robe before he came barreling through. Elijah and Ren were on his heels and cast an apologetic look in her direction before stepping inside.

"Sorry," Ren said, running a palm over his shimmering head, "We were having lunch and he just yelled something and ran here."

"We tried to stop him," Elijah added.

Ruby waved them off, "No worries. We're used to it."

She gestured for them to come in, realizing too late that Zag was already sprawled next to a bare-chested Liam on the bed, pointing excitedly to something on a map he'd brought in. The knowing glance Ren and Elijah exchanged made her face burn as she realized how their state of undress must have looked. Their personal activities were apparent to everyone in the room. Everyone but Zag it seemed, who continued to talk excitedly at Liam.

"Girl, you have got to see this! I figured it out!" He beckoned her to come closer, "We've been following this dude in a circle. All over the country! And it's just getting us closer to Westerlake!"

"Yeah, we know. Ruby already figured that out," Liam said.

"Well, obviously! She's the queen bee," Zag beamed and pointed back to the map, "but do you know why we're on this morbid little treasure hunt?" He knocked a pen against the paper, waiting for her to answer.

"No?"

"Ha! Well, you won't like it, doll. I mean, it's brilliant, but for sure you won't like it."

"Zag, will you stop with the theatrics and please just get to the point?" Elijah yawned and rolled his eyes.

"Ugh, fine. So, we know the murders are all near the water, right? Well, I started thinking– why the water? Why not anywhere else? Seems totes random, no?" He paused to look around the room before continuing, "So I did some digging, got Ray on board, and turns out that these spots here," he drew large circles around the places where they had found the murdered Elementals, "are like energy centers of sorts."

"Meaning what, exactly?" Ren asked.

"Not sure yet. Not technically. But who knows, this mumbo jumbo is more Twilight Zone than science if you ask me. Whatever! Anyway, these parts here where our homeboy left the bodies are exactly where the Aether Plane has the most contact with the real world. I couldn't get that weirdness out of my noggin! Energy centers, murders, circles. Sounds like a freakin' ritual!" Zag threw his hands up in excitement, "And guess what? It is!"

"It's what? A ritual?" Liam asked, leaning in closer to the map, the duvet slipping dangerously closer to his waist level. Ruby had to look around to make sure she was the only one paying attention before nudging him to cover up.

"Yep! Some weird thing from eons ago. Turns out that if you end an Elemental life in each one of these energy sucks and close the ring," he drew a circle around the map for emphasis, "some big doorway thing is supposed to open."

"A doorway where?" she asked, turning the map around to face her.

Zag knocked the pen against his head before tucking it into his shabby hair, "That, I have no clue of, milady. I was lucky I could even dig this stuff up. But I know it has something to do with Westerlake. Ray said the plane was the the most accessible there. Like it had the most energy out of all the other–" he thought about the word to use, "ports. Yeah, I like that!"

"Zag! Pay attention!"

"Right! Sorry! But yeah, that's basically it. Circle, murder, energy ports, Westerlake is in shit."

With his last statement, the room fell silent. She was afraid to look at their expressions out of fear of falling apart. They'd played directly into Demas' hands. He had strung them along and they had followed him; *she* had followed him. All the while the real danger was threatening their home and she had allowed it to be left completely unprotected. If Demas and the deities were to attack right now, they had no chance of survival. Sure, the knights and AetherBorns would put up a fight but she doubted it would be enough. Not if he caught them by surprise.

"We have to warn them. Elena is on her way back there, she can start securing the center with the rest until we make it back," she said, silencing the thoughts she didn't want to hear. "Zag, can you let everyone know?"

He nodded, folding the map under his arm before rushing for the door.

"Zag!" She yelled after him, "You did great. Thank you." She watched him give a final salute and disappear into the hallway.

"We'll call our people back home. Have them meet us in Westerlake," Ren said.

"Guys, I can't ask you to do that."

"You're not. We're offering. Besides, I've never been to Westerlake. I hear it's beautiful!"

Their eyes met and she smiled, only for a moment before her lips turned downward and a sadness settled across her face.

"Yeah, I'd live and die there."

CHAPTER 42

THE LIGHT SHE SAW BEFORE

Elijah followed Ren outside, trying to keep up with his pace and almost dislocating his shoulder on the door frame. The door closed behind them, the slam sending a rush of adrenaline through the room, followed by an immediate hush.

She tossed her suitcase on the bed next to Liam and started dumping her clothes into it in a rush. "Why do you think Westerlake is so important?" she asked, cramming a pair of jeans into the pile.

"I'm not sure. But there has to be a reason for so many Elementals to end up there," he noted, following her lead and beginning to pack himself. "That can't be a coincidence."

"I wonder why there of all places."

"Maybe they like the pizza, I'd stay just for that! We

have the best slice in the country!" He laughed but stopped as soon as she shot an unimpressed glare in his direction.

"I'm serious."

"I know. But I don't know what to tell you. As far as I know, there's been generations of Elementals being born in Westerlake for as long as anyone can remember."

"Since Westerlake was formed?"

"Probably even before that!" He announced excitedly, "My dad once told me that when our grandparents first started building the center, people died in the tunnels on the regular. Like it was cursed or something."

"And they still kept trying to build there?"

"Yep. Maybe something drew them to the place."

"Like whatever that energy is that Zag was talking about. Something from the plane."

"Could be."

"Well, it's a start at least." She rubbed the back of her neck, "We should see if I can find the portal to the plane when we get back."

"And do what if you do?"

"I don't know. Get Demas in there or something."

Liam's body tensed next to her. "And then what?" he asked, eyes fixed on the edge of the bed.

"Then I kill him."

The silence lingered like the scent of gasoline in an alley. When Liam finally spoke, his eyes were a shade of green she hadn't seen before. She tried to discern the meaning in them but he'd built a wall to keep her out. "That's suicide."

"What other choice do I have?"

"How about choosing not to attack a murderous deity?"

"You know I can't do that." Her hand grasped his, "Things are different now."

"You definitely are."

"What's that supposed to mean?"

"Ever since we started this whole wild goose chase you've been changing. It's like you don't care about anything but him and his deities."

"Liam, he's going to kill everyone! That's his big plan. I can't care about anything else right now. I have to stop him!"

"What if you can't? What if he just goes on killing Elemental after Elemental? You going to keep chasing him around the country?"

"No. Like I said, I'm going to kill him."

"By yourself? You're going to go up against four deities all by yourself?" His hand jerked away from her, "Look, I know you're an AetherBorn and have the sword or whatever but you're not invincible. And you're not that strong."

"Well, I was really hoping that the rest of you would help out."

"The rest of who, exactly? The ones in the center?

Do you mean the kids or the AetherBorns you brought in who are afraid of their own shadows? Who is going to be strong enough to do this with you, Rue? Do you even have a plan?"

He stood in front of her. His body blocked the rays of sun coming through the sheer curtain and it made the hotel room remind her of his sleeping quarters at the center. How she wished to be there right now and not stuck in this strange town– and in this conversation.

"Look," he continued, "I love you and I will follow your little butt wherever you go but I hope you trust me enough to believe me when I tell you that you need a plan. One that's better than 'I'm going to kill him'. You had to watch me die once, please don't make me go through that with you."

Ruby's heart broke. She'd been so preoccupied with everyone's safety that she hadn't stopped to think about how her actions might affect him. Of course, he was upset. If he wanted to rush in and get himself killed, she'd be furious. She ached for him. She wanted to tell him that she was sorry. That she would be careful. That he had nothing to be worried about. But her eyes failed to focus on him, gazing instead over his shoulder, into the small beam of light that escaped into the room.

HER GAZE TRACED *the direction of the light, following it to the wall. It was dark but she could still see bits and*

pieces of the room. Blood covered every inch of it. Every-
thing around her was coated in its red thickness. She
looked down at her hands, vibrating from the sight of
them. It was as though someone had sliced open her
arteries and painted the world with their contents. Her
attention slid back to the light she saw before. By the time
she realized what it was, it was gone.

"RUE? YOU THERE?" Liam asked.

"Huh? Uhm, yeah. What happened?"

"You zoned out for a second."

"Oh. I think I just had a vision."

"You did? What did you see?"

She wanted to describe it but there were no words. She wasn't even entirely sure what she saw herself. "Blood," she said, "a lot of blood. And–" she paused, glancing back to the window, "I think I saw a portal."

The warmth of his hands on the back of her legs relaxed every tense muscle in them. She let out a breath that had been caught in her throat for what seemed like an eternity. Her fingers ran through his thick hair, settling to cradle his head in her lap. She tried to remember some detail of the vision but the only straw she could grasp was the blood. So much blood.

There were too many questions washing over her. So many that she had to steady herself just to breathe.

Stay here. Stay with him. Don't go back there. She recited, hoping to avoid another vision without success. Before she could take another breath, she was back in the blood room. Staring at the portal with eyes wide as saucers, clueless as to where it might lead.

CHAPTER 43
DECIDE

Ruby felt like she had spent half her life on trains. The shaking, the whirring, the sudden jerks in her seat had become like a ritual for her. Each squeal of the wheels against a rusted track silenced her rustling thoughts, sending her back into the car, half reclining in front of Zag and Ray, who were more than a little friendly. She heard Zag say something resembling a joke, sending Ray into a whirlwind of laughter. The AetherBorn's hand landed on his forearm and stayed there, lingering playfully.

Oh, for Christ's sake! Are they flirting?

She remembered these moves. Her and Liam used to play the same games. Now the only moves Ruby could think of involved the dagger and a very dead Demas. She replayed the thought in her head, hoping the blood she saw in her vision was his.

"I'm going to get a cup of coffee," she said, pulling up the drooping waistline of her jeans.

Zag offered a half nod in her direction, but that was as much attention as she got from the two. Shaking her head, she closed the car door behind her. No one needed to see that.

The train jolted, sending her into the side railing. She cursed under her breath but kept walking. She thought about finding Liam – Cyril had pulled him away some time ago for elder business, and he was likely bored to tears by now – but having this one moment alone seemed precious, and she didn't want to part with it.

Carefully making her way to the main car she felt her footsteps slow. She was a few doors away from Jake's seat and tried to use whatever positivity she had left to wish for the door of his car to be closed.

It was wide open. *Figures.*

Ruby turned to look in, slowing her steps yet ready to get away as soon as time allowed. Jake was slouched in the seat, his hand twirling a vape pen thoughtlessly, gaze to the window.

"Finally kicked the habit?" she asked and watched his head jerk to face her.

"Nope. Forgot to charge the battery last night," he said with a smirk. He pointed to the empty seat in front of him. "Need some company?"

Not really, she thought but came in anyway.

He sat up, tucking his feet in to make room for her. "So how are you feeling?"

"Ugh. I guess you want to talk about my little freak out."

"We don't have to."

"Yeah, right! I can see you're dying to talk about it. It's fine. I think I owe you an explanation."

"So, this whole thing with my dad," he chewed the bottom of his lip until it flushed, "what happened there exactly?"

"Other than what I said already?"

"Okay, I don't need the attitude. Just tell me what happened, geez."

She twirled a piece of hair into a point. "Sorry. Every time I talk about it–" she paused. "It's just hard, that's all."

"I know, Rue, but he's my dad. I deserve to know."

"Remember before the treaty? When you came to see me, and I told you about my plan?"

"When you made yourself a martyr for my dad and Elena," he said.

"Yeah, that time," Ruby fidgeted in her seat, rearranging herself to sit on her hands to avoid biting her nails. "I did that right after I went back."

"In time, you mean?"

"Yep. My original plan didn't exactly go to plan."

"How did you even figure out how to do that?"

Her mind disconnected as thoughts of that day flashed by. She remembered the surprising pull of the sword, its power sinking into her. Saw the room spin in front of her again just as it did that day to carry her back through time. Then, like a bullet, it struck her. The image of Cyril slicing Liam's throat, his eyes falling life-lessly in her direction, and the blood. *All* the blood. "Let's just say I had motivation," she finally said.

"You mean my dad killing Liam."

"I'm sorry, Jake. I know you want him to be a hero. I can't un-see it, I wish I could."

Jake slid off one of his loafers and rested a leg on the seat. His gaze left her, softly landing back at the window and the passing view of the landscape. "I get it, you know," he said in almost a whisper. "The connection between you two. I get it more now, I think. Living through something like that, you decide pretty fast how you feel about someone."

She wondered if he was remembering his brother's death at that moment. His face offered no clues but something in his tone made her feel like he wasn't just talking about her and Liam.

"I still love you," he continued. "That won't change. Ever. But I get it now."

Ruby wasn't sure what to say. Instead, she leaned in and reached for his hand, offering a gentle squeeze. His face didn't budge but she continued to hold his hand, her own gaze drifting to the window to join his.

Sometimes how you feel about someone doesn't need any deciding at all.

CHAPTER 44
ONE BY ONE

The floor was slick beneath her bare feet. She took a calculated step, sliding a little before regaining her balance. Her hand reached for a wall to hold but caught only a handful of glittery air instead. Ruby had a feeling that she was back in the Aether Plane. When she opened her eyes, the mixture of glitter and black fog around her only confirmed it.

She took a few more steps forward, almost falling each time.

"What the hell is that?"

Ruby looked down, trying to discern why it was so difficult for her to move. The floor was covered in a dark liquid, not plasma, but something just as murky. She knelt down, sliding her finger against it and lifting it up to her face. The liquid dripped down her hand, getting brighter with each touch of her skin until its color changed entirely. Not plasma, but blood.

She looked down to the floor again and stifled a scream, seeing the deep red spread from her stained feet, rolling over the ground beneath her until the edges of eternity.

Following its trail, she braved another step, then another, splashing more of the blood over her legs. She trudged through it, feeling its thickness in between her toes but not stopping. Ruby walked for hours, until her legs could no longer carry her, until she was shaking and almost every inch of her legs was reddened and stained. Her next step sent her tumbling on all fours and yet she crawled forward, splashing blood on her chest, her neck, her face.

Her eyes were tired and ready to close but she pried them open, concentrating on the path in front of her. She could see an edge on the horizon, a cliff of sorts. The blood that led her here fell off it like a waterfall.

Ruby crawled to the edge and looked down, following the flow of the liquid that oozed slowly down the rocky cliff walls. From her vantage point, she could see where it hit the bottom and continued onward. Flowing slower now like nothing more than a peaceful river. She wanted to fall into it, let go of her grip on the edge and allow the blood to carry her away.

"What is this place?"

She strained her eyes to see further. Past the edge and

the bloody trail, far beyond to the glowing red in the distance. *Ruby squinted to bring the light into focus. It was unlike anything she'd seen before and even from this far away she could tell it must be brighter than a million light bulbs. It was spreading slowly, first a thin vertical red line, then wider and brighter.*

Not a light, *she thought*, a door.

She was looking at a large door in the distance. It was bright and dreadful and final.

And it was opening.

RUBY HAD ALREADY SHAKEN off her vision when Nola came by to see her. As much as she relied on her power of sight, the visions she'd been having lately had offered nothing but morbid visuals and riddles. Either she was losing her touch, or she had finally gone crazy like her grandmother.

She wiped the sleep from her eyes and waved for Nola to sit beside her, hopeful that she wouldn't ask too many questions.

"Did you see Liam out there?" she asked, "He's been gone forever. Starting to think he ran off on me."

"Yeah, 'cause that boy isn't whipped at all," Nola said, trying to force a smile without much luck.

"Oh, God. What's wrong? And don't say nothing, I know that look."

"Have you seen the news?"

"Uhm, no. I haven't checked my phone in a while." She reached for her back pocket and pulled out her cell phone.

"Maybe don't then." Nola put a hand on the phone and lowered it to her lap.

"You're starting to freak me out. What's going on?"

Her black eyes narrowed. "There was another murder. In Falkirk."

"Falkirk? That's just a few hours from Westerlake. Who?"

"A family. All Waters."

"I thought Zag said there was only one Elemental in Falkirk. We were supposed to warn him!"

"They weren't from Falkirk," Nola lowered her eyes, "They were visiting. From Westerlake."

"What? Who?"

"The Achedeons."

Ruby's chest tightened. Her breaths sharpened into needles in her lungs. She tried to open her mouth for air but barely succeeded. "They were–" She gasped, "They had–"

"A daughter. Six years old."

"How? Wait, no. Don't tell me. I don't want to know."

She wasn't just going to kill him. She was going to cut every limb from his body first and watch him bleed out in front of her. But not before she made him watch as she did the same to his family. She was going to hunt them down, one by one, and slaughter them. Deity or not, they would pay for this.

The train car door slid open and Liam walked in. From the look on his face she could tell he had just found out about Falkirk. His hair was a mess and she guessed he had spent the walk back running his fingers through it to calm himself down.

"Have you heard?" he asked and stood in front of her, holding her face in his hands and completely disregarding Nola.

"Yes. Nola just told me."

He nodded toward the other AetherBorn in the room as if only just noticing her. "We need to tell Elena to get everyone to safety. We're almost at Westerlake, hopefully we'll be back in time."

"He's not in Westerlake. Not yet."

"What do you mean? It's the only place left in the circle to hit."

"He's still in Falkirk."

"Rue, how can you possibly know that? This was the last stop before completing this morbid ritual. At least that's what we thought before, no?"

"It is. But he's not done yet."

"Why?"

"Because he's waiting for me. For all of us. This wasn't just another murder. He knew what this would do. How it would affect me."

"You think this son of a bitch killed a child just to get a rise out of you?"

"That's exactly what he did. And it worked."

"And so he's what? Just waiting for us back in Falkirk?"

"Yep. So, let's not keep him waiting long."

Nola peered at her from the corner. "What exactly are you planning to do once we get there?"

"I'm planning to finish this. It's time we do some killing of our own."

CHAPTER 45
FALKIRK

Their procession down the financial district of Falkirk was a sight to see. With Ruby and Liam leading the herd, closely followed by the elders and the rest. They resembled a makeshift arm, or at the least, a very small parade. She was proud to lead them down the skyscraper lined streets, holding her head higher at each turn and breathing deeper with each step that brought them closer to their final destination.

There was no way to know for certain that Demas would be waiting, but something about the way she was beginning to feel made Ruby think that she was correct to assume it. The dagger's powers intensified steadily, forming an ache in her stomach that could only be explained by a mixture of anticipation and fear.

She marched them further.

Past the busy, rush hour streets of the metropolis. Past the bustling happy hour bars. Glancing back only when the streets became quieter and the roads opened up to signal that they were getting closer.

The sun was beginning to set, and the heat of the afternoon had almost subsided, leaving only slight beads of sweat on her brow. One good thing about chopping off most of her hair was the added bonus of never having to worry about having it cling to her wet face.

When it was clear that the hustle of the city was far behind them, Ruby slowed her pace. The Achedeons were found in a car lot right outside of the downtown core, and they were inching closer to it with each step. Her eyes spotted the tall, mesh gate a few blocks down, and she dug her heels in, halting the group behind her.

Liam's attention snapped to her, quickly understanding the pause.

In a few minutes they would reach the lot's entrance. She could only hope that the cops had already abandoned the premises for the night. They would need to get inside without drawing too much attention. She could see from where they stood that the perimeter of the lot was secured with two cameras and an excess of police tape. Zag and Leah did not waste time, strapping their minds into the trees on either end of the building to pull the branches inward until they covered the camera lenses.

Getting past the alarm was a more difficult challenge. They needed to creep behind the building and attempt to disarm the system without setting it off. When they were out of sight from the main street, she popped open the alarm box, only to be pushed aside by Ray. A few cut wires later, the kid was grinning back at her, holding out the motherboard of the alarm system like a tribute. Ruby hated giving her credit but having Ray around might prove to be useful after all.

She waved Jake over and gestured to the door handle on the gate. Without a question, he placed his hand on it, freezing its interior mechanism. The ice expanded, breaking apart the joints of the handle and a quick jolted twist sent it shattering to the ground. The sound of the frozen metal hitting the concrete made her jump, hoping the sound did not attract attention. She slowly pulled the gate, careful not to swing it wide open, and snuck inside the lot. When she was certain the place was abandoned, she peered back through the metal at Liam, gesturing for him to lead the rest of the group in.

Her heartbeat through her thin shirt and Ruby imagined it breaking through her ribs and landing at her feet. Taking a deep breath in she reached down and pulled out the dagger from its holder. She rolled her fingers around the handle, tightening them until they were as red as the sunset behind them.

Another quick glance and she began to make her way deeper into the lot.

Time to end this madness.

CHAPTER 46

THE GAMES AND THE TOYS AND
THE FUN

T he back of the car lot stretched across the entire length of the block with cars stacked above one another on mechanical hoists. They walked in pairs down each of the rows, surveying the car collection as they passed.

It was quiet. Unnaturally quiet.

She could see Leah trying to connect to local animal life, her face wrinkled in concentration as she walked. When she caught Ruby's gaze, she shook her head. The lot had been emptied of all life.

"He's here," she whispered to Liam out of the side of her mouth. He nodded and intertwined his fingers with hers.

A few minutes later, they stood in front of a wall of cars with lanes leading right and left. Liam squeezed her hand gently and gestured right. She followed, waving the tip of the dagger to indicate the direction to the group following behind.

She was starting to feel like they were walking in circles when the dagger pulsed in her hand and sent a sharp pain to her gut. They made another turn to the right and Ruby walked face first into Liam's back. He stopped in his tracks in front of her, shielding her partly with his body. Ruby peered over his shoulder and took a definitive step forward.

"I told you they would show up, brother." Demas sneered from in front of a silver Honda. "Looks like you owe me a drink. Again."

Eros half reclined on the hood of another car to the left of Demas and looked bored with the company. "I'm getting tired of these stakes, next time, I'll pick the wager," he said, his brilliant blue eyes finally looking up and resting on Ruby. "Well, hello there," he purred. "Love the hair!"

She said nothing and rolled her eyes in return.

"And what, pray tell, would you like to wager?" Demas asked.

"How about a heart? Or an ear? Something fun." A voice sang from behind a row of cars.

The darkness parted, illuminating a tall, female figure. The woman slowly stepped forward, creeping closer to Demas until she was at his side, her arm resting on his shoulder.

Ruby's mouth drooped open as she stared at the most beautiful woman she'd ever seen. Her straight black hair flowed down her shoulders, landing just above the curve of her behind, and she flipped it lightly with her hand to reveal a striking set of white-grey eyes. Eyes that held Ruby's gaze and twinkled with mischief. She was wearing a long black dress with a slit on one side that reached the top of her hip, the perfect doorway for her long, tanned legs.

"I'm guessing you're Nyx," Ruby said, trying not to sound in awe.

"Of course! Where are my manners?" Demas spun to grasp the woman's lower back, ushering her lightly forward. "Ruby, darling, I'd like for you to meet my sister, Nyx. Your little Elemental books likely describe her as the Deity of Night."

"That's all?" Nyx asked, her full lips curving into a wicked smile, "But I am so much more than just one thing. How I hate to be described as such!"

"I know, sister dear. Maybe you can fix that later."

Ruby unhooked her hand from Liam's and took another step forward. "Enough of this crap! We didn't come here for chit chat."

Laughter rolled over them. All three deities were cackling at her words which only made her angrier. She would have lunged at their throats right then if Liam hadn't tapped her foot, urging her to wait.

"Oh, you're right! She's quite the little thunder! I

can see why she entertains you so!" Nyx howled, still snickering.

A tinge of fire rustled in her fingers. She was sick and tired of being talked about like she was some toy. Like she belonged to these three and they could do with her as they pleased. She'd defeated Demas before; she'd do it again. And she'd take the other two down with him.

"Enough, Demas!" She yelled, "You wanted me here. I'm here. Your little plan didn't work. I didn't fall apart; I didn't run away. None of us did. You killed that child for nothing, you pathetic piece of garbage!"

Nyx raised a finger and traced the space between her and Ruby with it. Slowly, a trail of smoke appeared at the deity's feet, creeping towards her. She could see it shed ash as it rolled closer, wrapping itself first around her legs, then further up her torso, until the smoke was stretched over her neck, tightening against her like a rope.

"It's Tartarus," Nyx said calmly, raising her finger an inch. The smoke tightened again and moved up, pulling Ruby up with it until her toes were barely grazing the ground. Until she was choking. "Respect your elders, child."

She tried to cough, pulling at the smoke with her fingers, unable to break free. Liam grabbed her legs and pushed her up, freeing her neck slightly, enough for her to inhale. She couldn't panic. She wouldn't allow herself to panic, not with the deities watching. She used her free hand to push against Liam's shoulder and raised the dagger to the smoke at her throat. Her eyes met Nyx, unafraid.

"My goodness, Nyx. Put her down before she slices her own throat with that thing. It's just a name." Demas echoed from behind his sister. There was another snicker behind him, and she guessed that it came from Eros. *Smug son of a bitch!*

With an indifferent nod, Nyx lowered her finger and sent Ruby toppling down into Liam's arms. She rubbed her neck and took a deep breath in as Liam set her on the ground. His grip on her tightened but she pushed him away, standing in front of the group again. Unmoved by what had just happened.

"It's about teaching them respect, brother." Nyx smiled, and it sent chills down the back of her neck, "Like we would with our own children. Isn't that right, Hemera?"

There was a rustle from the darkness that Nyx had emerged from, followed by a few light steps before another woman appeared in front of them. She was younger than the rest, though it was nearly impossible to guess the actual ages of the deities. Her blonde hair glistened in the sunset and Ruby instantly recognized her. The messenger from the hotel in Sherfield was none other than Hemera, daughter of Nyx.

"You!" Ruby yelped.

Hemera looked down as if embarrassed by the

recognition. Ruby took in the sight in front of her. Four deities, in the flesh. They resembled a perfectly cast lineup of movie stars. Each one more tragically perfect than the other. So relaxed and yet so powerful. She wondered how it would feel to kill them. To rid the world of such beauty. Would she be relieved to go through with it or would guilt set in when it was done?

"You seem baffled," Demas said.

"I just don't get it," she spat back. "You, I get. You disgust me but I get it. But them? What the hell do they get out of helping you? Didn't you make all of us in the first place?"

"Oh, not us!" Eros jumped off the car hood, landing on his thick legs. "You all were everyone else's problem. I told them not to do it, but they were all about the games and the toys and the fun."

"So why bother coming here?"

"Because of the games and the toys and the fun." He winked in her direction, "there's a lot more to play with here."

Nyx lifted another finger, this one pointing at Cyril. The smoke flew towards him, grazing across his cheek and slowly making its way down the top buttons of his shirt. "Well, that's most definitely true," she smirked.

Disgusting, Ruby thought and waited for Cyril to slap her advances away. He did nothing of the sort, choosing instead to smile back at her. *Was he enjoying this? The bastard.*

She was done. Demas' family was no better than he was, and she didn't come here to get to know them. More so, she didn't want to. The only thing she needed to know was how to kill them.

A light hit the slight curve of the dagger, reflecting a rainbow of colors onto its blade. She ran a finger over the edge and rooted herself into its power. On either side of her, Liam and Jake followed queue and gathered their own powers. She couldn't see them but was certain the rest of the group was doing the same.

The dagger shook beneath her grip and encircled it with her strength. First in black fog, then in plasma. She let it grow from her hand like a suit of armor, channeling every emotion she had. The anger, the pain, the disappointment. All of it breathed new life into her as she pictured herself wrapped tightly in her powers. She opened her eyes, blacked by plasma, and stared at Demas.

She could have sworn that she could see the slightest speck of fear in him as she charged forward. Ready to tear him apart.

CHAPTER 47
A CHANCE

Ruby sliced through the air, her body barely visible beneath the plasmic shield that oozed behind her as she ran, leaving a trail of plasma in her path. When she was halfway to Demas, she lunged, using all the force in her legs to catapult herself in his direction. Her legs shook when she landed in front of him in a crouch and slashed the dagger across his thigh. The plasma seeped into his leg, immobilizing him briefly. She took her chance, rising to stand and swiftly punching him in the stomach. Demas slid back, his back hitting the hood of the Honda behind him, still holding onto his cut thigh.

She pounced, dagger in hand, ready to strike again. She fisted her other hand, throwing it forward to release a splash of plasma that soared at him, reshaping into an axe that barreled directly at his chest.

"Die!" she yelled, allowing herself a second to breathe.

She inhaled, almost biting her own tongue as the axe exploded in mid-air, sending a splash of plasma to the ground. Her gaze turned to her right. Quickly taking in Eros who stood just feet away from her, arrow and bow pointed. Ruby ducked, knowing a shot was coming her way but she was too slow. The tip of the arrow cut across her arm. Blood soaked her sleeve within seconds.

"Rue!" she heard Liam shout behind her. His footsteps quickened and she knew he was running to her rescue.

She waved him off. "I'm fine! Stay on Nyx!"

The dagger vibrated when she raised it, painting a wall of plasma in front of her.

"Nola! Ray! I could use your help here!" she yelled.

Fog encircled her feet and when she turned, the AetherBorns were at her side. Their hands moved quickly. Spirals of atmosphere rang through the air. They were machine guns of black fog.

Demas crouched beneath the shots giving her a chance to drop the wall. She moved quickly, reaching for Eros, her arm shooting a plasmic chain at his feet. When the chain made contact, she jerked her hand back and pulled, knocking him down to the ground.

Her head jerked back. "Dominik! Ren!" They rushed to her side, "Can you hold them?"

They nodded and turned their attention to Demas and Eros.

Her feet spun. Both arms up, she willed the dagger's powers and took a shot at Nyx, whirling two blasts of plasma in her direction. Each blast spun through the air, sharpening its tips until two swords were spiraling at the deity.

Nyx used her smoke to block one of the swords but the second caught her by surprise. She hunched over, wailing in pain, and tried to pry the plasma out of her side.

"Thanks," Jake smirked and nodded to Cyril and Liam.

The three circled her, cutting her off from the other deities. Their hands twirled and danced as fire and ice hit her crumpled body. Behind them, Elijah and Sealie worked together to gust blazes of fire in a wall around her.

"Babe? You're good here?"

Liam cast a side glance in her direction. "Yeah. Don't worry! Help Leah!"

Without losing time, she ran to a row of Toyotas on her left where Zag and Leah were struggling to hold down Hemera.

Each attempt they made was met with a block. Rocks and dirt exploded as Hemera shot blasts of fire at them, shielding herself with a wall of light with her other hand.

Ruby ran faster, fog trailing behind her like a jet taking off. She collected flames into her hand and pushed them out at Hemera's shoulder. The hit twirled the deity to the side, her eyes disoriented from the shock. Ruby signaled to Zag, motioning for him to hit her other side. He moved quickly, launching one of the concrete blocks forward. The block leveled Hemera, her hands breaking her impact as she dropped to the ground.

The earth shook and Ruby watched as Leah ripped the concrete beneath one of the vans next to the deity. She raised her arms, pulling the concrete and the van up with them. With a quick flick, she sent the van flying into Hemera, trapping her underneath it.

The deity shrieked, trying to pry her leg from under the car without success.

"Holy shit, sis!" Zag's mouth gaped. "You're a freakin' superhero!"

Screams echoed through the car lot. Not her people's screams; the deities. *We got them!* She couldn't believe it. There was a chance they could end this. They could go back home.

Ruby let a smile sneak in as her attention turned to where she left Demas.

She barely heard Liam yell her name when the air around them shivered, the blinding sound sending her to her knees. Ruby's smile vanished as she watched the walls of cars around them crash down like metal sand.

CHAPTER 48
ONE WAY TO END

Her ears still rang from the explosion. She rubbed them with both hands, her fingers reddening from the blood that leaked down her neck. Her vision had just started to come back into focus and she tried to survey the lot.

What happened?

Wrecked cars were everywhere. Crowding the lot like corpses in a flooded cemetery. She scanned the wreckage, her eyes finding Liam in the midst of the dust in the air. His back was turned to her, but she could see the smoke around him from where she lay. It was spiraled around his entire body, a python of death squeezing him dry. She shifted her attention to Jake and Cyril, similarly caught in Nyx's grasp. She couldn't spot Elijah or Sealie, but she was certain they were just as trapped.

"No!" she gasped when she saw Jake stop struggling, his body going limp in the smoke.

Ruby scrambled to get up, her head felt like it was in a vice and she lost her balance, falling on all fours. She struggled against the vertigo and the continuous ringing in her ears. Raising one foot at a time she came to a crouch, willing herself to stand.

Another bang rang out and something ripped into her. Her body convulsed, falling back to the ground. She reached for her shoulder and side, running her fingers across the arrows that protruded from them. *Eros!*

Her head slumped to the side, too heavy to hold up and tried to rip the arrow heads out of her flesh. In the distance, she could see Dominik on the ground, Nola cradled his body yelling something.

Suddenly something moved in the rubble.

Something dark and almost transparent but she was sure she saw it glide in her direction. Either that or the arrows did their job and she was dying.

Ruby shook her head, sending the balls in her skull rolling back and forth. Her eyes watered and she used one bloody hand to wipe them. Pressuring herself to focus.

The shadow moved again. Faster this time. She wasn't dying after all. It flowed at first, then dipped lower and lower until it was touching the concrete ground. As it got closer, the shadow solidified. First the feet, then the legs and torso and finally the face. Thin and angular with a sharp nose and thin lips made for cursing. Demas.

He walked to her lazily. Ruby counted the slow, wretched steps. *One, two, three.* He paused and smiled, like he had won some prize in a lottery. *Four, five.* She heard him laugh and stand over her. *Six.*

"My last offer still stands," he hissed. "Help me right things."

She raised her head slightly and spat blood at his feet. "Go to Hell!"

"Tsk, tsk, tsk. Not yet, Ruby, darling."

His fingers twitched and she was instantly in agony. Her calves felt like they were being sliced by a million knives. She looked down to see a darkness swallowing them. Slowly swallowing her whole. Her hand searched the ground, trying to find the dagger. Nothing.

The darkness thickened, moving up her legs now, ripping her to pieces. She palmed at the cement, feeling nothing but rock and shards of metal. Then suddenly a clang! Her hand pulled in the direction of the sound, landing on the dagger's hilt. She gripped it desperately, raising herself half off the floor.

I have to cut my legs off. It's going to eat me alive! She thought and stabbed the blade into her right leg.

Ruby's scream burst through the car lot. Her tear stained face was red with pain and poor attempts to breathe. *What the hell was that? Why did I just do that?* She shook her head again. Had she gone insane?

Still from above her, Demas laughed. Chills ran down her arm.

He's in my head. He's changing my thoughts.

Growling, she snapped the dagger and reached for his leg, hoping to rip a piece of his flesh off. He took a step back, sending her hurling over herself and rolling unto her side. Her shallow breaths mixed with tears and saliva and she almost choked on her own cries. *This is it. This is how we die. I did this. I caused this.* She raised the dagger to her throat. *There's only one way to end this.* She could feel the tip of the blade push into her skin, but she didn't stop. Not until she drew blood. Not until she could hear Ray's voice calling to her. "Ruby! Stop!"

Ray ran to her, black fog emerging from her hands as she neared, putting up a wall between her and Demas. She grasped her free hand, yanking to get her attention.

"Snap out of it!" She howled, "Get a grip on yourself!"

She didn't listen, only pushing the blade deeper. The tears hit her neck and mingled with the blood before continuing to fall down her body.

Ray shook her more, trying to get the dagger out of her hand. When that didn't work, she stretched out her hand and brought it down across Ruby's face. Her knuckles met bone and Ruby's head snapped to the side, the dagger falling in her lap. She turned to Ray, wide eyed and furious.

"Did you just actually punch me? Whose goddamn side are you on, Ray?"

"You were about to off yourself, loser." Ray pointed at the bloody dagger in her lap, "You're welcome."

Her thoughts were wild. She vaguely recalled what had just happened, but it was like she was drugged. That bastard had crept into her brain and controlled her. He violated her mind and what's worse, he enjoyed it. She picked up the dagger and jumped to stand, forgetting her previously shredded skin. As soon as she made the sudden movement, the pain shot through her. Her legs buckled, her shoulder went numb, and she stumbled back, falling unto Ray.

"Use me," Ray said and clasped her hand.

Ruby didn't need to be told twice. She tightened her grip on Ray and activated the dagger. Her body channeled the AetherBorn's powers, sucking her dry of them. As Ray surrendered, she got stronger. Strong enough to get up again. To keep fighting. She released Ray's hand, letting her tired body slide to the ground. As Ray closed her eyes, the fog dropped. Revealing an empty car lot behind it. Empty with the exception of Zag holding Leah's lifeless body in his arms.

CHAPTER 49

WHY NOT KILL US?

"Can you stand?" Liam tried hoisting her over his shoulder. He was barely able to move himself and from the way he winced when she leaned on him, she was sure some of his ribs had been broken.

She swallowed hard, pushing the pain in her legs out of her mind. "I think so."

They were moving slower than a worm on asphalt, but she had to get to Zag and Leah. Her eyes burnt watching him stand motionless over her body while Cyril performed chest compressions. Even from here she could see Leah wasn't breathing. Her chest was completely still and the blue in her lips made Ruby realize she hadn't taken a breath in quite some time. The ash around her was another dead giveaway.

"Nyx?" she whispered when they were closer.

Liam nodded, wrapping his arm around her.

"Zag, I'm so—"

He held up a hand, his eyes glued to Cyril and Leah. There were no words on his lips, no reaction to their surroundings, it was as if his world stopped when Leah took her last breath.

From the corner of her eye she spied Ray limping to his side and slipping her hand in his. There was a gentle squeeze and more emptiness. The two of them stood there staring down, Ray's eyes reddened with watery, tears drawing lines down her dirt covered cheeks.

Cyril looked up and shook his head and her world collapsed.

She turned around letting the tears flow freely, choking on them and her own bloody spit. She couldn't look back, couldn't see Zag collapse over his sister's body, couldn't grieve her death. Instead, she hobbled away. Her body covered entirely in blood and plasma that continued to burn through her flesh. She was a creature of death and loss. She was nothing at all.

Liam was right behind her, steps away if she needed him.

"Is—" she choked out. "Is she the only one?"

"Yes. Dominik is still unconscious, and Ren's arm is broken. The rest are beaten up, but they'll survive."

"Good."

"Rue, are you—"

"Please don't. Not right now." She ran her hands

through her hair, painting it a matching shade of red. "Why did they leave?"

"Who?"

"The deities. Demas. Why did they just leave? Why not kill us?"

"I don't know. I don't know anything anymore." He stopped, not expecting her to turn around. "I got Zag, go sit down for a minute, okay?"

Giving no answer she nodded, the back of her head was the only inclination that she heard him. She needed to get away from here as soon as possible. She could already feel the fog rustle in her chest, pressuring her to lose it, to let it out. She was a ticking bomb of power that needed to be contained.

She turned down a line of cars that were still in their original formation, undamaged by Demas. Reaching a shaking hand to a door handle she gave it a stiff pull. No luck, the door was locked. She tried another, the van's door creaked and gave way, swinging open to welcome her in. Ruby climbed into the driver's seat and closed the door behind her. When she was sure it was locked, she rested her hands on the steering wheel and let out a low-pitched growl. Her breath wavered but she steadied it, continuing to raise her voice until she was screaming.

Her knuckles were swelling as she punched every surface she could reach. Shaking and screaming until her throat was sore and her arms were ready to burst. She flung her head back in the seat and took a deep breath before opening the van door and prying herself out.

Ruby was able to take another breath of air before an arm reached around to cup her mouth and pull her back behind the cars.

HEMERA LET GO of her mouth carefully and stepped back, letting her spin around, dagger drawn. She raised her arms up in defense.

"I'm not here to hurt you."

"Just to kill me like you killed my friend?"

"I didn't kill anyone," she flicked a blonde curl behind her ear. "That was Nyx."

"Your mother, you mean?"

"Yes. I suppose that's what she likes to be called here."

"Here?"

"On earth. It's not exactly the same where I'm from."

"Where's that exactly?" Ruby looked her over, disgusted by the sight. "You know what, never mind. I don't care. What the hell do you want?"

Hips angled, Ruby fisted her hands and let the fog escape them. Her mind raced, landing on Leah each time. *How dare she? How dare she show up here after this?* She wanted to hurt her. No, to kill her. Ruby's fists raised, the fog around them shifting to fire. "Give me a reason not to burn you right this second."

The deity bit her lip and leaned her curvy bottom on a car door. Unlike her mother, she was dressed casually in jeans and a tee that hugged all the right places. Ruby wondered how well the two got along. Mostly she wondered if Hemera would shed tears when she killed her mother.

"I want to help you."

"Oh, this should be good!"

"I really do."

"Why does everyone who betrayed me and almost killed me want to help all of a sudden? Is this some goddamn joke? Am I being recorded for a reality show?"

"A what?"

"Forget it," Ruby rolled her eyes. "Why would you want to help us at all?"

"Look, I don't expect you to understand but I care about Ny– My mother. And until now, I did everything she asked me to."

"So, what changed?"

"This isn't right. Killing children is not right, no matter what their reasoning is."

"Sorry, you want me to believe that you actually have a conscience?"

"Yes."

"Ha!" She threw her head back to laugh, "That's freakin' rich! You assholes just killed someone!"

"I know. I'm sorry about your friend."

"I don't give a crap if you're sorry!" Ruby raised the dagger and got ready to fight.

"But I am sorry! About all of it! What they're doing here, what they're planning to do, it isn't my choice. I would never choose this. I–"

"What do you mean 'planning to do'?" she asked, lowering the dagger to her side. "Do you know why they're doing all of this?"

Hemera nodded, sending her thick curls bouncing around her shoulders.

"You wanna fill me in?"

"They're heading to the abandoned library in Lakeside."

"Why?"

"To open a portal. Demas wants to open the Gates of Tartarus. He wants to destroy your entire world."

CHAPTER 50

THE GATES

The perplexed faces of the elders anointed the coffee table of Elena's living quarters in the Elemental center. They reminded Ruby of gargoyles guarding the ancient churches in Europe, each one conveying a different emotion. The bruises all over their faces did not help the visual. She tried not to laugh as she looked around the table, knowing how serious the situation really was. By the time she got to Liam's somber expression, she was almost in stitches.

"He wants to open the gates of Hell?" he asked finally.

"Tartarus," she answered, glad to have relief from the stifled laughter in her throat.

"Isn't that the same thing?"

"Not exactly," Harvey interjected. "Technically, there is the Underworld, I think that might be what you're thinking of. Tartarus is thought of to be an entirely different area well beneath it."

"It's all very vague, of course." Myriam added and folded her hands in her lap.

Ruby glanced at Liam to see if he was satisfied with the answer. He still seemed confused, so was she. "Wherever or whatever it is, I don't even know if it's true. We're not exactly going to trust a deity."

"But what reason could she have to lie to you?" Cyril asked.

"How about to get me to fall for whatever Demas actually has planned?" she fired back, venom on her lips. "For all I know he sent her to talk to me."

"It's possible but I think we can trust her." Nola said, "Opening the gates in the old library would align with the ritual Zag uncovered. There's a good chance that this is the portal the circle would create."

"How much do we know about Tartarus?" Liam asked.

Harvey and Myriam exchanged side glances. "Not a large amount."

"But it's not looking good?"

"When has opening gates to anything been good for us?" Ruby sighed, "I just don't understand why they didn't kill us all when they had the chance."

That silenced the elders. Each one looked for a distraction, suddenly fidgeting with their hands and rearranging their legs. Cyril was the first to break the tension and she wished he would have kept his mouth shut.

"Because they need you for something."

"For what? And why me?"

"I'm not sure. But it's the only thing that would make sense. Perhaps it's the sword they need and you're the only one that can wield it—"

"So why not just kill me and take the sword?"

Liam winced at her side and she regretted not choosing better wording.

"That I do not know. It is quite difficult to sever the connection between an AetherBorn and the sword, at least from my experience."

"But not impossible?"

"No, not impossible."

"So, they could? Kill me for it, that is?"

He looked up from his lap. "Yes."

"So, if it's not the sword," she took a deep breath, letting the air sit at the top of her lungs before breathing out. "Then it's me. Somehow they need me for this garbage."

"Great," Liam growled, "just great."

She couldn't disagree with him. She was sick and tired of being some ploy in Demas' plans and yet somehow, she always ended up in the middle of them. She almost wished that he would kill her and get it over with so she could stop living in constant fear. If only it were that easy. Too many people depended on her for their safety, at least if he still needed her for his pathetic plans, she had some time to figure out how to stop him. And keep everyone safely away from him. For now.

"I don't think we should trust Hemera," she said. "But I do think we should use this information for now."

"You sound like you have a plan," Elena said, her tone vividly cold.

I guess she's still pissed at me.

"Not yet. But I will. Just need a bit more time to figure it out. But if he's not going to kill me, I suppose I have the time after all."

She smiled.

Liam frowned.

"Now that we're back home," she changed the subject, "we should probably figure out what to tell everyone."

"You mean about–" Harvey whispered.

"Leah." Her eyes burnt at the mention of her friend. "When is the funeral?"

"Tuesday."

"Has anyone talked to Zag?"

Myriam straightened the folds in her skirt and cleared her throat. "He's been avoiding all of us."

"So not just me then?" she said, her mouth a thin line. "I'll go talk to him today."

"Maybe you should give him some more time, Rue?" Liam asked.

"We don't have more time. Not if we want to live."

With that she nodded to them and got up to leave. Her steps were heavy the entire way to the door. She dragged one of her legs behind her, still unable to put pressure on it without causing her wounds to bleed. She tried to concentrate on the pain to keep her mind from racing. It was circling like a hamster in a wheel, always landing to one place. Leah's body in the car lot. Her blank stare. The way her head wobbled from side to side as Cyril performed the compressions. She would never forget that image and as long as she lived, she'd make sure Demas wouldn't forget it either.

CHAPTER 51
LOBSTER TRAPS

R uby's outstretched hand hovered over Zag's bedroom door for a few minutes before she finally willed herself to knock. Her knuckles barely met the metal, and she was about to knock again when Zag's voice rumbled from inside.

"Come in."

Her chest rose and fell as she tentatively slid the door open. Zag was sitting down on his bed, surrounded by books and papers. It looked like a hurricane blew through his bookshelf, landing him perfectly in the eye of the storm.

"Uhm, what's going on?" she asked, trying to make sense of the mess.

He tucked a pencil into a half-bun of red hair and looked up. "I'm trying to figure out how we can trap them."

"The deities?"

"Yah, girl! We can't hurt 'em, we can't kill 'em. So, what's left? We're gonna have to trap 'em!"

"That's great but–" she hesitated, "Zag, are you sure you're alright?"

"More than alright. I'm really close!"

"Not what I meant."

He paused writing, the pencil making a dark mark in the paper as he pushed it down. "I know what you meant."

"And?"

"And I need to keep working."

She said nothing. She understood him perfectly. If she had lost a family member, the last thing she'd want is to be reminded of it. There was nothing she could do for Zag now except to help him forget, even if for a brief moment. Besides, she could do the remembering for both of them for now.

"Ray's been helping with some of this stuff. Wanna see?" He shoved a pile of papers her way.

"Uhm, sure. Ray, huh?"

"What?"

"Nothing. You two are pretty chummy."

"Sorta. She's nice."

Her mind flashed back to Ray's hand in his at the lot. "Just be careful, okay?"

"Yah, okay." He rolled his eyes, "So you wanna know what this is or what?"

Ruby nodded her head and sat next to him, flipping through the pages in her lap. From what she could tell, they looked like the drawings of a crazy person. Somehow resembling her grandmother's journals from her time in the hospital. If there's one thing Ruby learned, it's that sometimes what might seem like gibberish could actually hold all the answers she needed.

"So, what is this?"

"Girl, what isn't it?" He tapped the pencil on one of the chicken scratches on the page. "I've been wracking my brain on how we can catch these bastards. I mean, no offense, but even *your* powers don't do much, and you're like the strongest thing we got going for us!"

"Cool. Thanks."

"Whatevs. So, I started thinking about that mirror room in the Aether Plane. You said they were like doorways, right?"

"Uh huh..." she tried to follow his logic without success.

"But Demas still needed you and the sword to open it. So, they weren't doorways. You follow?"

"What were they?"

"Cages. Sorta. Like lobster traps."

"Okay, you lost me."

"Lobster traps are like funnels. Kinda sorta. The lobster goes in but 'cause of the way the traps are made, they can't get out."

"Right," she nodded, still lost. "So, you want to lobster trap the deities?"

"Hell, yeah, I do! The mirrors are the traps. They could get in, but they need you to get out. Lobsters!" He smacked his hand on the papers, sending a few strays to the floor.

"But the mirror room won't work anymore. Whatever happened when I stole their powers when I was there must have broken this trap thing. Otherwise they never could have gotten out in the first place." She chewed dead skin off her lip and slouched down.

"Who says we need the room?"

"Okay, you lost me again."

"We don't need the room; we just need the mirrors."

"Hello? Reality check. The mirrors are in the room!"

"Girl, we don't need those mirrors. We just need *a* mirror."

Her eyes formed into saucers and she had to forcibly close her mouth. "You want to make your own plasma mirrors."

"You got it! We'll need your powers of course. And Nola and Rays. I think if you can connect to the plasma and use that to form the doorway, then the girls can keep the connection to the plane open until we can put the trap together."

"So, when they pass through the plasma, we'll

redirect them into a part of the plane that has no other portal access." She said, finally understanding.

"Exactly! The plasma will stop them from getting out and since there are no other portals, they'd be stuck!" he hollered.

"And Ray knows the best place in the plane to do this?"

"She says she does."

"You really think this could work?"

"Yo! I don't even know if we can make these mirrors. But it's worth a shot."

She pushed the papers off and bolted up. Excited but scared at the same time. If they could make this happen they would save everyone! "But how do we even get them into the mirrors?" she asked, suddenly deflated.

Zag flashed a set of teeth. "Every lobster trap needs bait."

"Zag!" She yelled and leaned in to kiss him on the cheek. "You're a freaking genius! Seriously!"

"I know," he blew a self-assured breath at his knuckles. "Oh, Rue?"

"Yeah?"

"Love the new hair."

"Thanks. Leah cut it."

His eyes lowered. He grabbed a random piece of his own hair, inspecting the dead ends. "I know. She was always great at that stuff."

CHAPTER 52
ON BOARD

R uby interlaced her fingers and pressed until
the blood rushed into them.

"Is everyone on board with the plan?"

The prolonged silence filling the center's library
worried her. She had half expected the elders to be leery
of the idea, especially Liam, but seeing Jake and Nola
dumb founded was starting to make her doubt the whole
thing.

She looked to Zag for support but even he looked
uncertain.

"So, you want to trust Hemera?" Liam asked.

"Not trust. Just use," she folded the corners of Zag's
papers in and out. "We just need to play nice with her
long enough to trap her in the mirror."

"And she's going to volunteer to get in there?"

Ruby rolled her eyes at him, "Obviously not. We

won't tell her she can't get out. Make it seem like we're using her to trick the rest of them."

"I don't know," Jake said, shaking his head. "This sounds like it could go south pretty damn fast."

Great! Now *these two agree on something!*

"She's our only chance right now."

"And you're sure we can't do this without her?" Elena asked.

"Honey, no." Zag yelped. His back straightened when he suddenly realized his mistake. "Sorry. Elena. We need her to get the others."

Elena shook her head and trained her attention on Ruby. "Can you walk me through it again?"

"Sure. We get Hemera in the mirror and use her to get Nyx to us. I have a feeling that won't be hard to pull off. We'll need to make sure there's only one way in so we can ambush her when she comes for her daughter. Once we trap her, we can worry about the other two." She paused to make sure Elena was following, "Use Nyx as bait this time. I doubt Eros will come alone so we need to be prepared for both him and Demas showing up together."

"We're caging them all?" Cyril asked.

"Not all of them. Demas doesn't survive this."

Another silence filled the room. Liam reached for her hand.

"I won't go through with it unless you're all on board," she said. "But I think we need to do something."

"And you think you can actually make these plasma mirrors or whatever?" Nola raised an eyebrow and leaned back in her chair; arms crossed.

"I'll need your help with that. Ray's too. But yeah, Zag thinks we can."

"Look, I don't know the first thing about this mirror room you were in but I'm assuming it can't be that easy to just make a cage like that."

"Oh, girl, it's the opposite of easy!" Zag said. "That's why she'll need both of you. If not more."

"Rue, how are you even going to connect to that much plasma?" Liam turned to her, concerned and unyielding.

"We'll need to be somewhere where I can have a better hold on the plane. I think I'll need to be almost in both places at the same time to make this happen."

"The old library," Jake whispered.

"It's the last place I remember having that much control over the plasma. It's also the only place I was able to pull that much plasma out." She remembered the plasmic rain she poured over the library hall when she came back from the room of mirrors. Looking around the room, she could see the ones that were there remembered it too.

"It's also the place that Demas is planning on opening the Gates of Tartarus," Liam snapped. "No way! Too dangerous!"

"Would it help if I told I want you there the entire

time?" she purred, hoping to sway him.

"Not enough for me to get on board with it!"

"Liam..."

"No, Rue. It's not happening. For all we know, they're already there and you're just, what? Going to show up with some picture frames and hope for the best?"

"They're not picture frames," Zag said, annoyed.

"And they're not there," she added.

"And you know this how?"

"Hemera told me."

"What? You went to see her again without telling any of us? How could you put yourself in that much danger? You said it yourself, we can't trust her!"

Crap. Should've led with that.

"I had to get more information. We didn't exactly have all the time in the world at the car lot," she glanced at Zag, who seemed unaffected by the memory. Either that or he was turning into an excellent actor. "And I was going to tell you, I swear."

His eyes narrowed and he looked away. This was not the end of this conversation; she was sure of it. She felt like an idiot. She had just smoothed things over with him and promised to be forthcoming only to mess it up again. Why hadn't she just involved him from the beginning? When this is all over, she would have to make it up to him big time. Just because Liam was an elder now didn't mean that she should treat him like she would the rest of them. He wasn't her subject; he was her boyfriend. What type of person forgets that?

"Ruby is right. It's our only shot." Cyril's voice almost knocked her off her chair.

Was he actually agreeing with her?

"I say we put it up to a vote. All in favor?" he asked and quickly raised his own hand.

Her eyes drifted from person to person as their hands slowly joined his. Elena, Myriam, Harvey. She watched as one by one the entire room had their hands high in the air. She turned to Liam who sulked in his chair, his hands fisted on the table.

"I can't do this without you, you know?" she whispered.

He didn't meet her eyes. One by one, he unlocked his fists and raised his hand slightly.

"Okay. So, we're doing this," she said to no one in particular.

There was a light shuffle as everyone lowered their hands back down. Some looked at each other, others stared at her with a questioning intensity. She wondered if she should say something encouraging, dredging her mind for words of strength and power. She had nothing. Instead, she slouched in her chair and looked down at her nails.

"Great," Liam said. "Just great."

I guess that'll do, she thought and finally took a breath.

CHAPTER 53
ON THE WRONG END

Four long hours later and she was back in the old library, huffing and puffing from overusing her powers. When the six of them first squeezed into the building through the small window Ruby nearly had an aneurism. Her body shook, a volatile reaction to her memories of the place. Now, however– while she stood covered head to toe in sweat and black fog– memories were the last thing on her mind.

"I can't do it!" she shouted, dropping her arms to her side.

The small amount of plasma she had managed to pull through dripped from her fingertips. It made nearly silent splashes when it hit the floor before disappearing in a cloud of black fog. The drops reminded her of the rain she had poured down the last time she was here.

This was somewhat like that except much more useless. She was useless.

"This is pointless; I'll never get it!" She slouched, "I never should have dragged you guys here."

Zag kicked the large silver frame on the floor and relaxed his shoulders. "Don't harsh this with your drama, girl! It'll work! We just have to readjust some stuff."

"Yeah, like this whole plan," she huffed.

He ignored her comment and nudged the frame again before getting back to his notes. His face scrunched and he was all but biting off the tip of his pen while he read over them. Nola, Jake and Ray huddled around him, each one trying to look over his shoulders.

"He's right, you know?" Liam whispered in her ear. His chest pressed against her back as he wrapped his arms around her middle. "You're being too hard on yourself."

"Someone has to be. I was so sure this would work and right now, I'm thinking we should just run off and hide somewhere and hope he never finds us."

"Yeah, but did you really think this would be easy? You can't tell me you honestly thought that you could reconstruct something you saw in some surreal version of reality with the snap of a finger. We don't even know how the mirrors work exactly."

"That's my point, Liam." She sighed, resting her palms on his warm forearms. "Whoever created the mirror room knew exactly what they were doing. It had to be an AetherBorn, I could feel her energy all over them but whoever she was, she was way stronger than me."

"You're pretty damn strong too."

"I feel like I'm trying to recreate a cake without a recipe. Just dumping in random crap and then wondering why it's falling flat."

"Yeah, but that's what's so great about you! You come up with these risky plans and yeah, they might not work sometimes, but when they do— it's freakin' magic, Rue. You're magic." He leaned in close, his breath tingling the side of her neck and making her knees weak.

"I thought you hated all my plans?" She teased, hoping that he wouldn't catch the blood rushing to her face.

"Only because they always put you in danger somehow."

"Well, you don't have to worry about that this time. I'm not doing much of anything it seems, so all safe here!" She lifted her hands in defense and rolled her eyes.

"That's 'cause you're on the wrong end," Ray's sharp tone rang next to them.

"Huh?" She ducked out from under Liam's hold and stood at his side.

"You keep trying to pull the plasma out."

"Isn't that the point?" Liam asked.

"No, pretty boy. The point is to make a trap."

Ruby didn't like her tone of voice. She especially didn't like that Ray seemed to know something they didn't and was wondering why she waited until this moment to share information. This kid was really starting to get on her nerves, it's like she was *trying* to look untrustworthy.

"That's what we're trying to do, Ray," she hissed. "Not sure if you missed the memo."

"Yeah, cool story." Ray brushed her purple bangs over her forehead. "Seems to me like you're trying to take whatever pathetic amount of plasma you can manifest and put it in the frame."

"I mean, that was the plan..." her voice trailed off.

"No offense, but that plan's real dumb."

"Let me guess, your genius hacker mind knows a better one?" Liam asked.

"Obviously."

"Care to share?" Ruby snapped; she had reached her breaking point with the kid.

"You said whoever made the Room of Mirrors must have been pretty strong, right?"

"Ray, how long were you eavesdropping on us?" She yelled, slapping her hands on her thighs.

"I wasn't eavesdropping. Get over yourself. You're not exactly quiet and we're in a library. The sound carries."

"Still creepy," Liam teased.

"Whatever. Anyway, that AetherBorn was one badass!"

"And?"

"And so were you when you were in there. From what Zag tells me, you were like a killing machine or something."

"I still don't see your point."

Ray breathed out an annoyed sigh. "Hello? What do you think you and the AetherBorn had in common?"

"The sword?"

"No, not that! I mean, yeah, that helps, but what else?"

She shook her head. She had nothing.

"The plane! You were both inside the plane!"

"Holy shit." She looked from Ray to Liam. "The kid is right. We're on the wrong side. We need to be inside the plane for me to have enough power to do this."

"You want to make another mirror room inside the plane?" Liam asked. "It won't work. Demas will never fall for it. He'll never meet you in there."

"Oh, we won't make the mirror in there."

"Sorry, I thought you said I'm right?" Ray sulked.

"You are. But so is Liam."

"So, what are you going to do exactly?"

"I'm going to open the portal. The one Demas opened last time."

"Oh!" Ray's eyes widened as she caught on.

"What 'oh'? What does that even mean?" It seemed Liam was not on the same page.

"She's going to split herself in between both places. Pull the plasma in from one end and push it out the other. God, you're slow!"

"Watch it, Ray!" she barked. "But, yeah, that about covers it."

"And you think that'll work?"

"I think so. But I'll need help."

"How much help?"

"About fifty AetherBorns worth of help. I'll need their power, it's the only way I can get enough juice to open the portal."

The excitement of actually being able to do this lingered at the tip of her tongue. She nearly jumped at the thought as she turned to fill Zag in. She wasn't useless. She was strong and she could do this. She repeated the words in her head over and over until she almost believed them.

"Oh, and kid?" she turned to Ray and nodded. "Good job."

CHAPTER 54
READY

"R ue! You need to hurry up!" Liam yelled, straining to help Jake and Zag hold up the frame. "They can't hold on much longer!"

She looked over them to the group of AetherBorns. Some were hunched over, some held the hands of those around them; all of them looked like she was sucking them dry, though she supposed that was a fair assessment seeing as how it was exactly what she was doing. Their powers flowed into her, the black fog rushing from their bodies into the dagger that vibrated in her hand. She could almost taste their energy in her mouth.

"I almost got it!"

Her short hair was plastered to her ears and forehead, darker in shade from the sweat that now coated it. She was squeezing the dagger so hard that she felt it might pop right out of her hands. The rise in power threw all her vitals into overdrive. Her heart pounded; her breathing was faster than that of a marathon runner, but she didn't stop. She was close to opening the portal, she could feel it.

What was it that Demas said last time?

The further you travel, the bigger the energy needed.

Well, she needed all the energy she could get right now!

A moan sounded, followed by a heavy thud. She didn't bother looking back, knowing that if an Aether-Born passed out there was nothing she could do to help them right now. The only way to help everyone was to get this portal open.

Sweat beaded on her brow and a rogue drop ran into her eye. She blinked the burn away, concentrating deeper on the space in front of her. The glimmer of light that started to push through.

So big, it starts to seep out sometime.

She heard Demas' words in her head. She was doing it! She was actually opening the portal to the Aether Plane! Not by accident and not without any knowledge. She was in full control.

Her lips parted and a hint of a smile formed as the light grew, opening the doorway large enough for her to step through.

"Mirror! Now!" She yelled and stepped halfway into the light, keeping the dagger exposed to the library.

There was no describing what her body was going

through. Ruby felt like all of her atoms were ripping in half, like the plane was pulling her into pieces. The part of her outside of the portal ached to be in while the part inside screamed to get out. She was at war in her own body. There wasn't pain, which shocked her to no small degree. Just a discomfort that could only come from one's energy being turned upside down and shoved back into their body. Her blood started to feel solid and she glanced at one exposed arm to see black veins run across it. *It's starting,* she thought and closed her eyes.

She pictured the plasma. Imagined feeling it on the tip of her fingers, twirling around her index finger and latching on like she was a chew toy. She pictured it flowing through her arm and into her chest. Into her entire body. Ruby willed the power of the plane to enter her. Willed it enough that it obeyed. She couldn't see herself, but she was certain that her eyes were pitch black and judging from the veins that covered her skin, there was not a single part of her left untouched by the plane's energy.

When she took as much power as she could hold, she pushed it into the dagger. Her back teeth anchored against each other, grinding down the enamel on her molars. The dagger grew heavy, pulling her hand down, but she fought against it, raising it higher and higher. The power rushed through her and she could feel it push her organs aside as it flowed. As it passed her, she changed it, filling it with her own energy, making it answer only to her.

There were whispers all around her and she was pretty certain that she heard Jake curse in astonishment. Ruby couldn't open her eyes for fear of losing her grip on the plane. Instead, she shut them tighter and pictured the plasma flowing out of the dagger and filling the mirror.

"Ruby!" Nola yelled; her voice closer than she anticipated. "Go!"

It was time.

She opened her eyes and stared at the plasma filled frame in front of her. She did it! She actually did it!

"Ruby!" Nola yelled again; her arm outstretched.

"Right, sorry!" She grabbed her hand and let the AetherBorn pull her out.

Ray was already at her side, the three of them feeding their powers into the portal to keep it open while Liam and Jake dragged the mirror in front of it. The moment of truth, she thought, time to see if Zag's theory was right.

As soon as the mirror was in front of the portal, the AetherBorns dropped their hands, letting the portal begin to close. It pulled on the plasma in the mirror, sucking it back into itself. Taking back its property. Jake and Liam gasped as the mirror was yanked out of their hands, flying back into the portal.

She kept one eye open, afraid that if she stared too

intently the portal would swallow the mirror whole and all their work would be for nothing. It didn't. The edges of the mirror slammed into the light and stopped like it plugged a hole.

Ruby folded her body in half, leaning her arms on her bent knees in a forward fold.

"I told you, Zag. You're a freakin' genius."

"And you're absolutely certain that they won't be able to get out?" Hemera raised an eyebrow at the mirror.

"Only I can activate the portal behind it. And only when I have the dagger," Ruby assured her. They only had a short while to test the trap before Nyx showed up, but she was certain that no one else could walk through. It was as though she had put a combination lock on the plasma when it passed through her. When they tried it out earlier, Ray nearly had a heart attack thinking that she was stuck in the plane before Ruby opened the portal again. "There are no other doorways in that part of the plane either. Ray made sure of it." She winked at Ray who stuck her tongue out before turning away.

The deity ran her long finger over the silver frame.

"Don't worry," Ruby lied, "I'll pull you back out."

Hemera's face froze. "Don't."

"Excuse me?"

"Don't pull me out. I want to stay with them."

"But why? It'll be like it was before. Weren't you sick of it? All alone like that for ages? Plus, this time, you'll have betrayed them. Pretty awkward, no?"

"I wasn't alone, silly girl. I was with my family."

"Still. Seems unbearable."

"At times. But you keep forgetting we're not like you. Time isn't the same for us. And trust me, we have ways of keeping ourselves entertained." She smiled and Ruby's blood froze. She didn't know what entertainment might be for a group of vicious deities and she never wanted to find out. "Besides," Hemera continued, "if they're locked up, maybe they'll start acting like themselves again."

"What's that like?"

"Nothing like what you've been forced to see, my dear." The deity lowered her gaze. "They were all so special. Fierce. Powerful. Absolutely brilliant."

"So, what changed? When did they–"

"Develop their taste for killing?" she frowned. "About the time Demas came here. It wasn't right away. They grew bitter over time, angry. At each other, of course. They blamed themselves for what happened to him. For how they treated him when they found out about Eirene."

"You mean locking him up in Tartarus?"

She nodded. "I wasn't there when it happened, but I know my mom and Eros fought against the rest of the family when the decision was made. They felt for Demas, understood his pain. They wanted to help him."

"So, what happened?"

"Majority rules. They didn't stand a chance. Neither did he." Hemera sighed, "When they dragged him to Tartarus, he cursed them all. Cut his ties and loyalty to the family, even my mom and Eros."

"So that's why they're helping him now? Guilt?"

"It can be a powerful weapon, even for a deity."

"And you?"

"In your world, I would be a good daughter."

"Even to a murderess?"

"Even to her."

Ruby bit the inside of her cheek and looked away. She didn't want to feel sorry for Hemera, much less for the rest of them but she could almost understand it. Not the murder and complete disregard for anyone's life but their own, but for the guilt of betraying their brother. Demas should be held accountable for every one of his actions, but in a way, they put him on this path. Them and the Elemental elders that killed Eirene. Its too bad Ruby wasn't around back then; she would have given them a run for their money. Her hands played with the locket that Hemera gave her as proof of her kidnaping and for a brief second, her heart broke for the deity.

"You ready?" she asked, pushing her remorse away.

Hemera fell silent for a moment before finding her

eyes. "I don't expect you to forgive him," She glanced briefly at Liam, "but I hope you can understand him."

With that, she turned her back and stepped into the mirror, her golden hair disappearing in the dark of the plasma.

CHAPTER 55
SOME WILL DIE

Ruby twirled the locket's chain around her finger then let it fall back down again. She'd been doing this for almost an hour, and her patience was wearing thin. Behind the rows of books, she could feel the restlessness of the Elementals and AetherBorns that joined them. Their sharp sighs echoed through the library's main hall, and each one made her wonder who it belonged to. Cyril? Ren? Sealie? She wrapped the metal around another finger.

Nyx should have been here by now. Maybe she shouldn't have trusted Hemera after all. Even though the deity did everything they asked. She called her mother, asked her to come alone, told her that they were unarmed and just wanted to talk. She should trust her. So why was there a knot in her gut right now?

Feet shuffled beside her and she turned to see Liam

get up from his chair. He arched his back before making his way to her. "She'll be here."

"When? Hemera called her an hour ago," she let the chain stretch down in her hold.

"She'll be here." Liam said again.

Her attention snapped to the back of the hall where Jake and Nola sat on the floor, both of them looking as bored as ever. Nola leaned her head back and closed her eyes. *Is this girl for real? She's napping?* Ruby shook her head and scanned the book stacks wondering how many others were asleep on the job. Between the center and those who came on Ren's request, they had managed to get almost three dozen fighters to join them. She knew the word 'fighter' was a stretch to describe them. With the exception of the knights, not one of them was fully trained for battle. Some had put in some practice time while Ruby was away, but she doubted it was enough to prepare them. She wasn't even sure *she* could win this, and she was the one with the dagger.

It would have to do. Maybe they could win solely on numbers alone.

"What if she doesn't show up?"

"Then we think of something else. The bright side is that you actually made the mirror. And we already have one of them in there."

"Yeah, unfortunately, not the right one," she sighed.

"Rue. Think positive please." Liam nudged her

elbow, "You made a plasmic mirror! That's pretty badass!"

She parted her lips, forcing a smile to her face. "Yeah, I guess that's pretty cool."

"You think she's alright in there?" He jerked his head to the mirror.

"She's fine. She just has to last long enough for Demas to get here."

"About that..."

"What? What about it?"

"Have you thought this out? I mean, I know you want you to end this and I know you made up your mind, but have you *really* thought this out?"

"You mean killing him?" She threw her hands up, "I have thought of nothing else but that. So yeah, babe, I thought it out."

"And what about them?" He pointed at the book stacks, "Have you thought about them?"

"Yes."

"And?"

"And what do you want me to say?" She lowered her voice, "That I'm sure no one will get hurt? That no one will die? I can't say that. Some will get hurt and some will die. We can't avoid that!"

He was quiet for a moment, then reached to press his palm against the curve of her back. "I guess we can't."

The locket dropped from her fingers one more time.

"I really wish it could be different. I'm doing my best here."

"I know. I hate that you're in this position. You shouldn't have to make these decisions on your own."

"Of course, I should! It's better this way. If we actually pull this off, they'll feel accomplished and powerful. And if we don't," she paused, "well, at least they'll have someone to blame."

"Wow. Being an AetherBorn really sucks," he laughed.

"You're telling me!" She pressed her back against his side, breathing in the musk of his cologne. "Hey, when this is ov–"

The short hair on the back of her neck stood at attention. They weren't alone, at least not for long. Her gaze focused on the empty spot in front of her.

"What is it?"

She pointed at the sliver of light that started to peer through the air. "She's coming. Warn the others."

Liam pulled out his phone, his fingers dancing across the screen. She could hear the rest of her group start to shuffle behind the bookshelves and wondered if they were as afraid as she was.

You got this, she whispered to herself.

The light grew and she watched it, mesmerized by its beauty. Both light and dark at the same time with sparkles fleeing from the air within it. Aether Plane air. She raised her palm to her forehead to block the rays peering through. They had spent so many hours in the dim library hall that the opening portal was almost blinding.

Through squinting eyes, she saw a leg emerge into the hall. Then another. Two long, slender legs peeking from beneath a sheer black skirt. Nyx.

Ruby nearly jumped for joy before realizing the portal wasn't closing. She glanced at Liam whose eyes were fixed on the light. When she looked back to face Nyx, her heart dropped to her feet, shattering every hope she might have had. The deity wasn't alone. From behind her pointed shoulders two more pairs of eyes stared back. Eros and Demas eyed the four of them with hostile grins on their lips.

"Darling Ruby, how lovely to see you again."

CHAPTER 56
WHY?

Ruby squinted.

"What? No fun little insults this time?" Nyx purred, twirling her skirt around the halls. "Come out, come out, wherever you are!" She sang, pointing her long finger to one of the bookshelves.

Hemera betrayed them. They'd prepared for this. Brought more people, made sure she was in the mirror for good, yet Ruby was still disappointed. The deity's final words made her think she might be on their side after all. *Once a snake, always a snake.*

She raised her arm and offered a small wave. One by one, her group appeared from the stacks. Each one of them ready, their powers sitting at the tips of their fingers. She'd never seen so many powers in one room. Fire, Earth, Water, Air, AetherBorn. All of them shining bright against the darkness of the hall. It was beautiful.

"Guess I don't need this anymore," she tossed the locket at Nyx's feet.

The deity cackled, bending to pick up the chain. "I'd bring my dear daughter out now if I were you."

"Or what?" She hollered, "You'll take on all of us? I doubt she told you how many of us were coming here. Take a look around! You think you can take us all?"

She pulled the dagger out and let the fog cover its blade. She was ready.

This time, it was Demas that was laughing.

"She didn't tell us anything, darling." He looked back at the stacks, "Time to stop the charade!"

From the corner of her eye she could see some of the powers extinguish. The Dalhurst Elementals lowered their hands, their faces followed. Ren let go of Elijah's hand and stepped forward. His eyes met hers and she could see his lips whisper something. *I'm sorry.*

"I told you what I knew. You have to let us go know. That was the deal," he glanced at Elijah whose eyes were wider than her own.

It was Ren! He was the one who betrayed them!

"Why, Ren?" Elijah pleaded. "Why would you tell them anything?"

His partner said nothing, his eyes still glued to Ruby. She didn't need to hear him say it, she knew why he had told Demas the plan. *The bastard threatened Elijah.* It was the only thing that would make Ren weak. She couldn't even blame him. If the tables were reversed and it was Liam's life on the line, she would do the same thing. She'd done worse to save the one she loved before.

"Yes, of course! Off you go!" Demas waved his hand dismissively. The Dalhurst team exchanged uncertain looks before taking a few steps back. Ren's hand was on Elijah's again, dragging him away from the hall.

"Still feeling confident, my darling?"

"Stop calling me that," she said, "and yes."

She grabbed a book from the table next to her and sent it flying forward, her dagger hand looped around, forcing a ball of plasma to encase the book. It picked up speed and barreled at Nyx. The deity lifted her arm, her oversized bell sleeves stretching as she blocked the book, tossing it to the side. From where Ruby was standing, the sleeves made it look like she had wings.

"Cute," Nyx said.

Ruby felt a flashing heat pass by her head and turned to see Liam thrust a fireball at Eros. He leaned to the side, avoiding the hit and reaching for his bow and arrow in one swift move. She raised her hands, glancing quickly at Nola to signal her to do the same. Before he could fire, they sent him flying back, spiral blasting black fog at his chest. His feet skid across the floor as if he was on ice skates until his back hit one of the shelves.

Upon impact, the Elementals near that shelf were on him. Waters threw ice ropes at his arms and legs while Airs worked together to get a grasp on his lungs. He was too strong, shattering their holds and shooting off arrow after arrow until he hit a target. She could see two bodies on the ground already but the rest persevered. Powers clashed and banged like fireworks.

At least they're keeping him busy.

She turned, ready to strike.

Nola and Jake had cornered Demas. Nola blasted atmosphere his way while Jake's hurricane raged around. Nothing touched him.

"He has his damn shield up again!" she yelled at Liam. "Keep him busy! I got Nyx!"

His expression was questioning, but he did as she asked. She only had time to blink before a river of fire spread from his feet to Demas' invisible dome. Liam's body disappeared into the flames, reappearing within moments on the other side of the hall, his fists pumping balls of fire at the dome.

Ruby ran in the opposite direction to where Ray, Dominic and Zag were attempting to block off Nyx. Pushing her towards the mirror with each hit. Her face was stoic and unconcerned. She blocked their powers effortlessly with one hand while her other pointed at them, smoke trailing in the direction of her finger.

Ruby sped up, her leg finding the top of a chair. She stepped on it mid run, using it to catapult her body in the air. She was flying now, dagger pointed, right at Nyx's back.

Die!

She felt victorious. She was about to end a deity.

Her feet readied to land, to absorb the impact of the fall when she was spun backwards. Her shoulder was on fire. She looked to the arrow that protruded from it then quickly to Eros. The deity grinned, shooting a quick wink in her direction before continuing to fight the Elementals he was busy with before.

"AAAAAH!" she roared, ripping the arrow out of her flesh. She tossed it to the ground, her blood staining the dusty carpet.

Nyx turned at her scream, the smoke in her grasp accelerating to find Ray and the Elementals. It wrapped itself around each of their throats and squeezed. Their eyes bulged and their bodies convulsed. Ruby could see their muscles tense. *She's crushing their windpipes!*

Jumping to her feet, she pushed the pain in her shoulder out of her mind and used the adrenaline to connect to her power. Binding her hands together, she pushed them forward, sending a blast of fog at the deity. The fog was about to make contact when Nyx shifted, her body turning to night. The fog blast flew through her, hitting a bookshelf instead and sending it toppling to the floor. Before Ruby could throw another hit, the smoke was around her. Its snake-like grip twisted and raised her off the floor, dragging her to the deity.

Not this again!

She hung in mid-air, feeling her organs start to convulse from the pressure. Her eyes felt like they were about to pop out of their sockets and her lungs were struggling to gain air. "I ca–" she gurgled before Nyx twisted her hand, squeezing harder.

The wound on her shoulder was gushing blood, dripping down her side and coating half her body in its dark red shade. She couldn't move her hands and her fingers were barely holding onto the dagger. Another squeeze and it would go flying out of her grip. She closed her eyes, accepting what was coming next. Accepting the defeat. The death.

The smoke loosened, just slightly at first then it was gone. She collapsed on the ground, her hand lolling to the side. It touched the plasma of the mirror and she jerked it away, feeling the plasmic burn on her fingers. She looked over to Nyx, who seemed shaken now, then over her shoulder.

Cyril's face was marked in concentration as he outstretched the palms of his hands at the smoke emerging from Nyx. She could see the smoke was no longer a fluid gas but thick like honey. *He's freezing her power!* Ruby thought and staggered to her feet.

"Ouch!" she yelped at another sudden burn on her wrist. She yanked her hand away, but something was holding her back, scorching her skin.

Ruby's attention jumped to her arm and the plasma from the mirror that engulfed it. Hemera's hand reached through the mirror, her plasmic grasp bubbling Ruby's flesh.

"Rue!" she heard Liam yell from further away.

She didn't bother answering. Her right hand twisted the dagger to point down and she reached over her shoulder. The blade ripped into the mirror, tearing the plasma open as she pulled it down. Hemera's hand let go and before Ruby could finish the cut, she was by her side.

"You better be here to help," she said.

The deity smiled and closed her eyes. she outstretched her arms to the side, her breathing slowing. Ruby's mouth gaped as Hemera's feet rose, levitating inches off the floor. Her blond curls flowed around her like she was submerged underwater and a brilliant, blinding light encircled her and Ruby both.

"Mother! Enough!" She howled, her voice entirely unlike the one she had before. It boomed through the library, making everyone pause to see where it came from. "It's time to go home now."

Nyx looked at her daughter, her face contorting, eyes filling with dark rage. The deity huffed a smoky breath, snapping her arms to her side and shattering Cyril's hold on her. Spinning on her heels, she was facing Hemera and Ruby. The anger around her was almost physical and Ruby shivered before clutching the dagger tighter. As Hemera lowered herself to the ground, the light shield shrank, leaving them once again unprotected. Ruby calmed her breathing and put her hands in front of her, coating them with black fog and readying to attack.

"You would choose her over your own family?" Nyx roared. "No daughter of mine would do that!"

"I am choosing you, mother. Come with me," Hemera outstretched a hand.

She felt sorry for her. Ruby Black felt sorry for a deity. She watched as Hemera's eyes begged Nyx to stop. Watched as she continued to beckon her forward with an open palm. Watched even as Nyx's gaze shifted to Ruby and she raised both arms in her direction. Ruby watched two streams of smoke whirl around each other, twisting into a thick braid of death, soaring in her direction. Watched Hemera push her out of the way and jump in front. Watched her body fold into itself and fall on the ground.

The light around her dimmed then disappeared entirely.

Hemera was on their side after all. She was on their side, and she died for it.

CHAPTER 57
TIME TO GO

"**D**AUGHTER!**" Nyx's voice rang as sharp as a church bell, shaking the library hall. The high pitch of it carried through the air, its frequency rising as it reached Ruby.

She dropped to her knees, pressing her palms against her ears.

One look at Hemera proved there was no bringing her back. Her face, once lit with the bright light of her power, was losing color fast and her eyes had rolled back into her head. She had fallen down in an unnatural position, her legs splayed beneath her while her upper body drooped sideways. The deity looked like a puppet whose strings had been cut mid-leap.

Nyx rushed to her daughter's side, shaking her roughly, trying to bring back some semblance of life. All without success.

Ruby felt Liam's eyes on her, and when she caught his gaze, she knew they were thinking the same thing. *We're totally screwed now.*

She jumped back to her feet, wincing at the pain in her shoulder when her arms leaped to the side. She needed to get away from Nyx, away from Hemera's body. Her legs shook with fear and adrenaline as she ran to the other side of the hall, closer to Liam and Jake. Closer to Demas. Glancing back, she could see Nyx still cowering over her daughter. Mourning her loss.

Up above, in the top level, Eros was wielding every bit of his power over her team. More bodies had been thrown on the ground. Some were hiked right over the railing from the impact of his arrows.

Death.

There was death all around her now.

She knew going in that not everyone would survive but this was something else entirely. It was a massacre. She had led them all into oblivion.

"Zag! Get Ray!" she yelled as she ran past.

When she reached Liam, her hands fisted and without hesitation she blasted fog at his shield. It strained at the hit and while she couldn't see its perimeter, for a split second she saw a dark shadow crack. It disappeared instantly as Demas strengthened his hold on it.

She blasted at the shield again, this time pulling more power from the dagger.

Another crack.

Zag and Ray reached her side. "Keep at it!" she yelled and watched them follow her lead.

Each hit of their powers splintered the shield more.

"We got him!" Jake yelled but before the smile fully formed on his lips, he was thrown back. His back hit the table behind him, and he crashed to the floor, shadows running away from his body.

Inside the shield, Demas laughed and extended one finger in the air.

One down.

There was no time to see if Jake was still alive. Her attention turned to Ray. "Where's Nola?"

The AetherBorn didn't answer. Instead she pointed to the top level. *Great!*

"We'll have to do this without her," she said and reached her hands back.

"Do what?" Zag yelled out.

"I need your powers. Ray, just like last time we were here! Show the others what to do!"

She didn't bother checking in. One arm outstretched to her friends, pulling out the power from their bodies. Whatever Ray showed them was working, she was getting stronger. The dagger felt it too, shaking and getting heavier in her grasp. She used the power and stretched her other arm toward Hemera's body, praying that her plan worked.

It did. *It's freakin' working!* She shouted at herself

as Hemera's residual energy flowed into her. The light mingled with the black fog, with her own darkness, until she was surrounded by a marble shield of fog and sun.

Ruby buried her feet into the floor and pointed her arms at Demas. For a moment, her body felt heavier than an army tank but then, in the blink of an eye, she was weightless. She could feel herself disconnecting. Her mind floating away from her body.

When she opened her eyes, she realized it wasn't just her mind that had been floating.

Ruby was a few feet off the floor. *Am I flying? No, not flying. What is that?*

Her eyes traced the black plasma beneath her, raising her like a peaking mountain. It swallowed her whole. Starting at her feet and all the way to the top of her head. There was no skin left, she was made entirely of plasma.

She could feel it in her blood, her breath, her very soul.

Nothing of herself remained.

Holy crap!

The fear of what she felt and saw pressed in, but she shook it away. This was good. Where there was plasma, there was power.

Her hands strained as she extended the black goo to Demas' shield. She encircled it and pressed, putting more and more pressure on the shadowed dome. The cracks started to form under the plasma. She pressed harder, feeling her breath slow down a little.

More pressure.

She used the the light shield, sucking its energy dry and turning it into plasma. Feeding its power into her hold.

More pressure.

Her arms shook.

Then pop!

The dome shattered around him, shadows flying out in every direction. She had popped his shield like a zit.

From her side, she could hear Liam's relieved laughter. Her hands moved quickly, pulling Demas into a plasmic hold. She could see him fighting against it but didn't let go. The goo stretched from her, drops as slow as molasses falling to the floor. When she had a good grip on his body she started to turn, dragging him along. His feet scratched the floor as she pulled him to her left side– towards the mirror.

Demas' eyes widened, and he stopped fighting her.

She might not get to kill him like she wanted but she needed to get him away from here. Away from her people. She pulled him quicker now, the plasma that stretched from her arms straining at the speed. His body flew past Nyx and Hemera until he was right in front of the mirror.

Ruby willed the plasma to carry her forward so she could be at his side. Her one hand held the grip on him while the other wielded the dagger. She raised her hand, slicing into the mirror, opening the way into the portal. Readying the doorway to Demas' prison.

"Brother!" Demas yelled.

She turned her head as an arrow flew by her, cutting the top of her ear mid-flight. The pain shrieked within her, but she held strong. Until she couldn't.

Her hand shook. She tried to keep hold on the dagger as much as she could, tried to keep slicing through the mirror to open the portal wide enough to push Demas in but she couldn't bear it any longer. Ruby pulled her hand out of the plasma, shock washing over her.

Eros's arrow had sliced her index finger right off.

Blood was everywhere.

It gushed from the wound, mixing with the black of the plasma into a morbid shade of brown. It dripped down her arm and unto the floor. Her scars had opened, bleeding as though they were gifted to her all over again. Ruby looked down, a gasp escaping her lips as she stared at the slip n' slide of her blood forming at the base of the mirror. The red pool vibrated, sending droplets of her blood in every direction. It looked like a dog shaking itself off after rain. As the blood shook it crept upward, inching closer to the mirrors edge.

She stared at it then moved her attention to her injured hand, turning it to get a better look. This was her vision. This is what she foresaw.

But if the vision was right and her blood was the answer then...

"NOOOOOOOO!" Ruby screamed, anticipating what was coming.

"Rue!" Liam ran to her, firing at Demas as he neared. He wrapped his palms around the wound, pulling away quickly from the plasma burns. She still had a plasmic grip on Demas, in shock from the pain and the blood loss. "You need to let go, Rue!"

She nodded; her eyes locked on his.

Slowly, her breaths evened our, and she dropped her hold on their powers. She breathed deeper, her mind coming back into the room. Another breath and the plasma started to loosen, letting her go until it was nothing but black fog around her. Liam pulled his tee off, wrapping it around her hand. The grey fabric soaked through, darkening with her blood.

Ruby's breath quickened again until she was panting. Her body was soaked in cold sweat.

To her left, the mirror groaned and creaked. She turned back to face it, watching as red light crackled though the darkness. Her blood had already made its way into the plasma in the mirror. The two intertwined until the mirror was filled entirely in her blood. Ruby's eyes widened as a wall of red stared back at her.

· · ·

THERE WERE only slivers of light at first, then entire rays, until the wall of her blood smoldered. The red glow colored her face as she stared. It was mesmerizing. The luminesce reminded Ruby of a retro lava lamp she had on her nightstand as a child. Back when she was afraid of monsters under the bed– before she knew those monsters were real.

The same red glow she had foreseen.

Demas' laugh drew her attention back to the hall. "Thank you for the help, darling," he sneered. "That AetherBorn blood is just what I needed."

The son of a bitch played us. Again.

"Wha–" she gawked, unable to finish the word. Flashes of the bloody waterfall and a glowing, red doorway ran past her.

"Nyx! Eros! Time to go!" Demas hollered, waving his arm over her, "Tartarus is waiting!"

CHAPTER 58

REMEMBER EVERY PART

L iam's grip on her tightened.

Her gaze was trained on Demas' self-assured grin and her thoughts boiled to the surface. She felt nothing short of pure rage. Not at him but at herself. The bastard was getting what he wanted, and it was her blood that helped him.

There was a scream from the top level, followed by a thud. She turned to see another body fall to the floor below; one of the knights.

Spinning her head back to Demas, she pushed Liam away with her elbow. He stumbled back, registering what she was about to do.

"Guys! A little help!" he yelled back.

Within moments Zag and Ray were by his side, readying their stance. She didn't bother looking at them knowing full well that she had no need for them right now. Her damaged hand was going numb, the loss of blood taking its toll on the rest of her fingers. She ripped off the bloody tee Liam had wrapped around her and tossed it at Demas.

The fabric had hit him square in the jaw, and he threw it back in disgust.

By the time he'd wiped her blood off of his face, she was in front of him. Her good hand ripped at the back of his head, clutching a fistful of black curls while she held the bloody dagger to his throat with the other. Even without a finger she could feel its strength in her hand. The pressure she put on her hand made the blood spill faster.

She had better make this quick before she passed out.

The power in her itched to get out but she held it in.

If she was going to kill him, she would do it as herself. She wanted to remember every part of this.

Her eyes met his, unblinking. She was so close to him that the jagged breath that left her lips reached his face. He was much taller than she realized, and Ruby was straining to stay on the heels of her feet. She pulled back his hair, bending him into her and thrust the dagger's blade into his skin.

She could feel the blade crush his throat and for the first time, his grin was gone. Replaced by something completely different. Fear.

Ruby pushed down on the hilt, deepening the cut.

Her arm turned sideways, readying for the final turn of the blade when she heard a cry from behind her.

"Watch out!" Liam yelled, spinning her attention to Eros and Nyx.

The deities had her in their orbit. Nyx's finger was raised, pointing in her direction. The smoke bellowed from her, rushing to strike. Eros was a few steps closer, one arrow mid-air while he readied another.

She looked back at Demas and smiled, slicing his throat.

The cut was brief. Ruby managed to run the blade halfway down before Liam tackled her. His thick body pushing her out of harm's way. She landed on her side, the dagger staggering to the floor as she fell, her hand unable to hold it any longer. Her head hit the tile floor and her brain rattled in her skull. She reached up to her hair, feeling a clump of wet in it. Her fingers pulled away, covered in blood. There was so much blood on her it was hard to tell where it came from.

She pressed her hands into the floor and tried to push herself up. Her eyes were losing focus quickly and she swiped at them with her palms, painting a red mask across her face.

Blinking rapidly, she tried to make out what was happening.

Somewhere in front of her Demas was crouched on the floor, his hand at his throat. Nyx had him lifted halfway and was dragging him into the red glow in the mirror.

"No," she whispered, barely making a sound.

Her hand reached forward to stop them, but it was too heavy to hold up. She let it drop to the floor, the rest of her body following. Beneath bloody eyelashes she could see two more figures following into the portal. Muscular arms wrapping around a limp body.

Ruby crawled, her legs splayed beneath her. Her fingerless hand leaving a trail of red in her path.

"NOOOOO!" she screamed as Eros dragged an unconscious Liam into the portal.

Red light filled the room, painting the library in the hue of her visions, then dimmed. The portal darkened, plasma filling the mirror once again.

They were gone.

CHAPTER 59
BACK HOME

"We'll get him back," Zag knelt at her feet, his usual dramatics down to a minimum. "We will."

She wasn't sure who he was trying to convince, her or himself. Ruby sat on a chair in the library, her elbows resting on her knees. Nola was at her side, making sure her injured hand was elevated until the ambulance arrived. She was against calling them, but Cyril assured her that they were on his payroll, so they'd keep quiet. She was starting to wonder if she was the only one in the city not under his thumb.

Her downward gaze offered no welcome and she wished everyone would stop trying to console her.

They lost fourteen people. Nine Elementals and five AetherBorns. Two of them her knights. Then there was Liam. She had no idea where he was and if he was even alive. The only hope she had for his survival was that Demas needed him to get back at her. Liam would live only if Demas was as much of a self-absorbed jerk as she thought he was.

And even if he lived there was no guarantee that Demas wouldn't hurt him just for the fun of it. They had dragged him into Tartarus itself. From what she knew of the place, it wasn't exactly a five-star resort.

She needed to figure out how to get him out. Fast.

Ruby curled her right hand into a fist, her teeth grinding at the sudden pain where her finger used to be.

"Hey! I said no moving!" Nola harped, pointing at the fresh blood that flowed from the wound. "You're no good to us if you pass out."

"I'm no good even if I don't," she scowled back.

Jake's hand squeezed her shoulder, light enough that she could tell he was afraid of hurting her. "Maybe you should get over yourself, huh?"

"Excuse me?" Her head spun back so fast it almost ripped right off her body.

"Just sayin', I don't remember the last time you sat around moping and feeling sorry for yourself."

"If you haven't noticed, people died today, and that tool kidnapped my boyfriend!"

"So, what are you going to do about it?"

She bit her lip. "I don't know yet."

"Ah! But you're going to do something. So, start there."

"Where?"

"Where you always start, Rue." He smiled, "Remember in third grade when I told you that you couldn't play basketball with us because you were a girl?"

"Uh huh."

"And what did you do?"

"Threw the basketball at your face and broke your nose."

"See what I'm getting at?"

"I guess."

"So, what's the plan?"

She straightened her back and started to lower her arm, but Nola gripped it quickly and pulled it back up, scowling. "For starters, I need to get this goddamn finger thing figured out. Can't exactly hit up Tartarus like this!" She raised her arm at him and rolled her eyes.

"Oh, this is going to be amazing!" Zag leaped to his feet, the sparkle back in his eyes.

"I'm gong alone."

His face dropped. "Like hell you are."

"Zag, I'm not arguing about this. We don't know what's down there. Is it even down?" She asked no one in particular. "It's too dangerous."

"Girl, I'm going. He was like a brother to me. I won't lose him too," he looked at his feet. "It's not your call."

Jake stepped into her peripheral. "Me too. No arguments."

"What? He's like a brother to you too?" she scoffed.

"No. But you're family. So, you're stuck with me."

"Me too." Nola added, "And count Ray in as well." She glanced at the AetherBorn who nodded before rolling her eyes.

"Not to interrupt but we'd like to help," a voice sounded behind her.

She turned halfway and cast a sideways glance at Ren and Elijah. She had heard they stayed behind to fight with the rest of them despite what happened.

"You've done enough helping for today," she hissed.

"Look, Ruby, I'm sorry. I really am," Ren said. "There is no excuse for what I did. I just couldn't risk Elijah's life. And I am mortified at how this turned out. But I want to make it right. Please."

Elijah unraveled his grip on Ren's arm and stepped forward. "I'm not happy with what he did but he means it. He'll do anything you ask but, in the end, it's your call. If you don't want us there, we'll leave."

She closed her eyes and let her good hand fall to the side, her finger grazing the handle of the dagger next to her. She wasn't sure what to do or how to move forward. She wished Liam was here, he was always good at helping her plot out her thoughts. She had no plan, no army, and her hand hurt like hell.

Ruby thought back to the basketball court. Her tiny body throwing the ball at Jake's face, all because of a game. Because he made her angry. Well, now she was more than just angry, and Jake had a point. She *was* going to do something. She would always do something.

She looked up, her back a little straighter, gaze more determined. Eyes as black as ravens.

"Looks like we're going to Tartarus," she said and found the dagger again. "We're bringing Liam home."

EPILOGUE

L iam's body was cold as ice which was uncommon for a Fire Elemental. His head pounded and he felt like he'd been kicked in the gut a million times. With a hammer. He wasn't sure how long he'd been lying on the floor but the numbness on his left side implied it had been at least a few hours.

He rolled over on his back and pushed his palms firmly into the ground, pushing himself up to sit. His hands felt suddenly warm and he looked down to see them covered in soot.

Well, this is different.

It was dark where the deities dumped his body and he tried to make out the layout of the place. It looked like a cave, the walls dark and rocky and spanning high enough up that he couldn't see where they ended.

Where the hell am I?

He grabbed a handful of soot, bringing it up to his nose. It smelt of fire and ashes mixed with something else. A metallic smell that turned his stomach. Blood.

Liam threw the soot back on the ground, wiping his hand on his pants. He was mildly regretting taking his shirt off to wrap Ruby's hand right now. Who knew what he could get hit with in this place.

Tucking his knees in, he pushed himself up to stand. The pain in his side from where Nyx's smoke fired into him was gnawing at his nerves, but it was nothing compared to the pain the two arrows sticking out of his thigh were causing. He squinted his eyes and tried to make out the fletching in the dark.

When he caught a glimpse of the edge, he reached for it with his right hand and snapped the end off. The dull pain vibrated to the back of his thigh and he bent over, fighting the vertigo that came with it. His left arm looped around the back, feeling for the point of the first arrow. Liam found it quickly– hard to miss a piece of metal protruding from skin.

His teeth gritted and he took a quick breath in before pulling the arrow out through the back. The pain was blinding. His breathing sped up so fast he could hardly keep up with it. His body shook and he bent forward, retching between his legs.

One more, he thought and snapped the second fletching.

Another pull and a few more bouts of vomit and he

was leaning against the cave wall, trying to focus his eyes again.

There was a rustle in the wall opposite him, followed by the sound of metal dragging on stone. He shielded his eyes as red light streamed into the cave. *A door! Someone is coming!*

Liam's eyes struggled to make out the shape, slowly focusing on the curvy figure in front of him. The back-lit, red doorway cast an ominous glow over her long gown. His eyes followed up her legs, past the unnaturally long, black hair, landing finally on her face. In the dim light of the cave stood Nyx, grinning at him from ear to ear, her white eyes twinkling with savage joy. Though it was hard to tell from his vantage point, he could swear that from behind her back, two shadowy wings emerged.

His rage rose to the surface, warming his once cold body with a fire only he could summon. Taking one great stride forward he lunged for her. His body soared through the air, almost majestic and...

Snap!

Something tugged at his neck, pulling him back to the wall.

The air escaped his lungs as he landed flat on his back. His hands reached for his throat, feeling for what had hold of him. Something slick and metal. His fingers moved to the back, feeling the metal encircle his entire neck. He whipped his head back, hearing the sound of the metal on the rock for the first time. He was too preoccupied with his pain before to notice...

The assholes chained me to the wall!

Nyx howled in front of him, her laughter echoing up the cave walls.

"Oh, brother dearest!" She yelled through the open doorway, "I think your dog wants to go for a walk!"

THANKS FOR READING!

I would love it if you could leave a short review of the book to let me know what you thought. You can post your review at any of the sites below and I hope you know how much I appreciate you doing this!

https://www.amazon.com/dp/B07V7XB3PT

https://www.goodreads.com/book/show/47867341-aetherblood

If you want to hear more about my books or be the first to receive news on sales and giveaways, sign up for the newsletter!

https://ansage.ca/newsletter-1

A.N. SAGE

AETHERWARS

THE AETHERBORN SAGA, BOOK 4

AETHERWARS, BOOK 4 OF THE
AETHERBORN SAGA

**To save the ones she loves, she has to give up
everything.**

AetherBorn and leader of the Elementals, Ruby Black,
never imagined that her blood could open a portal. Let
alone a portal to Tartarus, a realm that is more night-
mare than truth — filled with death, torture, and
unspeakable horrors.

When her boyfriend is captured by Demas, the self-
appointed wicked King of Tartarus, she knows there is
only one thing she can do. Ruby must gather an army
and form unlikely alliances to save her boyfriend and
destroy Demas for good.

But war is a fickle thing, especially when the lives of
everyone she loves are on the line!

Will Ruby be able to destroy her mortal enemy and

save the love of her life? Or will the evil-filled world of Tartarus engulf her whole?

Everything is put to the test in the final chapter of The AetherBorn Saga. With lives on the line and worlds to save, can our strong heroine survive what's coming for her?

BUY ON AMAZON NOW!

https://www.amazon.com/dp/B087NV4C9D

ALSO BY A. N. SAGE

Kartgega- Kartega Chronicles Book 1

https://amzn.to/2YFSekp

Kartgega 2.0: A Star Reborn- Kartega Chronicles Book 2

https://amzn.to/2ZhT7yR

AetherBorn- AetherBorn Saga Book 1

https://amzn.to/31tCAdB

AetherQueen- AetherBorn Saga Book 2

https://amzn.to/38mMGyJ

AetherWars- AetherBorn Saga Book 4

https://amzn.to/2Vtz2US

AetherBorn- The Complete Saga Box Set

https://amzn.to/31tmMYE

ABOUT THE AUTHOR

A.N. Sage has spent most of her life waiting to meet a witch, vampire, or at least get haunted by a ghost. In between failed seances and many questionable outfit choices, she has developed a keen eye for the extra-ordinary.

Since chasing the supernatural does not pay the bills, she dabbled in creative entrepreneurship, marketing and retail management. A.N. spends her free time reading and binge-watching television shows in her pajamas.

Currently, she resides in Toronto, Canada with her husband who is not a creature of the night.

A.N. Sage is a Scorpio and a massive advocate of leggings for pants.

For more books and updates:
www.ansage.ca

Connect on social media:
Facebook Group:

https://www.facebook.com/
groups/945090619339423/

Instagram:

instagram.com/a.n.sage/

Twitter:

twitter.com/ANsageWrites

Facebook:

facebook.com/ansagewrites

Pinterest:

pinterest.ca/ansagewrites

Goodreads:

goodreads.com/author/show/
18901100.Alexis_N_Sage

Amazon:

amazon.com/author/a.n.sage